THE BULLAUN STONE

By Jan Flynn-White

THE BULLAUN STONE

Digital Edition Published by Jan Flynn White Literary Enterprises

http://www.janflynnwhite.com

ISBN: 978-0-9966582-0-1-Digital
ISBN: 978-0-9966582-1-8

Cover design by Heather McCorkle of McCorkle Creations
http://heathermccorkle.wix.com/mccorklecreations

Acknowledgements

There are so many wonderful people whom I would like to thank. First, my brother, Jerry, whose love of all things Irish was the inspiration for my book – hope I made you proud. Thank you to my sister-in-law, Sherrie Barrett Flynn, who is the embodiment of the meaning behind the Barrett coat-of-arms. Thanks to my kids – Courtney, Luke, and Bekah – who didn't roll their eyes (at least not in front of me) when I told them I was writing a book. And heartfelt thanks go out to Vickie Petty and Susan Weaver, who read my book in its rawest form and still loved it.

I would be remiss if I didn't send kudos to Jodi Henley, Mary Buckham, and Jodie Renner for writing such fantastic craft books and conducting workshops to share their wealth of knowledge to budding authors. Thanks, also, to Bryan Cohen, whose 'how to' podcasts have been extraordinarily helpful to self-publishers like me.

A very special thank you goes to my awesome editor, Yelena Casale, for helping tidy up the wayward bits and pieces of my manuscript, and for introducing me to Heather McCorkle, the fabulous cover designer who captured the heart of my book and made my vision a reality.

And finally, to my wonderful husband, Gary – no words can express my gratitude for your patience, love, and support.

Table of Contents

The Bullaun Stone

Chapter 1

She ran her fingers across the top of the dust-covered wooden doorframe and found the spare key. The house smelled of lemon-polished floors and dried lavender with a ghostly hint of warm gingersnaps fresh out of the oven. *Maybe it won't be so bad*, Kate told herself in an attempt to slow the anxious thumping in her chest. But the sudden jangle of the kitchen phone set it to beating double-time again.

"Who is this?" the voice on the other end demanded.

"Kate McKenna. May I help you?"

A sigh of relief was audible through the wires. "This here's Peg Flanagan. You remember me?"

How could anyone forget Peg? She'd moved into the rundown clapboard on the farm next door the summer before Kate's senior year in high school. Short. Stocky. Full of spit and vinegar was how Grandma once described her.

"I sure do," Kate said. "Is everything okay?"

Peg chortled. "It is now. You 'bout had me scared to death. I was standing at the sink washing some dishes and saw headlights in the driveway. When a light came on in the house, well, I reckoned I better call and see who was over there, 'cause I know

Pearl has been in the hospital for a week now and last I heard she might be there awhile."

"Yes, ma'am, I'm afraid so. She called me this morning. Asked if I could come help with the garden and run her booth at the market. I'm sure she thought she'd be home by now. I stopped in at Memorial to check on her but didn't stay long. She was…she looked…" The lump in her throat made it nearly impossible to finish. "I mean, she's real weak."

Peg clicked her tongue. "Sorry to hear that, hon. You let me know if I can do anything to help, you hear?"

Damp handprints stained the black receiver as she eased the phone back onto its cradle. The muscles of her stomach began a slow twist.

Stop it, you can do this.

She sucked in a deep breath, wiped her palms down the sides of her jeans and picked up the handle to her suitcase, determined to make it to the bedroom without another emotional intrusion. But a glimpse of the black and white photo, half-hidden behind the other knick-knacks on the mantle, crushed her resolve and deflated her lungs. A young girl, around seven years old if she remembered correctly, with a riot of cotton-colored curls stood on the running board of a 1936 Nash. One hand lifted in a wave; the other clutched a homemade rag doll.

Kate's favorite picture of her mother.

Don't you do it. Don't you cry. If you let it start…

She obeyed the stern admonition and managed to swallow the tears, but couldn't stop the pain that sliced through her heart, reopening the wound that refused to heal.

The hallway ended abruptly. Grandma's bedroom was on the right. Kate pushed open the door on the left and groped her way to the nightstand. The faint glow from the double-globe parlor lamp did little to warm the room that had once been her mother's. Kate always hoped this ascetic transformation had taken place after Mom moved out.

A large four-poster bed dominated the room. Left just enough space for the plain wooden dresser and ladder-back chair. The only spot of color hung above the headboard. The Barrett coat-of-arms. A crowned lion crouched atop a red and white striped shield. Below the shield, a ribbon proclaimed the family motto: "Frangas non Flectes: virtus probitas." Grandma said it translated to "Unbowed. Unbroken. Honor and Courage."

Kate heaved the blue vinyl suitcase onto the bed and flipped up the catch. She stared blankly at its contents while her thoughts wandered. Not once, in all the summers she'd spent here, not once had she ever seen her grandmother ill. Others her age had retired, but Grandma was still up at dawn. Working in her garden. Preparing dried herbs to sell at the flea market to supplement her social security. Sure, it was ridiculous to think she was invincible, but that's how Kate always saw her.

At least until now.

She shook the thought from her head and began pulling out the jumble of cutoffs, t-shirts, and underwear, which she crammed into the top drawer of the dresser. Jeans and short sets went in the next. The bottom drawer, she discovered, was already filled with colorful scarves, lace handkerchiefs, and butter-soft kid gloves. Remnants of a more genteel era. She picked up one of the gloves and ran it across her cheek. It still held the faint, flowery fragrance of her grandmother's perfume and brought back memories of playing dress up in the drop waist dresses and T-strap heels packed away in Grandma's cedar chest. A tiny smile fluttered the corners of her mouth. As she folded the glove lovingly back in place, she caught the burgundy outline peeking from under the white silk squares embroidered with delicate lace. Pushing them aside, she uncovered a small, leather-covered book.

Her fingers traced the elaborate roses etched into its cover. She held it to her nose – old vellum, musty with a hint of vanilla. The thin metal clasp gave the illusion of privacy, but it wasn't locked. Property of Pearl Jean Barrett – 1923, flowed across the page in an elegant script. She read the first entry.

> *May 12 –My life is moving fast, like a train bereft of its engineer, barreling forward with no brakes, nothing to impede its travel or inhibit the skyrocketing speed at which it thrusts forward. I have so many thoughts that are swirling around in my head, so much going on. It feels like this summer is going to be a huge turning point in my life, so I bought you, Dear Diary, to record it all.*

Kate closed it thoughtfully.

Grandma was born in '03, so she'd have been about my age.

A part of her wanted to read it. See what a young woman in a small town in the '20's would write about. Then again, they were her grandmother's private thoughts. How would she feel if somebody had access to *her* private thoughts? She shuddered and reached to place the book back where she'd found it.

Then hesitated.

In that brief instant, curiosity overruled conscience.

Kate skimmed through the pages. Some days only a sentence or two had been written. Others contained lengthy treatises full of thoughts and ideas. There were clippings from magazines, newspaper articles, a swatch or two of frayed fabric. Lodged almost dead center of the book, she discovered a sepia-colored photograph and a piece of folded parchment. She pulled the picture out first. Odd, she'd been through stacks of old photos, but had never seen this one. Kate recognized her grandmother right away. She looked so young, sitting there on the bench, legs crossed demurely at her ankles. Gloved hands clutched a small bouquet of roses. Her dress appeared to be of white satin and a stole, created from a filmy, gauze-like material, draped around her shoulders. Her dark hair hung in a loosely braided chignon that followed the curve of her neck. Kate studied her grandmother's face; slender with a broad forehead, a slim nose and full lips that curved into a gentle smile. Long, thick lashes framed the eyes that gazed up at the young man whose hand rested on her shoulder.

He looked nothing like the pictures of her grandfather. Thomas McKenna had always been a somber-looking gentleman with horn-rimmed glasses and a narrow mustache. This man's straw hat tilted at a rakish angle. His shirt sleeves were rolled up, plaid vest unbuttoned, and what could only be described as an impish grin lit up his face. Kate swore she could see the twinkle in his eyes. She turned the picture over.

"All my love, Aidan" was printed in bold letters and below that, a date. May 23, 1924.

Who was Aidan? Kate shrugged and stuck the picture back in the diary and pulled out the note. Fingertip-shaped smears stained its edges and the ink splotched and blurred in a couple of places.

My dearest Pearl,
You have my heart. Don't take my soul as well. I beg you to reconsider your decision. Words cannot express the depth of my passion for you, nor can they express the measure of my agony at the thought of not having you with me always. Please meet me at the bridge tonight at nine o'clock. I must explain to you about the gift I left under the willow tree. I will be waiting anxiously.
Until we are reunited, Aidan.

Beautifully written but heartbreaking.
Kate couldn't imagine getting a note like this.
Correction.
Didn't want to imagine it.

That would mean letting her guard down, letting someone get close, maybe even loving them.

And we all know how that turns out.

Kate swallowed hard and placed the note back beside the picture and laid the diary on the nightstand. She ruffled her hair with her fingers. The back of her neck prickled with heat. She needed some fresh air.

It was only a couple of steps to the French doors that led to the backyard patio. The heavy fragrance of roses and honeysuckle floated into the room. Like a balm, it washed away the ache in the back of her throat, and at the sight of the weeping willow, her taut shoulders relaxed. The tree had a whimsical look tonight. Lightning bugs twinkled in and out of the draping limbs, and slender fingers of fog swirled around the trunk and up towards the top.

The corner of Kate's mouth shaped into a half-grin.

She remained in the doorway, listening as the sounds of summer glutted the night air. The incessant chirps of crickets and cicadas were interrupted by the occasional hoot of a barn owl or the deep croak of the bullfrog's bellow. It was noisy. But in a peaceful way, she thought. Not like her cramped apartment near the university, where the walls were thin, and she could hear everything. Cars as they drove past on the street below. The pounding beat of loud music from the nearby coffee house. The canned laughter from her landlady's blaring sitcoms. That suited Kate just fine. The noise was a distraction. It filled her head, so there wasn't room for the darker, sadder thoughts that tried to invade.

A sudden gust of wind swept past her, slamming the hallway door shut. A cold shudder ran the length of her spine.

Don't be ridiculous, it was nothing.

But that nothing had flipped open the diary to the last page. Its scrawled entry caught Kate's attention.

June 28 - I am so tormented right now that I have become quite ill. I cannot eat, I cannot sleep. Mother will not cease to interrogate me. Yesterday I was at my wits end. I screamed at her in tears, pleaded with her to let me be. Father called Doctor Cullen who prescribed a sleeping draught for me. I am sorry I have caused such despair for Mother and Father, but I cannot tell them what happened, cannot tell anyone why I

That was it.

Tiny shreds of paper clung to the binding where the remaining pages had been torn out.

Kate reread the passage. She could almost feel the agony ooze its way through the ink and into the diary. What could have happened to make her grandmother that upset?

As much as she wanted to find out, the emotional day was taking its toll. And this diary wasn't something Kate wanted to rush through. She wanted to savor each word, every description, every thought. She placed it back on the nightstand beside her and sank her head into the pillows. Squeezing her eyes shut, she muttered a desperate plea, "Help me. Just help me get through this."

Kate was jarred awake the next morning by the disorienting awareness that she wasn't in her bed back at the apartment. She lay with her eyes closed and let her thoughts drift while her heartbeat slowed. This wasn't how she'd imagined her return would be. Not under these circumstances. A spasm of guilt squeezed her chest when she thought of Grandma's phone calls and letters. Encouraging her to come back for Thanksgiving or Christmas holiday. Kate used college as an excuse – she was studying to keep her grades up, doing research for her term paper – but she always suspected Grandma knew the truth.

Or a portion of it anyway.

After a quick shower, she slipped into her cutoff jeans, a worn t-shirt and Keds. The fragrance of morning glories and jasmine greeted her as she stepped onto the front porch.

'This is the house I was born in. This is the house I'll die in,' Grandma always swore.

Not yet, Kate prayed, *please not yet*.

She found a wheelbarrow in the barn. Removed a stack of canvas tarps, replacing them with a rusty hoe, a hand fork, and a spade. The gate latch to the chicken-wire fence surrounding the garden was rusty and crooked. Kate had to wriggle it several times before it finally lined up so she could open it to step inside.

Grandma's herb garden didn't just supplement her income. It was her pride and joy. Kate could see it in the tidy rows of basil, thyme, lemon balm and lavender that sprouted from the fertile soil. Tucked into the corner under a vine-covered arch, a porch swing strewn with quilted pillows swayed in the mild breeze – an inviting shelter for when the withering Texas heat became unbearable. The old scarecrow in the middle of the garden seemed more a cliché than a deterrent, judging from the sparrows that perched in a straight row across its shoulders. And there was a new addition. Wooden posts were stuck into the ground every four to six feet. Plastic pipes with tiny holes ran suspended between them. The bright green water hose snaked its way across the yard, connected to the pipes. A watering system. *Pretty cool idea*, Kate congratulated her grandmother's ingenuity.

Due to some overcast days and unseasonably mild temperatures, the plants weren't affected by days of neglect. Weeds, on the other hand, had used the situation to their advantage. Clumps of henbit sprouted everywhere, and towheaded dandelions dotted the soil. Kate didn't like to use garden gloves. They were too stiff, too clumsy. Besides, she liked the way the dirt felt as it sifted through her fingers. How, at her touch, the herbs released their fragrance, clinging to her hands like a primal perfume.

She worked until the sun broiled overhead. Sweat trickled its way down the small of her back and glistened on her arms. She was tired, and her stomach complained that nothing in the pantry or fridge sounded appealing. Plus Grandma didn't keep soft drinks in the house, and Kate missed her Coca-Cola fix. She thought a minute. What about the little mom-and-pop store up the road?

Only a couple of cars were parked in front of Donovan's. The store had begun to show its age. Whitewashed wood had faded to silver. The roof was a patchwork of tin and rust, pockmarked from years of battering hailstorms. Kate picked her way down the uneven sidewalk, past the fire-engine-red drink cooler plastered with decals advertising Nehi Grape, Chocolate Soldier, and RC Cola.

"How y'all doin?"

The gray-haired lady behind the cash register gave her an exuberant greeting as she pushed open the screen door.

"Good, thanks. Just need to pick up a few things."

The cashier peered over her glasses.

"You're Pearl McKenna's granddaughter, ain't you? My, how you've grown. You remember me? I'm Margaret. Margaret Donovan."

"Yes ma'am," Kate nodded, smiling. "You used to give me free ice-cream sandwiches if I could finish three books during summer vacation. Probably have you to thank for my love of reading."

Mrs. Donovan beamed. "I'll be danged. I haven't had that nice a compliment in a month of Sundays. Well, you let me know if you can't find what you're looking for." She shook her head and muttered again, 'I'll be danged."

The store hadn't changed. Wooden shelves sagged under the weight of canned goods. Cloth sacks of flour and sugar were stacked in piles along the front wall. The floors were still gray, unpainted concrete, although tiny cracks had begun to spread throughout, immitating the thin threads of the spider webs that escaped the straw bristles of Mrs. Donovan's broom.

The right wheel of her cart squeaked in protest as Kate walked the aisles pulling cans and boxes off the shelves, checking items off her mental grocery list. At the butcher counter, Mr. Donovan shaved thin slices of honey-baked ham and cheddar cheese onto the white, waxy paper.

He handed her the packages.

"Anything else?"

Good question. Maybe some fresh vegetables and fruit?

Kate stood in front of the bin of oranges, contemplating its tall, pyramid shape. A setup for disaster. One false move and she'd bring down the whole display.

She reached for an orange near the top of the stack.

"I don't think I'd go for that one."

Kate's face warmed from the unwelcome flush of heat that always accompanied embarrassment. Exactly who was the stranger insinuating himself into her decision making and questioning her choices? She turned; brows raised.

Dressed in a white t-shirt and low-rise Wrangler's, he stood several inches taller than she. A shock of sandy-brown hair swept across his forehead. Almost covered his eyes. *And that would be a shame*, she concluded, *because he has the most beautiful Hershey-chocolate eyes...*

She yanked her thoughts back into focus.

"Why not?" she countered, with a lift of her chin.

"It's simple engineering. See, if you pull this one out," he waved his hand at the orange she'd reached for, "it takes away the support. The result wouldn't be pretty, I promise."

He searched the stack, chose four plump, ripe oranges and held them towards her.

"I'd go with these."

"Thanks." She deposited them in a paper bag and nodded over her shoulder. "So are you responsible for this accident waiting to happen?"

A grin deepened the dimples in his cheeks.

"Nah, I'm a pharmacist over at Clarke's Drugstore. Name's Mike Sheehan."

He thrust out his hand and grabbed hers in a hearty shake.

"Oh. Well, I …I'm Kate McKenna."

"McKenna. You any relation to Mrs. Pearl?"

She'd forgotten that in a small town, everybody knew their neighbors and that her grandmother was considered a bit of an icon. Lifetime resident and former head of nursing at Memorial.

"I'm her granddaughter."

He walked beside her as she steered her cart towards the checkout counter.

"You gonna be in town for a while?"

"Yeah, I, uh, I'm here to take care of the house and garden until she gets to come home from the hospital."

"Man, I was real sorry to hear about Mrs. Pearl getting sick. They got any idea what's wrong?"

His question was innocent enough, but the visual of her grandmother lying fragile in the starched white bed brought on an unexpected swelling in her throat. She ducked her head and used her thumb to try and blot the wetness that seeped from the corner of her eyes. Her response was a strangled, "Not really."

Mrs. Donovan rang up her purchases.

"That'll be $10.42."

Kate fished a twenty out of her pocket and laid it on the counter.

"You okay, hon?"

The sympathy in Mrs. Donovan's voice sent Kate's emotions over the edge. Her lip trembled. She grabbed the grocery bags and, eyes averted, mumbled a polite "everything's fine, thanks," as she hurried from the store.

Tears clouded her vision and kept her from seeing the rise in the sidewalk. Her toe caught the corner. Paper bags split, and groceries flew as Kate stiffened her elbows, preparing to meet the pavement. Instead, she fell hard against the broad chest of Mike Sheehan.

"Whoa." His arms steadied her. "Are you okay?"

The familiar warmth spread across her cheeks as she took a step back and nodded.

"Uhm, yeah, sorry," she stammered. "I'm such a klutz."

"Guess it's lucky I followed you out." He held out some bills and coins. "You forgot this."

Her change. She thanked him and stuffed the cash into her pocket then knelt to collect her scattered groceries.

That couldn't have been more humiliating.

She glanced sideways and watched as he disappeared back into the store, thankful that her hair fell forward, shielding her face like a curtain while she tried to regain a modicum of dignity.

Moments later Mike returned with new paper bags. He held one out to her. She could barely meet his eyes, still stinging from embarrassment, but she managed another "thanks," before cramming items haphazardly into it.

"Count Chocula?" He picked up the box of cereal. Kate reached for it and he continued, "I didn't take you for the pre-sweetened type. I figured you'd be more 'Wheaties, breakfast of champions.'" He curved his arm upward, flexed his bicep, and flashed her a grin.

Kate shook her head and tried to ignore the quickening pace of her pulse.

"If you knew me better, you'd know I don't have an athletic bone in my body."

Another dimpled smile.

"Does that mean I might get a chance to know you better?"

Was he serious?

She brushed his question aside with a nervous laugh and shoved the groceries into the back seat. Mike held the car door while she climbed behind the steering wheel. She thanked him again and started to close the door, but Mike hadn't moved. He shifted his weight and ran his fingers through his hair.

"I know we just met, but with your grandmother in the hospital, seriously, if you need anything, just let me know. You can always find me at Clarke's."

She nodded and with a little wave, backed out of the parking space. A swift glance into the rearview mirror showed Mike, still glued to the curb, watching as her hand-me-down Nova pulled onto the highway. The corners of her mouth turned up in a smile that froze, then wilted when her heart reminded her, *you can't be hurt if you don't care.*

Right.

Just a momentary lapse.

Her back straightened, and she gripped the steering wheel in a chokehold as she followed the asphalt road back towards her grandmother's house.

By the time she finished up in the garden, a dark blue wall of clouds had gathered in the north. She shut the gate, her spirits as weighty as the wheelbarrow full of weeds she dumped in a pile beside the barn. Those clouds carried the makings of a serious storm, and tornado season wasn't over yet. She hurried to replace the tools and went inside to find a weather forecast on TV.

Dust covered the Zenith console, and the strips of aluminum foil wrapped around the rabbit-ear antennas didn't instill much confidence. Kate knelt in front of the television and pulled the knob anyway. Hissing static and a scrambled screen confirmed her suspicions.

Hungry and anxious to hear about the weather, she threw together a sandwich and sat listening to the radio she'd relocated to the kitchen table. Wolfman Jack's canned program played in the background until Kate heard the official-sounding voice of the local newscaster. She cranked up the volume, straining to catch each word through the intermittent crackles.

"Skies were overcast across North Texas early this morning as an unusual cold front boundary began to approach the region from the north. A line of storms developed along this boundary throughout the morning. Temperatures before daybreak were in the upper sixties ahead of the front and in the upper fifties behind the front. Winds are generally from the south at ten to twenty miles per hour, but will switch to the northwest behind the front. By late evening, storms are expected along the Sherman, to Fort Worth, to Hamilton line. The main threat anticipated from these storms is large hail and damaging winds."

From Sherman to Fort Worth to Hamilton... Wasn't that north and west of where they were? That meant the worst of it might miss Ardee. Kate peered out the kitchen window. Sheet lightning flickered an erratic pattern behind the gray-green clouds.

A déjà vu moment. Something about green clouds. What was it? The answer was so close, but the thread that would have connected her to it remained invisible.

A rumble of thunder rolled through the house. Rattled the window panes along with Kate's nerves.

She hated storms.

And it looked like a storm was headed right in her direction.

A crash of lightning jolted Kate from her dreams, but it was the steady thud on the rooftop that made her tumble out of bed in a panic.

Hail.

She glanced out the French doors, eyes widening as each flash punctuated the damage to the garden. The beat of her heart matched the pounding on the roof when Kate realized if she didn't act quickly, Grandma's means of support would be destroyed.

Chapter 2

Kate shimmied into her cutoffs and tugged on the shirt she'd tossed over the chair last night. She fumbled to tie her Keds. Why wouldn't her fingers cooperate? *Come on*, she urged, and securing the laces in sloppy loops, she bolted out of the house and sprinted toward the barn.

Think, Kate, think.

Surely there was something in the barn, something she could use to help shield the crops. Lumped in a pile near the door were the tarps she'd taken out of the wheelbarrow. Tents. She could make tents by draping them over the irrigation poles, securing them to the wooden posts. She heaved them into the wheelbarrow and began rolling it toward the garden. Already unwieldy, the extra weight of the canvas tarps made the wheelbarrow almost impossible to maneuver. On top of that, hail was accumulating so fast the yard looked as if it was covered with white marbles. And it was just as treacherous, she discovered, when her foot slipped and twisted sideways. A searing spasm shot up her calf. It brought tears, but she blinked them away with a frantic prompt – *never mind that now, just hurry.*

Whips of hair, possessed by the gusting wind, lashed savagely across her face as she fought to unhook the crooked latch.

With a heavy grunt, she kicked the gate open and dragged a tarp to the closest row of herbs. Hail pummeled her head and shoulders with icy fists, but she was resolute. Feet planted squarely in the mud, she grabbed the end of the tarp and began lifting it towards the nearest post when a sharp blow glanced off her cheek. Fingers of pain dug into the right side of her face. For an instant, her vision tinged with red. Kate dropped the tarp and reached up to touch the gash opened by the jagged chunk of ice.

Keep going, her brain prodded, *you can't quit now.*

A crimson smear stained the edge of the canvas as she grabbed it again. By now, the rain and hailstones had begun to pool in the tarp and weigh it down. She gave it a jerk, but her arms buckled.

"Try harder," she screamed in rage and desperation. With a low growl, she pulled again. The effort helped drain rainwater from the side, easing the tarp's weight. Encouraged by the bit of progress, she tried draping it again, but her arms gave way. It just wasn't going to happen. She didn't have the strength to carry out her plan.

The earth tipped a little to the right, her pulse began to thrum loudly in her ears, and the whole scene started to drag, like playing a seventy-eight vinyl on a turntable at thirty-three-and-a-third speed. Kate sagged against a nearby post. Her fingers uncurled slowly from the canvas, and it slipped to the ground.

I'm sorry, Grandma, so sorry, she repeated as tears and blood mingled, washed downward by the restless torrent.

The sharp crack of lightning and the tingle from ion-infused air interrupted her narcosis, and she gave an involuntary jerk, instinctively raising her head in its direction. Her heart and limbs froze. The tall silhouette of a man stood just a few feet away, cloaked in a dark raincoat; a black fedora pulled low on his face. Before she could process a response, he leaned over and picked up the tarp, tossed it across the misting pipes and secured it to the nearby wooden post. Then he signaled Kate to fasten down the ropes on her side.

Wake up Kate, whoever he is, he's here to help.

A surge of hope launched her into action.

The clatter of hail and booming thunder silenced any attempt to talk, but Kate understood what to do. Together, they were able to cover most of the garden in less than ten minutes.

Kate hurried to tie off the last cord determined, despite the storm and the throbbing in her right cheek, to try and thank the man who had come to her rescue. But the next burst of lightning left her temporarily blinded. When her pupils became accustomed to the dark, she searched again, but her savior had disappeared.

She gave up and hurried to the protection of the back patio, where she scanned the garden once more, just in case he was still around. But no one was there. And it looked like the hail was letting up. Maybe with the help of the stranger and a little luck from Mother Nature, the herb garden would survive. She blew an exaggerated sigh of relief and leaving her shoes and clothes in a muddy heap, went inside to clean up.

A little while later, Kate emerged from the shower; hair wrapped up in a towel. She pulled a clean t-shirt gingerly over her head, careful to avoid the red slash that reflected back at her from the bathroom mirror. At least the bleeding had stopped. Kate dabbed ointment on the wound and applied a bandage.

The featherbed, with its white chenille bedspread and fluffy down pillows, had never looked more inviting. She started to smile but stopped when her cheek cried out in agony. With a whimper, she slipped under the covers, ready to crash for the night. But her face and ankle ached, and her brain was still at work dissecting what just happened.

Who was that guy? How did he just happen to show up like that? How much damage had the hail done before they were able to cover the garden?

"I'm too tired to think about it anymore," she groaned out loud and buried her head in the pillow in an attempt to end the cerebral debate.

It was another thirty minutes before Kate's body and mind agreed to compromise and settle down long enough to allow her a few hours of rest.

The crumpled wad of sheets and blankets confirmed her fitful night's sleep. Kate's first attempt to crawl out of bed resulted in a Charlie horse in her left calf. She flexed her heel and massaged her leg. Managed to work it out and hobble her way to the bathroom. She grimaced at her reflection. Dark hollows rimmed her eyes, and that bandage didn't cover the purple bulge that accompanied the cut. A few stitches might have been helpful but too late for that now. She applied a clean dressing, careful to avoid pressure on her tender cheek.

Her muscles screamed again as she pulled on a pair of shorts and eased into her denim work-shirt. *Can't help it*, she argued with them, *gotta get outside and get those tarps off the plants.* Downing a couple of aspirins, she plugged in the percolator and headed out to the garden. Had the rescue efforts been enough to save it?

It took the better part of an hour to untie, drain and roll up the tarps. Then she had to replant uprooted seedlings. There were a few casualties, but overall the damage didn't seem too bad.

As she rolled the wheelbarrow full of tarps towards the barn, Kate glanced down. No amount of bleach would get that black clay soil out of her Keds. Her legs were caked with mud. It stuck to her hands and forearms. She could even feel the muddy splotches that dotted her face. Her shoulders ached, her back ached, and the sweat that trickled into her eyes burned like fire.

She dropped the wheelbarrow handles.

Forget about the tarps, I'm going inside to take a shower

She took her irritation out on the barrow's front tire, giving it a kick with all the energy she had left. That's when she heard footsteps crunching across the gravel drive.

"After the storm last night I wanted to check on you," Mike called out.

A flush of red scorched across Kate's cheeks. She was a mess and he'd just witnessed that little tantrum. Was she doomed to present the worst possible side of herself to this guy?

If the earth had cracked open and devoured her right then and there, she'd have been happy.

But Mike had gone out of his way to make sure she was okay.

At least she could pretend to be hospitable.

"I need to run through the shower real quick. But if you want to hang around a few minutes, we could have a cup of coffee."

Mike wore black slacks and a white shirt; a wide, red tie knotted around his collar. Headed to work, she guessed, so she added, "I mean if you don't have someplace you need to be."

"Sure, that's no problem," he said. "I'll hang out 'til you get back."

Kate hoped he didn't catch her deer-in-the-headlights reaction. She hadn't anticipated him taking her up on the offer.

She was back within ten minutes. Wet hair pulled into a ponytail, a clean bandage on her cheek; she carried two cups of steaming coffee. Mike leaned casually against his El Camino. The closer she got, the more his smile broadened. Kate wasn't used to the kind of admiration she read on his face. It was all she could do to keep from ducking her head in embarrassment.

"I wasn't sure how you took it, so it's just black."

"Black is fine. I hope you don't mind me coming out. It's just that we didn't get much hail in town, but I heard y'all got hit pretty hard out here. Baseball-sized in some places."

As she handed him a mug, she noticed the smile was gone, replaced with a look of concern. He reached out to lift her chin.

"What happened to your cheek?"

The tiny hairs on her neck prickled. She took a step backward and shifted her gaze away. She wasn't trying to be rude. It was just... his touch. And that look...

"Oh, that's just from my carelessness. I was trying to cover the plants last night, and this big chunk of hail hit me because I was stupid and didn't think to put on a hat."

"I can get you a good antibiotic ointment if it doesn't heal up soon," he said, apparently undaunted by her recoil.

"Thanks, that's real nice of you. So," she took a drink from the mug while her mind rummaged around for a change of subject. "You, uh, got a chance to scope things out, what do you think?"

"Looks like you saved most of the plants." He nodded towards the pile of tarps. "You did that by yourself?"

"Well, you see there was this–"

Kate stopped. How weird would it sound if she told him about a guy who appeared out of nowhere to help, then disappeared before she could find out his identity?

"I mean, uh... it was this, you know, adrenaline rush – where you get the strength you didn't know you had."

Sounded unconvincing to her ears, but Mike didn't question it. He nodded, "I've read about those incidents."

He glanced down at his feet then looked up with an apologetic grin. "Do you mind....uh, can I ask..." he took a step closer. Now he was within inches of her. She caught a whiff of fresh soap, Niagara starch, and peppermint. There was a slight stirring in her core. It was an unfamiliar feeling, an odd combination of both elation and fear.

"What's that perfume you're wearing?"

Kate gave him a blank stare. She hadn't used any perfume after her shower. She sniffed her wrist first, then the bend in her elbow.

"I'm not wearing any perfume, but I guess I do sort of smell like the basil and lavender I had to replant this morning."

"Whatever it is, it's amazing," his head dipped towards her neck and he inhaled deeply. "If you could bottle that fragrance you'd make a fortune."

Kate's pulse quickened slightly. She wanted to be offended by his impulsive behavior but found it a bit of a turn-on. Started an emotional tug-of-war, and she wasn't about to lay odds on which side would win.

He took another sip of coffee and glanced at his wrist.

"Hey, I gotta run, but I wondered, would you... Would you like to get a bite to eat sometime?"

She hated being caught off-guard, especially right now. The psychological state she'd been in the past few days had left her feeling vulnerable and not thinking clearly. And she needed time to sort out these new feelings she'd been experiencing ever since she met Mike. She gave a nonchalant shrug and a careless glance to the side.

"Guess that'd be okay."

The brush-off. Yeah. That should send a message. It had always worked with intrusive men in the past.

"Great," he said, "I'll call you soon."

This time it was Kate's turn to stand and watch, dumbstruck, as Mike backed his truck around and took off down the dirt road towards Ardee.

Who is this guy and why does he want to go out with someone like me?

Someone like me? She repeated to herself. What's wrong with someone like me?

Damaged goods, echoed back at her.

She turned on her heel and went inside to dress for a visit to her grandmother.

Her stomach began to twist as she eyed the brick and glass monolith.

Hospitals.

Monuments to human frailty.

Kate wished she had inherited at least a little bit of her grandmother's positive outlook on medicine and healing. Since the accident, she could only see the darker side.

The one that left her motherless.

Her heart lurched along with the elevator that crawled upwards to the third floor. Grandma was so weak last night, how would she be today? Kate took a big gulp of air before giving the door to Room 312 a hesitant push.

The blinds were raised, allowing ample amounts of sunshine to spotlight the floral bouquets and get well cards that lined the ledge of the large window beside the bed. Her grandmother, propped up by a mountain of pillows, sipped clear broth from a cup. Tension slid from Kate's shoulder, and her face broke into a broad grin as she leaned over the guardrail to kiss her grandmother's forehead.

"You look like you're feeling better this morning."

"Oh, I am." She returned Kate's grin, but the tremor in her hand, as she placed the cup back on the hospital tray, didn't go unnoticed by Kate. "Doc Anderson says I'll have to stay for a while. I keep having bouts of nausea, and my chest feels tight. Had me on oxygen earlier, seems to have helped stabilize my breathing. They can't find an explanation for any of it. In all my years of nursing, I've never seen a group so confused about symptoms. You know how doctors are, though, there's no way they'll let me go home until they find out what's wrong." She reached to pat Kate's hand. "How are things at the house? And what did you do to your face?"

Kate pulled a chair up close to the bed, reassured her grandmother that everything was okay and did her best to convince her that the cut was just a surface scratch. She didn't want any unneeded anxiety added to her grandmother's condition. That's why she'd already made her mind up not to mention the appearance of the mystery man, either. Strangers dressed in black that showed up out of nowhere, even if they were there to help, probably wouldn't instill a sense of ease. Instead, she quizzed her grandmother about the dried herbs for Saturday's market and if there were any special instructions she needed to know about caring for the garden.

The lines that tightened around her grandmother's mouth relaxed as she explained how to judge which herbs were ready to sell. As for gardening, there were little nuances. Like pinching the flowers off the basil so they wouldn't get woody. Checking the thyme beds for ants that liked to build beneath the fertile soil. Soon, though, her eyelids began to droop, and her voice became thin and wavering.

"Okay, Grandma, that's probably enough to get me through for now. Oh, and Peg offered to help too. I'll be fine," Kate said, with enthusiasm she didn't feel. "You need to get some rest."

"Thank you again for coming. I know it was hard, but it means the world to me."

Kate caught the tremble in her grandmother's voice. Leaning in to give her a hug, she pressed her face against her grandmother's cheek. It was damp. Tears? A dull ache squeezed her chest.

"I'm sorry, Grandma. I'm sorry I didn't come back sooner. But I'm here now. You just have to get well, okay?"

This, she gripped the steering wheel with white knuckles, *this is why coming back is so hard.* It wasn't just the reminder of her mother's death. She'd been so absorbed in her grief it never occurred to her to think what an awful blow it must have been for Grandma.

Mothers weren't supposed to outlive their children.

And instead of clinging to each other for comfort, Kate had managed to push her only remaining family member out of her life.

She swallowed the lump that threatened to close her windpipe and sought solace under her favorite refuge. The willow tree. A warm breeze blew through its tendrils, ruffling them like a mother fondly tousling her child's hair. Kate allowed herself a faint smile as she recalled the countless summer afternoons she'd spent on the limestone slab under the willow. Book in hand, a plastic tumbler of Grandma's sweet iced tea sitting lopsided in the bowl-like depression that had worn into the slab's surface.

Leaves and debris from last night's storm camouflaged the stone's surface. She started to brush it aside, but her hand came to a swift stop when it collided with a fist-sized rock that protruded from one of the depressions. Kate mouthed an 'ouch,' shook her wrist, then knelt beside the large slab and picked up the rock to examine it. It was dark gray, nothing uncommon about that, but upon closer inspection, she saw several emerald-colored lines layered throughout. The bottom was flat and polished, but the top was still coarse and uneven. What it was doing in the hollow was puzzling, but she just shrugged and –

"How's it goin' missy?"

The surprise interruption startled Kate, and she dropped the rock. It fell back into the depression, splashing big droplets of muddy water on her face and down the front of her blouse. She jumped to her feet, hands clutching her chest.

"Peg, you scared the crap out of me."

Peg's flaming-red hair, now streaked with gray, escaped with frizzled abandon from the ribbon that held her ponytail in place. Her smile was big and toothy and revealed a startling lack of dental hygiene. But it was sincere.

"Sorry about that, hon. I just wanted to come by and check on you. See how you fared after the storm last night."

Kate dabbed at her face with her sleeve, but the muddy water had already soaked through the bandage.

"That's awfully nice of you, Peg. Would you like to come inside?"

After settling her at the kitchen table with a glass of iced tea, Kate changed from her stained clothes into a tank top and cutoffs and put a clean bandage on her cheek.

"Doctors still haven't figured out what's wrong with your grandma yet?" Peg questioned when Kate joined her in the kitchen. "That beats all I ever seen. Next time you see her, you tell her I hope she gets better real soon."

"Thanks. I sure will. Did you get much damage from the storm?"

Peg opined she'd have to replace the tin roof on her barn and cut up the fallen oak tree for firewood, which she offered to share.

"And that was a pretty handy idea of yours 'bout using them tarps to protect the plants. Though how you was able to pull it off is beyond me. No offense, but you're a city-gal. I wouldn'ta thought you had the strength to do that all by your lonesome."

Kate gave a sheepish grin and shrugged her shoulders. Still felt funny telling anyone about the mysterious stranger who'd helped her.

Peg drained the rest of her glass and wiped her mouth with the back of her hand.

"Reckon I better get back home now. Them chickens ain't gonna feed themselves."

She ambled towards the door, insisting Kate call if she needed any help getting ready for market. They stepped onto the porch.

"I'm not one to meddle, hon, but if it was me, I'd read up on my Irish history. Some people don't concern themselves with learning 'bout their roots. But you," Peg squinted, gave Kate a knowing look. "Yep, might help you out a bit."

Kate inwardly kicked herself for not paying more attention when she'd accompanied her grandmother to market. Back when she was younger, it was all about eating cotton candy and corn dogs. About playing Swing the Statue and Red Rover with the other kids who were stuck spending their Saturday entertaining themselves while their parents tried to make a little extra cash. So today, her mission was a self-taught crash course on herbology. She sorted through her grandmother's drying pantry. One by one, she held the different plants to her nose, inhaling their rich bouquet to familiarize herself with their individual scents. Thank goodness Grandma had labeled them. And there were bits of notebook paper, stuck to the wall with thumbtacks, where she'd jotted down notes – basil tea as a natural painkiller, thyme infused water for coughs, lemon balm makes a calming tea, lavender relieves headaches. It gave Kate an idea for the market. She could fill sachet bags with the dried herbs and attach labels that told how they could be used.

Eventually, her stomach grumbled, reminding her she hadn't eaten since breakfast. An omelet sounded delicious and easy, and working in Grandma's garden had inspired her. She grabbed an apron from the hook behind the pantry door. The flowered one with the deep pockets so she could carry the garden scissors.

She walked each row to reassure herself that the hail hadn't injured them too badly. She raised her face to the sky while her heart offered its thanks. Then she pulled out the garden scissors and snipped several tender basil leaves, squeezing them between her thumb and forefinger to release their scent before depositing them in the apron pocket. When she reached the row of lemon balm, Kate clipped a sprig and rubbed it on her wrist and neck. She closed her eyes. The citrusy fragrance fill her head with visions of Grandma's lemon icebox pie topped with mile-high meringue and tangy lemon slices until a rustle in the brush on the other side of the fence disrupted her calm. She glanced across the rows of lavender, halfway expecting to see a rabbit or some other small varmint come darting out. Instead, her jaw slackened as she fixated on a structure, barely visible behind the tangle of trumpet vines and mesquite trees.

To her recollection, no one had ever lived on the property other side of the creek. Kate always assumed it was an abandoned, overgrown field. So what was this? She scaled the chicken-wire fence, but the thick undergrowth would pose a problem. Better to come back when there was more daylight, and she was wearing different clothes; a decision reinforced on her return when a jagged piece of wire grabbed her apron. She lost her balance and toppled to the ground, landing hard on her backside. She got to her feet rubbing her hip.

Am I the only one in the world who can turn gardening into a health hazard?

Kate shook her head and limped her way back to the house. The aroma of sautéed onions, mushrooms, peppers and herbs permeated the kitchen. The result was a decent omelet that smelled and tasted amazing. Then again, maybe she was just hungry. Kate attacked the food, cramming unladylike forkfuls into her mouth. Just as she closed her lips around the last bite, the phone rang. She jumped slightly in her chair. Was every call going to be like this? A mixture of hope and anxiety?

She was surprised to hear Mike's voice.

"Hey, Kate, I know you have a lot of work to do tomorrow, getting ready for market. But I thought maybe we could get together and have dinner tomorrow night. I could answer any questions you might have about the market. Or maybe you need help loading the truck?"

That's right. She needed to take the truck. Her Nova was too small to hold the boxes of dried herbs and who knows what all else she'd need for the booth. Problem was, the Ranger was a standard shift.

"You know..." she hesitated.

Just ask for Pete's sake.

"I could use your help. I've never driven a stick before, and I know your El Camino is three on the column, just like the Ranger. Do you think you could teach me how?"

"Be glad to." His voice sounded eager. "It isn't that complicated. You just have to get a feel for when to shift and not grind the gears. But there's one condition."

Oh gosh, she braced herself, *here it comes. The condition.*

She could hear his smile through the phone lines.

"You have to let me take you out to eat afterward."

She lowered her head in defeat. He had her over a barrel. She deliberately heaved a loud sigh into the mouthpiece.

"Okay," she said, hoping her tone carried a marked lack of enthusiasm.

"Great. I'll see you tomorrow."

His cheery response told her he hadn't picked up on, or maybe had decided to completely ignore, her hint. After they'd hung up, Kate stood at the kitchen sink, kneading her shoulders. Already strained from hoeing, the increased tension from the conversation with Mike had her muscles begging for a hot bath.

She floated in the tub until the hot water turned tepid, and the lavender bubbles became a patchy froth. Wrapped in a damp towel, she ran her hand across the steam-frosted mirror. Peeled back the bandage to examine her injured cheek.

For a moment, she forgot to breath.

The cut.

It was gone.

Chapter 3

She grabbed the sides of the sink and leaned in for a closer look. Turned her head to examine one side of her face, and then the other. Tentative fingers swept across her cheek. Not only was the cut gone but the smattering of blackheads had melted away into baby-soft flesh.

What the heck was happening? Sure, she'd heard of miraculous healings, but those usually involved saints and occurred eons ago.

Not in Texas.

Not in the twentieth century.

She waited for the quivering in her stomach to subside and her legs to feel less like rubber bands before she made her way back to her room to collapse onto the bed. She grabbed the closest pillow and pulled it over her head, clamping it tightly against her ears. Like that was going to shut down the 'why's and how's' that bounced around her brain like a silver marble in the hands of Peter Townsend's pinball wizard.

A distraction.

She needed a distraction or she wouldn't get a wink of sleep.

Grandma's diary.

She turned on the lamp, fluffed the bed pillows against the headboard and settled back to read.

May 24 - I am practically giddy with excitement and hope. Today I received my acceptance to the Texas Regional Hospital School of Nursing. Mother and Father were not pleased but seem resigned to let me pursue my dream. I think they have doubts, but they haven't felt the compassion to help the infirm as I have. I believe I can make a difference in people's lives. It is an enormous responsibility, but I feel I am up to the challenge.

Several pages were devoted to preparations for school. In the margin, Grandma had penciled in a 'things to do list' and had written the words 'wardrobe, shoes, uniform,' and a question mark 'cost of books?' On the opposite page, she'd pasted a picture cut out of a brochure. The corner window was circled; 'nurses dorm, my room' the notation.

Her grandmother's narratives were so detailed it was like being transported back in time. Kate could imagine how she must have looked as she described her dress.

June 20 – Caireanne and I are going to the fitting today for our Founder's Day dresses. She chose a light green frock, with ruffles and a peplum made of Georgette crepe and satin. It brings out the color of her eyes and blond hair. I wanted the turquoise silk crepe with the lace tunic and sleeves. I think the color suits my complexion, and I have chosen the dearest of hats to go with it. It's the same fabric as my dress. A thin swirl of netting circles the band and Mother gave me a peacock feather, which I pinned on the side with a broach. The festival sounds like it will be quite exciting this year. Caireanne and I are working the refreshment booth with the Women's Auxiliary League. I simply cannot wait.

The next few entries described their preparations for the Founder's Day festival, but it was the page dated July eleventh that made Kate sit up straight.

> *Last night at the Festival Caireanne, Cassidy, and I were ladling cups of lemonade to customers when the nicest boy came up and introduced himself. His name is Aidan Kavanagh.*

Aidan Kavanagh.
Now she was getting somewhere.

> *He is new to the area, having come here straight from Ireland and is staying in town with Clive MacMurray, who I think might be a distant relative. He is tall and handsome, with dark brown hair and piercing blue eyes, and so polite and sweet. He stood at the booth and talked to us until our shift was finished. Then he looked straight at me and asked if he could escort me around the square. ME! I was so surprised. I glanced at Mother, who watched the exchange, and she nodded her approval. Aidan and I strolled the square, stopping now and again to visit the booths. He wanted to play some of the carnival games and win me a prize, but I wouldn't allow it. I don't want anyone to think of me as one of those 'easy' girls, accepting gifts from a virtual stranger. After about an hour, he excused himself, admitted he was tired and had business to attend to, but said he would come by tomorrow and ask Father's permission to escort me to town. I had such an enjoyable time. I cannot believe*

that I am this anxious to see him again. I hope I will be able to sleep tonight.

She read the next few entries. Found a date she recognized. August twenty-fourth. Grandma's birthday.

August 24 – I am quite unsure of my feelings right now. Aidan asked if he could come by and see me because he had a birthday present. I thought it quite endearing and assumed it would be a book of poems or maybe some ribbons for my hair since he does seem to have exquisite taste in fabrics and clothing. We sat on the front porch swing, and he pulled out a small, foil-wrapped box, encircled by a red ribbon. When I opened the box there lay the most cunning ring I have ever seen. The gold band forms into hands that clasp a heart in the center. A crown perches atop the heart.

Aidan called it a Claddagh ring, and told me its story, explained how to wear it. If worn on your right hand with the heart facing away from you, it means you are willing to consider love, but your heart has not yet been won. If worn on the right hand with the heart facing inward, it means your heart is now taken. On your left hand facing out, it means you're engaged. But if you wear it on your left hand with the heart facing towards you, it means you are married, and two hearts have now been joined forever.

A ring seems a bit formal at this point in our relationship, but he begged me to wear it. I think Father and Mother would disapprove of such a gift, so I told him for now the best I can do is keep it and consider his words.

Aidan promised to be patient and wait until I felt comfortable in his feelings toward me. He picked up my left hand and with the slightest brush of his lips, kissed my third finger. He said that my finger would remember his kiss, and the love and devotion of it, and would soon draw the ring there, because that's where it rightly belonged.

Kate closed the book. It sounded like this Aidan loved her grandmother. So why did she break off the relationship?

Just add it to the list of mysteries.

She turned off the lamp, tried to turn off her thoughts as she burrowed her head into the pillow. But she couldn't resist running her hand one more time across her now-flawless cheek.

At nine a.m. on the dot, Kate was at the door of the five-and-dime. A short while later she deposited a large bag of items onto the kitchen table.

Time to put her ideas into motion.

She secured several stems of dried lavender together with rainbow colored ribbons. Eye-catching. They would dress up the booth and be an easy way to sell by the bundle. Next, she tied the handwritten labels to little sachet bags filled with dried herbs. She allowed herself a late lunch break then spent the remainder of the afternoon labeling Mason jars.

When she finally finished it was already five-thirty. Just enough time to get ready before Mike arrived.

Kate was tempted to wear jeans and a cotton shirt. That way it wouldn't feel like a date. Instead, she caved and chose a flirty, deep turquoise, short-sleeved sundress. Princess-cut bodice that tapered at the waist, smoothed across her hips, then flared out, ending with a ruffle that fluttered around the hem. She stood in front of the mirror nailed to the bathroom door and did a little twirl to reaffirm that it wasn't too short. Mom used to rag on her about the length of her dresses, but everything was short when you were five-foot eleven in a world where the average woman's height was five-foot-five.

A touch of mascara and a dab of lip gloss later, Kate opened the door.

Mike emitted a low whistle.

"You look great."

She gave him a grateful smile.

"First things first, I guess." She handed him the keys to Grandma's Ranger. "Thanks for agreeing to show me how to drive a stick. But please, no laughing."

Mike explained how the gearshift worked, talked about the clutch and its function. Then he got behind the wheel and drove a while, showed her step by step when and how to change gears. Kate's turn. Mike was a patient teacher and didn't laugh, not even when she struggled to move the stubborn gear into second. He covered her hand with his and forced the stick into position.

"There you go. Don't be afraid to give it some push. You won't hurt this tough old truck."

Kate tried to ignore the crazy tingling sensation in her fingertips and the fact that her stomach was turning cartwheels just like it had the last time she'd ridden the wooden roller coaster at the state fair.

After ten minutes of winding down narrow dirt roads between neighboring pastures and farms, she headed back to the house.

"I have a place in mind to eat," Mike said. "There's this little hole-in-the-wall diner not too far from here. Got the most delicious burgers and Texas fries around. And they have homemade root beer."

"What are Texas fries?" Kate asked. "I've never heard of them."

"Seriously? Wait til you taste them. Cheesy, spicy. They're incredible." He was practically drooling.

The Dairyette *was* a hole-in-the-wall. But the floors were clean and the waitress friendly. They sat across from each other in the red vinyl booth, sipping root beer from frosty mugs. Kate didn't feel as self-conscious as she expected. She'd never met anyone laid-back as Mike. Conversation was easy.

"So, your dad was in the Air Force and your folks live in Colorado now. How did you wind up in Ardee?" she asked. "It's off the beaten path, and you don't strike me as a small-town kinda guy."

He chuckled. "I had insider help. My Aunt Cass. She's actually my great aunt, and she's lived here all her life. When the drugstore owner, Mr. Clarke, had a heart attack they needed someone to help out. And this other guy that works there, George, well, he's no spring chicken either and had some health problems of his own. So Aunt Cass convinced Mr. Clarke to give me a shot. I'd just finished my pharmaceutical fellowship, but he gave me a chance, and here I am. Been here, I guess, about six months now. What about you? You don't look like a small-town kinda girl, either," he tossed her words back at her.

"Funny you should say that because I *was* born in a small town. Rose City, Michigan."

Mike gave her a quizzical look. "What part of Michigan is that in?"

"Upper Peninsula. About an hour and a half from Lake Huron."

"Okay, gotcha," he nodded.

Between bites of juicy cheeseburger and Texas fries – which Kate found out were fried potatoes smothered in sautéed onions, jalapenos, and topped with melted cheese – she shared bits about her childhood.

"Mom raised me on her own. I never knew my dad. She didn't talk about him much," Kate shrugged. "They were divorced when I was still a baby. That's why my last name is McKenna. Mom went to court and had them change hers back to her maiden name. Changed mine too." She took a sip of root beer and continued thoughtfully. "You know, Mom had a gift for making bad situations seem okay, so it didn't feel odd not having a dad. I'm sure it was tough, but she was a hard worker, and money always came through when we needed it, so I didn't feel like I was missing out."

She stared at her straw, twirled it to stir up the last remnants of her drink.

"One time, Mom worked the soda fountain in a drugstore. Once a month she would give me a dime. Told me I could spend it on whatever the fountain served. 'Course back then ten cents was a big deal. And there was a world of sweets out there waiting to be explored. I got dipped cones, soft drinks and candy bars, a malted milkshake. Which I hated, by the way. But my absolute favorite was the ice cream sundae, swimming in chocolate syrup with whipped cream and a cherry on top."

Are you done being Chatty Cathy, she chided herself, appalled that she'd shared so much. She looked up to see Mike studying her face. His lips upturned in a gentle smile. Kate ducked her head and concentrated on the last of her burger.

"Your mom sounds like a great person. Where does she live now?"

After a while, you'd think it wouldn't hurt as much to answer.

Her voice was as dispassionate as she could make it.

"My mother died here three years ago. It was the summer I graduated from high school." Lowering her eyes again, she began to pick at the remaining fries. "I, uh, I haven't been back here since, until Grandma called and asked if I would come help her out for a while."

"That must have been hard," he said in a reverent tone.

Silence hung like a low fog over the table. Kate crossed her ankles and shifted slightly sideways, braced for the next question or the inevitable *'I'm so sorry,'* although it was usually Kate who felt like *she* should be the one to apologize for bringing pleasant conversations to a standstill once she told them about Mom.

Another second or two passed with no words exchanged. Kate looked up. Mike was watching her, his head tilted slightly in her direction, fingers laced together. Waiting. Okay, now she understood. It was her call. She could take the conversation anywhere she wanted. She sucked in a breath.

"I think I have everything for tomorrow," she said tentatively, just to make sure she was reading him correctly.

"I could come early and help you load stuff if you need me to," Mike offered.

Pressure off. The tension melted from her shoulders and she exhaled softly.

"I think I'm okay." She stacked her silverware and napkin on the empty plate. "I need to wrap up a few loose ends, but other than that, I feel pretty good about it."

She smiled at the girl who brought their check and began to clear their table.

"Mike said you had the best burgers around and I loved the Texas fries."

According to the black script embroidered across the bosom of her pink uniform, the bottle-blonde's name was Kimmie. She gave them both a wide-open grin.

"Thank you, sugar. Hope that means y'all come back real soon."

Mike walked Kate to the front porch and waited while she unlocked the door. She turned to say goodnight.

"I'm glad you had dinner with me tonight. I had a good time." He reached for her hand and gave it a squeeze before releasing it.

"I did too, and thank you again for showing me how to drive a standard. I think I have the hang of it, but we'll find out for sure tomorrow."

"Don't hesitate to call if you think of something," Mike said. Then he took a deep breath.

"You know, I wasn't going to mention it, but that cut on your cheek. From the hailstone. How did you? I mean what?"

He cupped her chin in his hand. Ran his thumb along her cheekbone.

"I only ask because... Well, there's no cut or bruise or anything now."

Crap.

Kate had forgotten all about that. She searched for a plausible response. Of course, there wasn't one. She tried to bluff an excuse.

"Yeah, how weird is that?" she shrugged. "I guess it wasn't as bad as I made it out to be."

Mike's forehead creased, and he opened his mouth as if to make a comment, then stopped, releasing her face slowly.

"Okay. Well, I hope you do great at the flea market tomorrow. I'll try to stop by on my lunch hour. See you then."

"Yeah, see you then."

Kate closed the door behind her, waited until Mike was out of hearing range then pounded her fists against the doorframe. That was a disaster. He knew she was lying, but how could she explain it? Even *she* didn't know how the cut had just disappeared.

Kate yanked her sundress over her head, wadded it up and fast-balled it into the ladder-back chair, causing it to tip back into the wall. Maybe she should have just been honest with Mike about the cut disappearing on its own. Let the chips fall where they may.

Why do I even care?

She wriggled a nightshirt over her head and threw herself onto the bed. He seemed so determined to be around her. Maybe it would have been a good test. She pulled the covers over her shoulder and burrowed further into the bed, sighing.

If he were going to bail sooner or later anyway, now would be the opportune time.

She awoke before sunrise on Saturday morning. Donning her formerly-white-now-muddy-gray Keds, Kate slipped outside to the garden. In predawn hours, it had an ethereal appearance. Tendrils of fog laced in and out of the rows of herbs. The thyme plant's tiny blooms nodded their approval, stirred by the light wind. The crickets and frogs had tired of their moonlight serenade and were silent. The birds hadn't started their morning chatter yet. Peaceful. Just what she needed. It was an important day for her. She wanted to do well. She *needed* to do well. Grandma was counting on her.

She made her way down each row, snipping off tender stalks with Grandma's fabric scissors because she'd misplaced the garden shears. She doused the plants in a bucket of cold water to keep them as fresh as possible. It would've been nice to linger and enjoy the sunrise peeping above the horizon, but she still had work to do before the market opened.

An hour later, Kate stood beside the truck, pleased at her accomplishment. All the dried herbs and sachets were stacked in boxes on the bed. Small Mason jars, filled halfway with cool water, held the fresh clippings. Those were in a box that would ride with her in the passenger seat. She ticked off a mental list of other items she might need.

Oh. I almost forgot.

Kate ran back into the house and removed the Barrett coat-of-arms from the bedroom wall, rolled it up and tucked it under her arm.

The flea market didn't officially open until nine o'clock, but the square was already teeming with activity. Vendors set up their merchandise, arranging their displays while catching up on the weeks' news. The scent of hickory wood and savory meat wafted its way across the parking lot from the barbecue stand. The air was filled with the smell of popcorn, cotton candy, and enthusiasm.

Kate's excitement morphed into misgiving. Her stomach tightened.

I can't do this.

For a minute, she considered turning around in retreat.

You have to; she chastised herself. *For Grandma.*

It reminded Kate of a dream she had once. She was walking down the hallway at her high school, wearing only a bra and panties. That pretty much summed up her feelings under the inquisitive scrutiny of the other merchants that watched her unload the truck. She pasted on what she hoped was a pleasant smile and nodded politely. She recognized a few faces, but they probably didn't remember her. Last time she helped at the flea market she was in Junior High.

A lot had changed since then.

This time her smile was sincere as she congratulated herself over the idea to display the coat-of-arms. She'd just reached up to loop the gold cord over a nail on the back wall when she sensed someone standing behind her.

"Barrett. You must be Pearl's granddaughter."

Kate turned to face a slender man staring down at her from pale gray eyes hooded by bushy, white eyebrows. His chalk-white hair was pulled back into a short ponytail secured with a black ribbon. Translucent flesh stretched tight across his face. His colorless lips were pressed together in a narrow line.

"Yes. She's in the hospital, so I'm—"

"I know where she is." He cut her off. "I make it my business to know. Perhaps I need to introduce myself. I'm the Mayor of Ardee, Darcy MacMurray."

He offered his hand in a half-hearted gesture, drawing back as soon as his fingers touched hers.

The exchange felt awkward. Still, he was the mayor, and she was representing her grandmother.

"It's a pleasure to meet you," she lied. "Thanks for stopping by the booth."

When the mayor made no effort to move, she attempted to politely sidestep. He didn't budge.

Great.

Cornered until he chose to allow her passage.

If the Mayor of Ardee was trying to make her feel uncomfortable, it was working.

His gaze went from the coat-of-arms back to Kate. His eyes squinted into thin slits, and he stooped over until his mouth was inches from her ear. His sour breath and words made her stomach tumble.

"You don't believe that nonsense do you, Miss McKenna? That a family crest reflects the true nature of its legacy? You have a lot to learn, Miss McKenna. A lot to learn."

She should say something. Defend herself. But his unexpected hostility had rendered Kate speechless. Her cheeks went hot, whether, from embarrassment or anger, she wasn't sure. The other merchants, who had stopped to observe the exchange, quickly busied themselves as Mayor MacMurray strode past and disappeared into the city offices on the opposite side of the street.

Peg's booth was adjacent to Kate's. She trundled over with a thermos and poured coffee into a paper cup.

"What in tarnation was that about?"

Kate shook her head and shrugged. Struggled to ignore the teardrops that collected on her eyelashes.

"Well come here and have some of this." Peg patted Kate on the back and handed her a cup of coffee and a napkin to wipe her eyes. "Mustn't let him get the better of you," she soothed. "You hold your head high and do what you need to do. You got a nice setup here, likely to attract a good many folks."

Peg lumbered back to her stall, mumbling to herself as she finished stacking jars of honey on the counter in front of her. Kate caught the words 'mayor shouldn't act like that' and 'better watch himself' and allowed herself a thin smile.

At least one person was on her side.

As the morning progressed, Kate was able to put the confrontation behind her. She enjoyed talking to potential customers, grateful she knew enough to answer most of their questions. Even some of the other merchants, when they realized who she was, approached her, complimented the booth, asked about her grandmother and sent their regards.

About noon, Kate noticed her fellow vendors laying out packed lunches. Why hadn't she thought of that? Her mouth was parched from all the talking, and her stomach rumbled at the smell of hot links and hamburgers sizzling on the grill. Maybe Peg would watch her booth so she could grab a bite to eat. She was about to ask when her peripheral vision caught Mike heading her way.

"Figured you might need these about now," he said, offering a brown paper bag and a Styrofoam cup.

After the lie about her cheek, Kate couldn't believe he was bringing her lunch. She dug into her pocket and pulled out a dollar bill and some change.

"How much do I owe you?"

Mike couldn't have looked more offended if she'd slapped him.

"You don't owe me anything," he said quietly.

"I, uh," Kate rocked back and forth on the balls of her feet. "I'm sorry," she said. "I'm not used to people doing favors for me." She lowered her eyes then looked up at him apologetically. "Thank you. That was awfully kind of you."

Mike gave her an 'aw shucks' grin that let her off the hook for the faux pas.

"You've sold a lot of stuff," he said, glancing around the booth. "Pretty good for a first-timer."

Between bites of her lunch, she told Mike about her morning and the conversation with Darcy MacMurray, still confused by his behavior.

"Why would he make a comment like that about Grandma's coat-of-arms? He was so hostile. And I've never even met him before."

Mike shook his head. "I've never had any dealings with him myself, to be perfectly honest. Guess that doesn't help answer your question."

"Not one to eavesdrop," Peg interjected, leaning against the low wall that separated her booth from Kate's. "But I seem to recall an incident 'bout the time your ma quit college. It was in the spring of her junior year. I believe there might've been some bad blood between Darcy and Kathleen."

Bad blood?

Mom?

Her mother was the nicest person you'd ever know. That didn't seem likely.

She opened her mouth to say so when Mike touched her shoulder.

"I guess I better get back to work. My break is over, and your business is picking up." He gestured towards the women who were checking out the sachets. "I need to get with you about herbs for the pharmacy, so maybe after the market closes we can talk?"

Kate never got another private moment to quiz Peg about what she meant by 'bad blood.' It was definitely something she wanted to delve into at a later date, though.

By the time six o'clock rolled around, Kate was exhausted. But the day had gone well. Peg, toting a cardboard box full of honey jars, stopped long enough to call out, "You did good, missy. Pearl would be right proud of you."

Kate beamed as she gathered the leftovers and carried them back to the truck. All packed, except for the coat-of-arms. Standing on her toes, she reached up to unhook it when a hand closed around hers.

"I can help with that."

Mike's lips grazed her ear when he spoke. She could feel the warmth radiating from his body. Smell the hint of peppermint on his breath. Kate prayed he didn't notice the goose bumps that suddenly popped out on her arms, or the fact that she wobbled when her legs threatened to become licorice whips.

Together, they lowered the tapestry.

"I... I didn't hear you come up," Kate said and fought back against the sensation from last night that started to rekindle inside her.

"You seemed lost in thought." He rolled up the banner, handed it to her. "You must have had a good day. Did you sell it all?"

"Oh, gosh no," Kate's laugh was self-conscious. "The rest is out in the truck if you want to come and pick out what you need."

Mike followed her, and together they sorted through the unsold items.

"Tell you what. I'll buy the whole lot."

She glanced sideways at him. Maybe she didn't have much money, but she wasn't a charity case. And she didn't like the idea of being beholden to anyone. Especially a man. Specifically, *this* one.

Jutting out her chin, she said, "That's not necessary. I'll just put them in storage for next week."

Mike shrugged.

"If that's what you want to do, it's okay by me. It's just that we have a display at the drugstore where we sell dried herbs. And I have this friend who's a chef at the café. He'd probably pay a nice premium for fresh herbs from Mrs. Pearl's garden. She has quite a reputation around town. It's like her stuff is... I don't know how to explain it. It's just – better. But, you know, it's up to you."

Okay, there's proud, and then there's stupid.

This was for Grandma. *Don't be stupid.*

When they finished unloading the boxes at the pharmacy, Kate followed Mike to his office. He pulled the chair out for her then sat down behind the desk and opened a zippered bank deposit bag. Kate scanned the room. The décor was predictable – brown leather chairs, a bookshelf full of medical and pharmaceutical books, a couple of beakers, an old mortar, and pestle. Not so predictable were the shelves devoted to books on stars and astronomy. A sundial and small star chart sat on the edge of his desk.

On one wall, along with his diploma, was a drawing of what appeared to be several stages of the moon. The other wall was the backdrop for a large celestial map, and in the corner a tripod supported an expensive-looking telescope. Kate got up to examine the map.

"It's from the 17th century – a Dutch cartographer, Frederik de Wit," Mike said. "He was famous for drawing and printing maps."

He came to stand beside her.

"The detail, the color, so precise. It's an amazing print."

"What about this one?" Kate pointed to the moon stages.

"Oh, yeah, that's Galileo. Brown ink-wash on watercolor paper. To me, it's the most interesting of Galileo's astronomical renderings. When I look at the moon, I wonder what was going through Galileo's head as he surveyed the lunar features all those centuries ago."

"How about the telescope? You use it often?"

"Sometimes I take it out to the country to get a better view of the sky. It's hard to see anything in town with all the streetlights. There's this spot I go to up north of here, at the state park." He nudged her. "You ever been star gazing?"

"Never. I wonder if Grandma's farm would be a good place to set up a telescope. We should do that sometime."

What happened to keep your distance? Her inner voice scolded.

"How about tomorrow night?" Mike said. "I don't have to work and it's supposed to be a cloudless sky."

Maybe she should take him up on it. Keep her from having to spend the evening alone in the deafening silence. Today, loneliness trumped resolve.

Mike stuffed some cash into an envelope and handed it to her. They walked back to the truck, and he opened the door for her.

"I'd say your first day at the market was quite a success."

Except for that rocky start with the mayor, it had been a great day. Gratitude bubbled up inside her.

"And a large portion of that is due to you," she blurted, and impulsively threw both arms around his neck and gave him a hug.

Mike wrapped his arms around her waist, returning the embrace; but instead of releasing her, he pulled her closer. His lips caressed her neck, trailing up to her face until they pressed against hers. It only lasted seconds. He loosened his hold and took a step back. Kate had to reach out to the truck to steady herself. What was she thinking, throwing herself on him like that? What man wouldn't take that as an open invitation–

"I'll call you later this evening, okay?" Mike said, interrupting her mental rant. "We'll make plans for tomorrow." His tone was so matter-of-fact. As if the kiss was nothing out of the ordinary.

She licked her lips and tasted peppermint. She couldn't think straight with Mike scrutinizing her, waiting for a reply.

"Sure. I, uh, I want to go by and see Grandma first and tell her how the day went. I should be home by eight, eight-thirty."

"Tell Mrs. Pearl I said to get well soon."

Kate crawled into the driver's seat and bent forward, letting her head bang onto the steering wheel. *Geez Louise*, she growled to herself, *why did she keep letting him get to her like that?* She would have continued navel-gazing, but the sound of a loud thump made her raise her head in its direction. The burgundy curtains that shielded the second-story window of the city hall shifted almost imperceptibly. But it was enough to raise Kate's suspicions.

Had someone been watching them?

The hospital was a ten minute drive away. Kate parked near the entrance and reached down to grab her purse off the floorboard. As she straightened, a tall, white-haired man pushed through the revolving door and strode towards the parking lot in her direction. Kate slouched in the seat and buried her head in her handbag, frantically rummaging for a pair of sunglass which she jammed onto her face.

She bowed her head, squeezed her eyes together and implored, *please don't let him recognize me*. Peering through her lashes at the side view mirror, she watched him fold into the Lincoln parked in a space behind her. She stayed hunkered down until the black car was well out of sight.

That was close.

No more encounters with the mayor until she could talk to someone and find out what happened between him and Mom.

On her way to the bank of elevators, Kate passed the gift shop. She paused to look through the window. The lone bouquet of lavenders and pink roses that stood drowning in a sea of stuffed animals and shiny Mylar balloons reminded her of Grandma's backyard. Kate had no choice but to rescue the spray, confident it would boost her grandmother's spirits.

She could barely suppress her excitement as she stepped off the elevator. Grandma was going to be so happy–

"Miss. Oh, Miss."

Kate turned. A nurse hurried down the hallway toward her.

"You're Mrs. McKenna's granddaughter, right?"

She gave a nod as the cadence of her pulse accelerated.

"We tried calling the house, but no one answered. We had to move Mrs. McKenna to the intensive care unit about an hour ago. She was suffering from ventricular arrhythmia and had trouble breathing, so her doctor thought it best."

The nurse paused.

"Your grandmother, honey, she's gone into a coma."

Chapter 4

The color drained from Kate's face.

"We tried to wake her," the nurse said, "but right now she's unresponsive."

"Unresponsive?" The air left Kate's lungs. "She's not..."

"Oh no, her vitals are stable. She's just unresponsive to stimuli. We've got her on oxygen, and we're giving her a saline IV with a broad-spectrum antibiotic. You can see her if you like."

Kate followed the nurse down the corridor and up the elevator to Intensive Care.

"Oh, I'm sorry, but those aren't allowed in the ICU," the nurse apologized.

Kate had forgotten about the bouquet she was unintentionally strangling with her right hand.

"You can have them."

She thrust the flowers at the nurse and pushed against the door.

"You're only allowed to stay for fifteen minutes," the nurse called after her.

Monitors emitted low hums and hisses. Plastic packets, hung from steel posts, carried vital fluids through snaking tubes to the needles in her grandmother's arms. Kate smoothed a wisp of hair from her grandmother's cheek, maneuvering the tubes and wires to hold her hand.

Kate chewed the inside of her lip. Was it true that when a person is in a coma, they can still hear you?

"It's me, Grandma. I came by to tell you things went well at the market today. I sold a lot of stuff and Mike Sheehan, that guy from Clarke's Drugstore, bought the rest. Peg sends her best wishes. So does Margaret Donovan. She dropped by when we were closing. Said you better get well and come home soon... " Kate's voice faltered. She forced a smile through the tears that blurred her vision. "...or her pecan pie was finally going beat yours at the Women's Auxiliary baking contest."

A short time later the nurse stuck her head in the door, reminding Kate her time was up.

"I love you, Grandma, I'll be back soon."

She gave her a kiss on the cheek.

"Please," she pleaded into her grandmother's ear, "please wake up."

Kate leaned her elbows against the hard wooden surface of the kitchen table, her face buried in her hands. A cup of lemon tea sat cold, untouched, on the table beside her. The once-comforting tick of the grandfather clock now amplified the emptiness that added itself to Kate's expanding collection of bruised emotions.

It was so unfair. Just when things were looking up, and Grandma was getting better. Now this. She wrapped her right arm around her waist to try and stop the anguish that had settled like a dull ache in the pit of her stomach.

I can't, she shook her head. *I can't lose her.*

The sudden ring of the phone sent an electric jolt down her spine.

What if?

She choked out her greeting.

"Kate it's Mike. Are you okay?"

She couldn't help herself. A quiet sob answered his question.

"I'm on my way. You can tell me when I get there."

A short while later, headlights lit up the kitchen. Without a word, Kate opened the door and let Mike into the living room.

He turned on the lamp, took Kate's hand, and led her to sit on the couch beside him.

"Why are you sitting here in the dark? Tell me what's wrong."

Tears and words streamed out in one sobbing breath.

"It's Grandma. I stopped in to tell her what a good day I had at the market and when I went to her room they said she was in the ICU and had gone into a coma and she looked so helpless lying there with all the wires and machines and they told me the doctor would call but he hasn't."

The rest came in a hoarse whisper.

"I'm just so scared of losing her. I don't think I can bear to lose another person that I love. I don't think I can bear to be alone."

Mike pulled her close, wrapped his arms around her trembling body. Kate buried her face against his chest, sobbing.

"I'm so sorry, really sorry you're going through this," he said, stroking her hair.

She stayed in his arms longer than she intended. It had been eons since she'd allowed anyone to touch her, much less hold her. And the firmness of his embrace insulated her, at least for a brief moment, from the fears that came crushing in –

Get a grip.

She bolted upright, untangled from his arms and wiped the back of her hand across her face.

"I didn't mean to lose it like that. It's just… She was getting better and now this."

"It's okay, I don't blame you. I can't imagine seeing someone you love in that condition." He smoothed away an errant tear that she missed. "Listen, a couple of the nurses from Memorial come into the pharmacy practically every day. Let me talk to them tomorrow and see if they know anything. Maybe I can ask them to check in on her and update you with any new information."

Next time the phone rang it was the hospital.

"That was Dr. Anderson." She sat on the edge of the couch and laced her fingers through her hair, pressing her palms against her temples. "He was nice and all, but they still don't have any answers as to why she went into a coma. It's the symptoms that are baffling him. Said they didn't make sense considering her medical history. They're running tests to make sure it wasn't induced by a heart attack or stroke, and he mentioned a couple of other possibilities, like blood clots and adverse reactions to drugs. But his initial evaluation doesn't support those ideas."

"What is it about the symptoms and her history that don't jive?" Mike asked.

Her forehead creased, and she chewed the inside of her cheek as she considered what the Doctor said. "He thinks it's highly unusual that someone with no history of heart problems or respiratory issues now has an abnormal heart rate and trouble breathing. They don't expect any test results back until tomorrow, or even Monday since they only have skeleton crews in the labs on the weekend. I guess it's just 'wait and see' for now."

"That's gotta be tough to hear," Mike said. "Is there anything I can do? Have you eaten? Can I go get you something to eat? There isn't a lot you can do right now, but not eating isn't going to help."

"I have zero appetite," Kate confessed. "You know, though, if you haven't had supper, I've got plenty of stuff here we can cook."

Her brows knit together.

"You like fried chicken?"

Fried chicken was comfort food.

Mike joined her in the kitchen. He mashed potatoes while Kate deep-fried the chicken and made cream gravy. Together they cut up tomatoes, cucumbers and lettuce for a salad. By the time they finished they could have fed an army, but that didn't matter.

Cooking had performed its therapeutic duty. Kate found her appetite.

She pulled a crispy chunk off a chicken leg and popped it in her mouth.

"So how'd you get interested in astronomy?" she asked.

"I'm gonna have to blame my dad for that," Mike said. "He bought me a telescope when I was in grade school. Used to take me and my brother, Gary, on camping trips. Just to get outta town so we could see the stars. And he religiously woke us up in the middle of the night every August to watch the Perseid meteor shower."

While they put away the leftovers and cleared the dishes, Mike entertained Kate with bits of astronomy trivia.

"Did you know that if you could put Saturn in a bathtub it would float? That's because it's less dense than water. And a day on Jupiter is only ten hours long – but on Neptune, one year lasts 165 earth years."

He paused long enough to dry off the dinner plates and place them in the cabinet. "They say the number of stars in the universe is greater than the number of grains of sand on all the beaches in the world. That means on a clear night, we can only see the equivalent of a handful of sand."

"How do you know all that stuff?" Kate asked.

"You're gonna laugh."

"I won't, I promise." Kate crossed her heart, smiling.

"Okay. Well when I was, like, a freshman in high school, my parents bought a set of World Book encyclopedias." Mike gave her a lopsided grin. "This is where you find out what a complete nerd I am... but I would lie in bed and read them at night. You know, just started with Volume A and read. I think it took the whole summer to get to Z."

"Aw," Kate punched him lightly in the arm. "That doesn't make you a nerd. It makes you smart. You know a little bit about everything. I kinda like that."

She twisted the kitchen towel in her hands, gathering her nerve to ask the next question.

"Uhm… Can I ask you something? What I mean is…"

Why did awkward get to make up such a big part of my DNA?

Kate took a deep breath.

"Would you like to hang out for a while?"

"Sure." Mike took her hand. Normally, she'd have flinched and found a way to politely remove it from his. But his touch was gentle and consoling. Right now, at this moment, it was exactly what she longed for. Some reassurance that things would be okay. He led her to sit on the couch.

"You know so much about astronomy, why did you become a pharmacist?"

Mike laughed ruefully. "Don't think I haven't asked myself that a hundred times. I guess mostly it had to do with my dad drumming it into my head I needed a job that was worthwhile. A career that would provide a steady living, not something frivolous. And since my grandmother came from a lineage of Irish physicians, I don't know, I thought I might have an aptitude for something medically related."

"Well if you ever decide to quit pharmacy work, you would be a great astronomy teacher."

And he was a great storyteller, too. Kate was satisfied just to let him talk, but soon exhaustion caught up with her. She tried to hold back a yawn, but a little 'meep' sound snuck out.

"Am I boring you?" Mike teased.

"No, not at all. I guess I'm just a little tired."

Mike checked his watch. "Oh man, sorry about that, I didn't mean to stay so long. You're so easy to talk to, and I like spending time with you."

He rose to leave.

Kate stood too, floundering for the right words. This was going to be tough, but she plunged ahead.

"I realize we don't know each other that well but right now the idea of being alone after all this feels unbearable. Could you, could you stay a little longer? Just for a bit?"

She squeezed the arm of the couch and braced for rejection.

Mike's expression softened, and he gave an understanding nod.

"Come over here." He settled back onto the couch, draped his arm across the back, and patted it. "Do you know the story behind the Apollo 13 mission?"

"I know 'Houston we have a problem,' but that's about it."

Kate sat next to him, tucked her feet up under her and rested her head near his shoulder. He began to relate the chain of events that led up to what he considered the most remarkable space flight in NASA history. Before long, Mike's words became a pleasant background hum and Kate allowed her body to droop against his. The last thing she remembered was the comforting beat of his heart as her head nodded against his chest.

She awoke the next morning to the steady tick of the grandfather clock. It took Kate a minute to realize she was still on the couch, a pillow under her head, crocheted blanket tucked around her.

Mike. He must have covered her before he left. She had a vague recollection now of him saying he'd call later. *What time is it?* She glanced at the hands on the clock. After ten. She never slept that late. Pushing the blanket aside, she stretched and experienced the rebellion of muscles unaccustomed to the physical exercise of the past few days. A hot shower and a cup of coffee. That's what she needed. She ambled into the kitchen. On the table was a scribbled note.

"Kate – glad you were able to get some rest. Take it easy today and be sure and let me know if you hear any news about your grandmother. I'll talk to you later." Signed simply, "Me."

She sat at the table and nibbled a piece of toast topped with Grandma's homemade strawberry preserves, plotting out her day. It was Sunday. Most of Ardee's residents were probably at St. Dominic's. Kate felt a pang of guilt. Maybe she should've made an effort to attend Mass. But she couldn't shake the visual associated with the chapel – a rectangular box dripping with red roses.

Instead, she showered and dressed for a visit to Memorial. On her way, Kate contemplated yesterday's events. Almost as disturbing as the news of Grandma's deteriorating health, was Mayor MacMurray's attitude. Why had he been so antagonistic towards her? Maybe Peg knew more than she let on.

The nurse gave Kate the usual warning about the fifteen-minute visit. It was all she could do to be polite, while her head screamed, *"What if it was your grandmother lying here in a coma?"* She glared at the nurse exiting the room.

Kate stroked her grandmother's hair as she reminisced aloud. "Remember the summer I got poison ivy so bad you had to take me to the doctor? He was going to give me a shot with the longest needle I'd ever seen. And you promised that if I didn't cry, you'd buy me an ice cream cone. I tried so hard not to. I think I was more upset about not getting ice cream than I was about the needle." She took her grandmother's hand. "You bought me an ice cream anyway. Said I was the bravest patient you'd ever seen." She gulped back her tears. "Just wake up, Grandma, please wake up and come back to me."

Kate was glad for the half mile walk to Peg's front door. The fragrant blend of wildflowers and fresh cut hay reminded her of summer afternoons that were too hot to do anything but lie on the thick St. Augustine grass and watch the clouds overhead transform. Sometimes they became white steeds outstretched in a gallop or pirate ships that sailed on azure seas, or handsome men, whose features twisted into goblin's faces as they shifted in the breeze. She squinted up at the sky and smiled at the round clouds that marched past in uniform rows looking remarkably like cotton fields ready to harvest. By the time she reached Peg's, most of the dejection she'd felt after leaving the hospital had disappeared; replaced with a smile.

Funny how your brain forges a link between a scent and a memory.

At least these memories were happy ones.

Peg must have seen her coming up the packed dirt driveway. She was standing in the doorway, a big grin on her face.

"Good timing," Peg called out. "I just finished canning some pickles and was about to sit a spell. Whew, I am worn out." She used her faded apron to wipe away the beads of sweat that trickled down her forehead.

"You go ahead and have a seat there. I'll be right out."

Kate sat down on a glider under the enormous red oak tree. Peg brought out a couple of metal tumblers and a pitcher glistening with condensation. She poured a glass of lemonade, handed it to Kate. Then filling her glass, she took a big sip and set the pitcher on a nearby wooden table.

"So how's it goin' missy? How's your grandma?"

Kate relayed the news about her grandmother's coma.

"And you say they can't find a reason why that happened, all of a sudden-like?"

"They've run tests, and nothing has shown up yet. Now we just have to be patient. Maybe she'll come out of it on her own."

"Well you poor thing," Peg clucked, "you've had your run of back luck, that's for sure." She took another chug from the glass. "I get the feeling you didn't just come to talk about your grandma. What's on your mind?"

Knowing the type of person Peg was, Kate took a direct approach.

"Okay. Well, first off – why did you tell me I need to learn more about Irish history?"

Peg settled back in her chair.

"Well, you know, it's like I said before, sometimes a bit of information can help you sort things out. Take our little town, built in 1873 by a group of Irishmen from The Peter's Colony. Named it Ardee, after a town on the banks of the River Dee. We may live on this continent, but our love of Éirinn is still strong."

Peg paused long enough to take another drink and swat away the fly buzzing around her head.

"So, your ma didn't tell you nothing about your ancestors? Your Irish background?"

"She might have mentioned it a few times, but never any real specifics. It didn't seem that important to her."

Peg snorted. "I know Kathleen was trying to run away from a lot of things she didn't care for back here, but you," she paused to lean in towards Kate. Her eyes, which usually looked like they belonged on a Penny Brite doll, narrowed into hawkish slits, "you'd best pay a lot more consideration to your heritage than she did."

Before Kate had time to react, Peg's mood shifted and she launched into tales of Irish lore, accounts of kings and heroes so intertwined it was difficult to sort reality from legend. Peg was a loquacious storyteller. Kate was fascinated by the legends, but it was the folklore that caught her attention.

"Banshee. Aye, that's a name that'll put the fear into you. She be the omen of death." Peg's voice lowered. "Lots of different stories you'll hear about a Banshee. Some say Banshees are seen or heard by one who's about to die a violent death, like murder. I've never heard her mourning call myself, but there's them who swear it's so piercing it can shatter glass. My ma said the Banshee made a sound somewhere between a woman wailing and an owl's moan."

She sat back in her chair again, causing it to bob along with her head.

"They say the Banshee will follow a family until every last descendant has died and been buried. Now you'll hear different opinions 'bout this, but old tradition says a Banshee can only cry for five major clans – the O'Neills, O'Briens, O'Connors, O'Grady's and the Kavanaghs."

Kavanagh. That name again. This visit was beginning to be way more informative than Kate thought it would be when she first sat down.

Peg emptied the pitcher, refilling their glasses. "I ain't boring you, am I? If I am, you just say so, and I'll shut my trap."

Kate shook her head vehemently. "Not at all. In fact, this is pretty fascinating. Please go on."

Peg continued telling stories about shape-changing creatures called Pookas, about the Dullahan – the headless rider who carries his head with him under his arm.

"Like in Sleepy Hollow?" Kate interjected.

Peg's head bounced up and down in agreement.

"Many believe that's who the tale was based on. And then there's the grogoch, bet you ain't heard of him. He's this little elderly man with a full coat of thick reddish hair. Likes to help with planting and harvesting, and housework." Peg paused to chuckle. "The thing is, you gotta beware of the sprites; they mean well, but they'll most likely just get in your way. All you have to do to be rid of him is ask a clergy member to bless the residence. He'll leave to go find someone else to bother.

"Now let me tell you about faeries. The true faeries. They're not tiny little creatures like Tinkerbelle," she scoffed. "They are the Tuatha Dé Danann. Descendants of the goddess Danu they are. Fierce warriors that are beautiful, powerful, hard to resist. Now it's said 'twas after their defeat by the Milesians that they was driven to the Otherworlds to live in Tir na nÓg."

Peg gave a dreamy sigh. "Tir na nÓg – the Land of the Young. It's where sickness and death don't exist. A place of eternal youth and beauty, and happiness that lasts forever. They say sailors and adventurers would stumble across it in their travels. Some folks even today believe there are faeries among us, ones who charm human beings and take them to live in Tir na nÓg. But eh, who knows," she shrugged.

Kate noticed that the shadows were tilting towards the east. She glanced at her watch, so caught up in Peg's chronicles she hadn't realized how much time had lapsed.

"I guess I better get home." She eased off the glider. "But, one more question. Can you tell me what you know about my mom and Darcy MacMurray?"

"Sorry, missy, don't know a whole lot more'n what I told you before. Whilst it's true I do know of Kathleen, we wasn't in the same grade at school. She was two years ahead of me. Smart, beautiful girl. Cheerleader. Homecoming Queen one year, I do believe."

The crease between Peg's brows deepened. "Now Darcy, he and Kathleen were in the same grade. He was different, that's for darn sure. Pale as a ghost. Even as a boy, his hair was white as snow. And them eyes. Almost no color to 'em at all. Darcy suffered his share of ridicule over it, no doubt about that. You know, back in the day, kids weren't as tolerant of them that was different. 'Specially in a small town. Most folks treated him like a freak and the ones that didn't, ignored him altogether. He was quite a loner. Smart boy, but no friends to speak of. Wasn't until they ran into each other at college that your ma and Darcy became friends."

"Wait," Kate stopped Peg, "Darcy and my mom were friends?"

"Oh yes' m, best friends. Thick as thieves they were. Came as quite a surprise that she'd become so tight with an outcast like Darcy McMurray. Kathleen hung with the popular crowd in high school. All they cared about was fast cars and cute boys and being envied by all the rest of us."

Kate thought she heard a taste of bitterness in those words. Peg got a faraway look in her eyes. For a moment, she seemed lost in the past. Her voice softened. "Always wondered why she bothered to hang out with that crowd. She weren't like them other girls. She was one of the few who didn't taunt Darcy. Can't say I recall a time when she was ever mean to him." Her pensive look turned dispassionate. "Again, not entirely sure what happened between 'em to make 'em go their separate ways." Then she shook her shoulders, and her mood suddenly switched to jovial. "Better hand in my gossip card if I can't do better'n that, right?" she chuckled and slapped her thigh.

"It's okay, you've helped a lot." Kate leaned over and gave Peg a squeeze. "Thanks for everything."

Kate sat on the porch, arms across her chest, staring out over the cotton field that neighbored her grandmother's property. Peg's comment about her mom being a cheerleader had awakened a recollection – Mom's cedar chest. It was where she'd kept keepsakes and memorabilia. Kate had stumbled upon it when she was a child. She'd started to rummage through the contents when Mom caught her. She slammed the lid down and ordered Kate never to touch her things again with asking. It was the only time Kate recalled seeing her mother truly angry.

It was after the funeral when Kate was going through her mother's things that she rediscovered the chest, hidden in the back of the closet. A rusty combination lock secured its contents. Kate remembered the day like it was yesterday.

She dragged the heavy chest out into the middle of the room. No matter that it left slender, claw-like scars as it scraped across the polished hardwood floor, rasping loud enough that the old windbag in the apartment downstairs thumped the floor with her broom handle – something she was known to do anytime Kate made a noise louder than a whisper. Kate was tempted to stomp her feet around a few times; the visual of Mom's disapproving scowl was the only thing that stopped her. Instead, she plopped down, cross-

legged in front of the chest and began to stare at it. The longer she stared, the more she could feel the rage inside begin its slow crawl up her spine, across her shoulders and down her arms, pulsating past her wrists until her fingertips started to itch and burn. Her vision narrowed, focused on the lock. It was her enemy. A nickel plated guardian with a black-and-white face. One more barrier to keep her from her mother. As if death wasn't enough, now this piece of metal and plastic was bent on denying her access to the only things she had left to connect her to the best friend she ever had...

Kate closed her eyes. *One, two three*, she began to count, slowly inhaling and exhaling in measured breaths. A trick she'd learned from one of the tried-and-failed grief counselors who'd attempted to help her deal with her mother's death.

Deal with, they'd said. What did they know? She had made sure to ask that question early on in the sessions, and their answers were unanimous. None of them had ever lost a parent. They could only spout platitudes and talk about using the right 'tools' to help her cope. She shuddered at the word. *Tools?* More like smoke and mirrors. Illusions that made everyone on the outside think she had come through just fine, while on the inside...

"We're done," she said aloud. Slamming the door on her rambling thoughts, Kate headed into the kitchen to pour herself a tall glass of ice-cold Coke.

With nothing better to do and time to kill before Mike came over, Kate decided to investigate the structure across the creek. She slipped into jeans and a long-sleeved denim work shirt, grateful for the added protection as she clawed through the brush and vines that blocked the path to the stream. After a few yards, the overgrowth thinned.

I can't believe it's still here.

The wooden bridge that spanned Boyd Creek.

She put her foot out to test it. Still solid. She ran her hands over the railing, worn smooth over the years. Her fingers found the initials she'd carved into the solid oak. She took another step. A family of turtles, who'd been sunning themselves on a nearby log, slipped into the water, disturbed by her unwelcome intrusion. As she crossed slowly, a flood of nostalgia washed over her. Kate had discovered the bridge the summer she turned ten. Grandma contrived a pole for her out of bamboo and kite string. Using a chunky piece of bacon threaded onto a safety pin, she'd spent endless afternoons, dangling it over the edge, waiting for the red and white bobber to disappear. If the catfish or crappie she caught were keepers, she'd bring them home, and Grandma would fry them up with a batch of onion rings for supper.

When she was a child, it seemed like the bridge had gone on forever. From an adult perspective, it only took a few steps, and she was on the other side. Several more strides brought Kate to the front of the building shrouded by ancient pecan trees. An old greenhouse. Abandoned, if the crooked door and broken terra cotta pots containing rotting plants were any indication.

How could she have missed this before?

One furtive peek around – no 'posted' signs as far as she could see. She gave the doorknob a turn. Didn't seem like it was locked, just a little rusty and stubborn. Another jiggle and she pushed the door open enough to slip inside.

It was like stepping into the canvas of a Matisse. The sunlit room was drenched with every pigment imaginable. Kate walked the path that ran its length, taking in the splendor. Boxlike containers overflowed with begonias, nasturtiums, bluebonnets, petunias and poppies. Baskets filled with impatiens, fuchsia, and verbena hung from the rafters, their blossoms cascading over the sides like rainbow waterfalls. One plot was devoted to roses of various colors and varieties. Cross-vines crawled up the support beams. Their tendrils spiraled towards the roof, showing off their orange trumpet-shaped blooms. The delicate, wax-like petals of pink and white orchids bobbed a floral welcome as she passed by. In the back of the greenhouse lime, apple, and lemon trees grew in old whiskey barrels. Tiny fruit hung like emeralds, rubies, and topaz from their branches. And the fragrance. Kate filled her lungs with the scent. Better than the perfume aisle at a department store.

The sound of squeaking door hinges shattered the enchantment.

Reminded her that she was on someone's private property without permission.

Her eyes flicked around the room, told her what she needed to know.

That 'someone' was heading her way, and there was only one way out.

The front door.

Great.

"Hello? I know you're in here. Show yourself," the 'someone' commanded in a deep voice.

She crouched beside the trees and tried to think up a graceful explanation. But graceful was not her forte. Especially when trapped. Best to just come clean and hope the guy was understanding.

She straightened, red-faced, and started babbling as she walked toward him.

"I'm so sorry. I live in the house behind here, across the creek. It's my grandmother's house, and I saw this building from our garden. I thought it was abandoned but when I got inside, it's just so beautiful, and I wanted to see it all and... Well, anyway, I apologize. I'll leave now."

She halted in front of the man she assumed was the owner. Six-foot-four at least. Dark brown, wavy hair curled around his ears and down the collar of his shirt. The prominent ridge above his eyebrows gave him the appearance of scowling, although he didn't seem to be angry. He had a slender, chiseled nose, high cheekbones, and full lips. Impossible to tell his age. His face was smooth except for the deep laugh lines that curved, like tiny crescent moons, on either side of his mouth.

He wasn't what she'd call an 'attractive' man, yet Kate found herself mesmerized.

He studied her too, with one brow lifted.

"You are Pearl's granddaughter. That would make you – Katherine," he said.

"I...I am," she stuttered, momentarily distracted by his lyrical accent. "But you have me at a disadvantage. You are?"

"Robert Doyle Kavanagh."

Tiny shockwaves traced their way through Kate's nervous system and made the tips of her fingers tingle.

Kavanagh?

Chapter 5

Robert Kavanagh's sapphire eyes locked with Kate's.

Intense. Unwavering.

Like playing a visual game of 'chicken.'

Kate was the first to swerve.

She looked down at her feet. Shoved her hands in her pockets.

"I'm sorry, I didn't... I mean, I hope you aren't mad at me for trespassing."

"Trespassing," he repeated.

Kate raised her head. Robert stroked his jawline. He appeared to be thinking.

"Well, you don't strike me as a hooligan. I'm sure you meant no harm. Indeed, I'm flattered that you were interested in my greenhouse. Come along then," Robert waved his hand. "Let's start at this end and I will tell you about my plants, and you can ask any question you like."

She walked alongside, only half-listening to his words, much more interested in her host than the plants. Now and then she'd steal a sideways glance. She had the weird sensation she'd seen him before. She just couldn't place where. When he paused to pull a couple of dandelions out of the petunia bed, Kate spoke up.

"So… how come you know who I am?"

"Do seanmháthair," he began, then stopped. A slow smile creased his face. "Forgive me. I sometimes forget I'm not at home. What I meant to say was your grandmother, the kind lady, spoke of you when I met her after acquiring this property. She showed me your picture. Told me about all the summers you spent with her." His voice softened. "Aye, I could see she loves you dearly."

Kate frowned, unsure about this stranger who knew more about her than she did about him. It put her on the defensive. She lifted her chin. Challenged him with her eyes.

"Yeah, well I used to fish off that old bridge," Kate used his words with emphasis, "all the summers I spent with her. And I don't ever remember seeing this greenhouse before."

"I would imagine not." Robert's laugh was deep and musical. "I only recently discovered the framework myself. It was obscured by moss and vines. But the underlying structure is stable. It simply took a wee bit of patience and labor to get it back into working condition. And it's perfect for my needs. Secluded. Quiet. And nobody knew about it," he said pointedly, "until now."

Kate couldn't handle that piercing blue stare.

They had reached the front of the greenhouse.

She grabbed the door handle.

"Really, I'm sorry. I promise I won't disturb you again."

Robert's hand closed around hers.

Was it her imagination, or did tiny sparks flicker off his fingertips?

She brushed the thought away with the shake of her head.

"On the contrary," he said. "I'm pleased to find someone interested in my flowers."

He gave the knob a turn and pulled open the door for her.

"It was a pleasure to meet you, Katherine McKenna."

Kate brooded over Robert Kavanagh all the way back to the house. Why did that last name keep popping up? And she was skeptical about his greenhouse story. But how could she argue? So much weird stuff was going on right now; he could be telling the truth. Then there was the nagging feeling that she'd met him before.

Too many questions, not enough answers.

At nine o'clock she opened the door and met a smiling Mike, telescope in one hand, picnic basket and quilt in the other. They walked together to a clearing near the cattle pond. Mike spread the quilt and positioned the telescope at its edge.

They watched as the sun bowed her exit, throwing kisses of orange and pink upward before she disappeared behind the cobalt curtain spattered with twinkling diamonds.

Mike pulled a bottle of chilled chardonnay out of the picnic basket.

"You are old enough for this, right?"

Kate resisted the urge to roll her eyes.

"I turned twenty-one last week. And you know they changed the legal drinking age to eighteen in '73, right? Besides," she scrutinized him, "you aren't that much older than me, are you?"

Mike popped the cork out of the bottle.

"Not that much."

He filled both glasses halfway and handed one to Kate.

"This is such a great night to see the constellations. Look," he pointed, "there's Libra. The scales, like in astrology. So your birthday was last week. That makes you a Gemini. Duel-natured, complex, conflicted between emotion and intellect. When I studied astronomy, I dabbled in astrology too."

"At least you didn't start with 'what's your sign'?"

Mike threw back his head and laughed. "No. I hope I'm not that obnoxious. You know, I do find the study interesting. There's a modicum of truth there, whether you want to believe it or not. And in case you're wondering, I'm a Libra. We're easygoing, sociable, romantic and charming."

"Oh brother," she said, but couldn't smiling at his little Cary Grant imitation at the end.

Mike scooted to the edge of the quilt near the telescope. "That's Ursa Minor – the Little Dipper." He pointed out the larger body in the formation. "That star at the end of the handle, that's Polaris, the North Star. It's the brightest star in the constellation. A supergiant – those are the most luminous stars." Mike grabbed her hand, pulling her closer to him while he positioned the telescope for her. "And if you think that's something, wait 'til you see the moon."

She caught a faint scent of patchouli, felt the heat of his body through her thin, cotton shirt as his arm circled her shoulder to adjust the telescope. How was she supposed to concentrate on the moon when her thoughts were orbiting around the body sitting next to her?

Mike lay back on the quilt, arms behind his head, searching the heavens.

"What are you looking for?" Kate asked.

"Shooting stars. If you see one, be sure and make a wish."

Kate smiled and took a sip of wine.

"So, tell me more about yourself," Mike said. "You say you moved around a lot. Why was that?"

"Not really sure." She chewed on her bottom lip and considered his question. "I always thought maybe Mom just had a restless streak. Or maybe she couldn't decide what she wanted to do with her life, so she did whatever struck her at the time. I'm sure she had her reasons, but it was rough on a little kid sometimes."

Mike's brow creased. "How so?"

Kate shifted on the quilt and began inspecting it, picking at a stray thread.

"I was relatively shy, then add the torture of always being the new kid. Always the outsider. It was hard to make friends because we never stayed long enough in one place to put down any roots. " She shrugged. "Anyway, I guess that's why it was always such a big deal to come back here during the summer. Grandma was my rock. She gave some stability to my inconsistent world."

Kate lifted her head. Mike was studying her face.

"What?" she asked defensively.

"Oh, nothing. Just thinking."

"Thinking what?"

"Thinking I wish I could tell that insecure little girl that she doesn't have to be an outsider. That it's okay to let people in. That there's someone right here who would love to be her friend."

This wasn't where she thought the conversation would go.

Tears welled up and threatened to spill onto her cheeks.

"Hey," Mike sat up and took her hand. "I didn't mean to say anything wrong."

"It's not you," she said softly.

Mike scooted closer, cupped her chin in his hand, coaxing her to look at him.

"I know this is a rough time for you. And I'm not going to pretend that I know what you're feeling. But I do want you to understand that I am here for you. In whatever way you need me."

His eyes searched hers. Eyes full of tenderness. Eyes that begged her to give him a chance. Without thinking, she leaned into him. Mike lowered his head, his lips pressed softly to hers. Her heart raced, and her breath caught in her throat. Abruptly, she pulled away, apologizing.

"I'm sorry. I don't know what I was thinking. You were… and I…"

Mike put a finger to her lips.

"Stop it, will you? You don't have to apologize for how you feel. And I'm sure not gonna apologize for how I feel. I think you're a smart, beautiful woman, and I want to spend time with you. As much time as you'll let me." His lips skimmed her cheek. "However, I do have to work tomorrow, so I probably need to head home."

Later, as she lay in bed, Kate considered Mike's words. He had sure tapped into something deep with his comment about the insecure little girl. How could he have known that was exactly how she felt? It was a scary feeling. She'd never opened up to anyone like that before and–

Keep your distance, her brain reminded her again, *he can't hurt you if you don't care.*

But he was so sweet and so determined to get to know her better. And she couldn't deny the physical attraction.

This was crazy-making.

She punched her pillow with her fist, then buried her face in it, fighting to quell her impassioned mental bickering. No wonder it was past midnight before she finally got the voices in her head to stop arguing so she could get some sleep.

Kate woke, gasping for air.

The dream was always the same.

She was four, maybe five years old. Her mother was walking down the sidewalk to the bus stop. Kate stretched out her arms to restrain her, keep her from leaving. But she was just out of reach. She tried to call out for her mother to stop, but only managed a squeak. Her attempts to run and catch up were useless; her feet anchored to the ground by some unknown force. It ended with little Kate standing there. Left behind. Heartbroken, as the bus took her mother away.

Silent tears dampened her pillow. The dream always left her feeling empty and frightened. Why tonight? Was that her psyche's way of reminding her how much it hurts to lose someone you love? And if so, was she willing to risk those feelings again?

The next morning's overcast pall with its steady beat of raindrops enticed Kate to snuggle under the covers longer than she ordinarily would. Mike had given her his business card last night with his home phone number written on the back.

"Call me tomorrow," he'd said after giving her a brief goodnight kiss.

He was working today, so she sure wasn't going to call him at the pharmacy. On the other hand, Peg had suggested Kate read up on history. Maybe she'd start with the history of Ardee. The library would surely have archived newspapers or journals she could search. And if she were already in town on another errand, it wouldn't seem out of place to drop in at Clarke's and say hi to Mike, would it?

How old are you?

Still, after her shower she chose a lime-green knit top and hip-hugger shorts. Spent a little extra time applying her makeup and arranging her hair. Good thing the Nova was under the carport. For now, she could avoid the rain shower.

By the time she got to Ardee, the precipitation had slowed to a light drizzle. At least she wasn't soaked when she entered the library. A tall lady with a salt-and-pepper perm stood at the front desk sorting a stack of index cards.

"May I help you?" she asked without raising her head.

"Yes, please. I was wondering, what would be the best way to find out about Ardee and its history?"

Mrs. Stewart, as the nametag identified her, looked up from her filing. "Our microfiche machine. It has information dating back to the twenties. I believe we even have a few documents from the late 1800's. Mostly pictures I think. Come with me, please."

After a brief rundown on how to work the machine, Mrs. Stewart left Kate to sift through the drawer of slides. They were stored in envelopes, arranged by year. She picked one out. 1923. A good place to start. The year Grandma began her diary.

She found an article dated July tenth about the Founder's Day celebration, accompanied by several blurry photographs, but she didn't recognize her grandmother in any of them. Switching to the envelope of slides marked 1924, she spotted a small blurb in the society section.

Mr. and Mrs. Edgar Barrett announce the engagement of their daughter, Pearl Jean, to Aidan Kavanagh of Leinster, Ireland. A wedding date has not been set at this time, but we extend our best wishes for a bright future to the happy couple.

Kate sat back in the chair. Her grandmother was engaged to Aidan? So that was probably the terrible decision she had to make. About breaking it off with him. And that must have been the reason for his note begging her to reconsider.

She scoured several more years' worth of slides and found an article from the fall of 1929 about Pearl McKenna, who had recently joined Memorial Hospital as their nursing administrator. The picture showed her grandmother, lips pressed into a thin line, dressed in her starched white uniform, standing stiffly beside a man Kate recognized as her grandfather. She thought of the picture in the diary. What had caused the transformation of Pearl Barrett from 1924 into Pearl McKenna of 1929? She was convinced the answer lay in those missing diary pages. Maybe her search was at a dead-end but her curiosity wasn't.

As long as she had access, Kate decided to look up another date. January 15, 1933.

Mr. and Mrs. Thomas McKenna announce the arrival of their daughter, Kathleen Barrett McKenna. Miss Kathleen weighs a healthy 7 lbs. 3 oz. and is 21 inches long. Congratulations to the McKenna family.

Kate's features softened. She touched the screen with her fingertips.

Mom, I miss you so...

Then her posture stiffened.

Don't go down that rabbit hole, Kate. Back to business.

She reached into her purse for a pencil and notebook to write down the date of her grandmother's engagement when she noticed him standing at Mrs. Stewart's desk.

Darcy MacMurray.

She gave a slight shudder and hunched over the microfiche machine, praying he would leave. Moments later the sound of footsteps ricocheted off the hard wooden floor, announcing his approach.

"Well, if it isn't Miss McKenna. A pleasure to see you again."

Sarcasm.

Kate was fluent in that language.

She rotated in the chair and opened her mouth to respond, but Darcy's gaze skimmed over her head, fixating on the microfiche screen.

"Now, isn't that sweet. Looking up mommy's birth announcement? And what other kinds of information are we attempting to glean from history today?"

He snatched at the pile of envelopes, riffled through the transparencies then tossed them onto the table, carelessly scattering them across the highly polished surface. Kate scrambled to corral the slides, but the mayor's icy grip stopped her. Her heart and shoulders flinched as his fingers pressed deep into her skin. He pulled her around to face him.

"You know what they say, don't you dear?"

Kate shrank back into her chair, eyes wide, vocal chords immobilized by his unexpected assault. Darcy's features contorted into a contemptuous smile. He leaned forward, and in sotto voce said, "Don't ask the question if you aren't prepared for the answer." Then he turned on his heel and stalked from the room, pulling the door shut with a crash that reverberated throughout the entire library.

Kate's scalp tingled. *Where was Mrs. Stewart during all this?*

The librarian had vanished. Kate fumbled to reorganize the slides and snatching up her bag, deposited the box on the front desk on her way out.

The drizzle was now a downpour. Kate didn't care. She crossed the street. Didn't notice the oncoming car until it skidded to an abrupt halt and honked. She waved an apology and sloshed through the running water to step onto the opposing sidewalk.

She sought shelter under the awning of Callie's Closet. Pressing her back against the wall, she took several deep breaths and tried to collect her thoughts.

No, she blinked away the drops that started to form on her eyelashes, *I refuse to be a victim of whatever mind game Darcy MacMurray is playing.*

Up ahead, the Clarke's Drugstore sign beckoned. She pulled open the glass door. Ordinarily, the blast of cold air would have been welcome in the June heat. Drenched to the skin as she was, it made her teeth chatter. She headed to the soda fountain at the back and sat down on a red-vinyl stool. The fountain clerk behind the counter stopped in the middle of filling salt shakers and cast a glance in her direction.

"I'd like a cup of coffee, please."

She fished a compact out of her purse and began blotting under her eyes. She looked up to see the teenager cemented in place. Kate followed his gape to her knit top, clinging to her breasts and stomach. She might as well have been naked.

"Now please?"

After that run-in with the mayor, Kate didn't have any patience left for teenage boys with raging hormones. She grabbed a handful of napkins, dabbed at the saturated material in an attempt to regain some modesty.

"You're soaked."

Mike kissed Kate's cheek.

She tilted her head. Gave him a look.

"Like I didn't know this?"

Mike laughed.

"Be right back."

The pimply-faced clerk placed a steaming mug of black coffee in front of her. She took a sip. Felt a bit better. Warmer anyway.

The clerk propped his elbows on the counter and leaned closer to her.

"Anything else I can do for you?" he said with a salacious grin.

In your dreams, Kate started to say, when she caught the familiar whiff of patchouli. Mike moved in protectively behind her.

"Back off, Jake." His words carried a threat. "It's not polite to harass the customers."

Jake stood erect and apologetic.

"Sh...sh...sure...sure man," he stuttered. "Hey, uh, don't mention this to my grandpa, okay? I need this job."

He retreated to the far end of the counter.

Kate stifled a laugh and rotated the stool to face Mike.

"You scared the crap out of that kid."

"Serves him right. Jake's a jerk, but he's George's grandson, so we tolerate him."

He held out a long sleeved, oxford-cloth shirt. She slipped her arms into it. The shirt swallowed her. She caught Mike suppressing a chuckle.

"I know it's too big, but at least it will keep you drier until you can get home and change. Here, let me help."

Mike lifted her arm so he could roll up the sleeve that draped past her hand.

"What happened here?"

Her wrist was red. Fingertip-shaped bruises dotted her forearms from the mayor's grip. She didn't feel like explaining. All she could think to do was play ignorant.

"I don't know," she gave him a wide-open, innocent look. "Must've done it while I was gardening."

"You need to be more careful." He moved a strand of damp hair from her cheek. "And you know, we sell umbrellas. Might want to pick one up before you leave today."

He winked at her.

After what she'd just been through with Darcy, Mike's comments rubbed her the wrong way. Condescending and very unfunny.

"Thanks for the advice," was her terse reply, and she jerked away from his reach.

Regret was instant when she recognized the shadow of hurt that crossed his face.

"I'm sorry, that was rude," she said. "I just...I'm not having a good morning, I guess."

"Well, there's your problem." His tone was forgiving. "It's not morning anymore. It's past noon. Have you had lunch yet?"

Kate shook her head, gave a slight chuckle.

"You're always concerned about my eating habits. No, I haven't had lunch, but I'm not hungry right now. This cup of coffee will be fine."

"Huh uh. Tell you what, I'm due for a break, why don't you go sit there and I'll bring you exactly what you need."

Kate picked up her mug and sat down at the small table. Glad to be away from Jake, who, even after Mike's warning, continued to sneak furtive glances in her direction.

Like I said – teenage boys and hormones.

She took another sip of coffee and looked over the cup's brim, just in time to see Mike carrying a large glass bowl filled with the most decadent ice cream sundae Kate had ever seen. Chocolate syrup drizzled down the sides, and plump maraschino cherries topped the artful flourishes of whipped cream. Multi-colored sprinkles and tiny chocolate chips spattered across it like confetti. He'd even scrounged up a couple of those little yellow plastic monkeys, the ones they put on the edge of the drinks from the drive-in. Positioned them in the middle of a mountain of fluffy topping.

Mike pulled up a chair to sit beside her.

"Your favorite from the soda fountain your mom worked at, right?"

She tried to get a grasp on her composure but had little success.

"I'm sorry," she shook her head helplessly and apologized. "I can't believe you remembered."

Mike reached across the table, running his thumb along her cheek to brush away one of the tears she'd fought so hard to contain.

"Of course I remembered. I remember everything you tell me. God, Kate, don't you know how much I like you?"

She made a pretense of examining the sundae. Didn't know how to respond. After a moment, she met his eyes and said softly, "I guess I'm beginning to."

The service bell sounded. Mike looked over his shoulder at the drug counter where an elderly couple waited.

"Sorry about that. Call me later? I get off work at six."

Kate nodded and took a few more bites of the sundae. Even if she'd had an appetite, she would never have been able to eat the whole bowlful. She left a dime and a nickel on the table for her coffee. With her hand on the door, she looked back at the pharmacy. Mike grinned and nodded towards the cardboard container that held colorful Totes umbrellas. Kate pointed at her clothes, mouthed "too late now," and waved goodbye.

The minute she got home, Kate took a shower. Tried to scrub away the scent of Darcy's tobacco-saturated suit that lingered in her nostrils as a repugnant reminder of their encounter. She slipped into her cutoffs and threw on her favorite t-shirt, one she'd had since high school – tie-dyed with a big green peace sign. Her private rebellion against MacMurray's hostility.

As an afterthought, Kate slipped on Mike's shirt. She buried her face in the sleeve, inhaling deeply. It smelled of starch and a hint of aftershave. A tiny lump bulged in the left pocket. She reached in and pulled out a wrapped peppermint candy. It reminded her of his kisses. She tore off the cellophane and popped it into her mouth with a goofy grin. Then she crawled onto the bed, propped herself up on the pillows, and retrieved her grandmother's diary from the nightstand.

> *August 31 – I must spend the day packing. Father is driving me to school this afternoon, as my first day of class begins tomorrow. Aidan came to see me last night. We spent an enjoyable time together. I must admit, but only to you, Dear Diary, that I am beginning to develop strong feelings for him. I find myself slipping the ring he gave me on my left hand, exactly as he said I would. It is as though I am compelled to wear it. Not in public, though, I fear Father and Mother's reaction. They seem to like him well enough, but I sense trepidation from them. Perhaps it's not Aidan himself; maybe they would hesitate to relinquish their only daughter to anyone. Only time will tell.*

Kate devoured the next few pages, imagining herself in Pearl Barrett's world. It was like reliving a piece of history. Her grandmother wrote about the hospital and nursing classes. About friends and patients. Most of the entries, though, were about her and Aidan.

> *December 26 – After I finished work this evening, I stepped outside for a breath of fresh air before dinner. I noticed someone standing beside a pale yellow car in the parking lot of our dorm. It only took me a second to recognize him – and it was all I could do to keep from running to him and throwing myself into his arms. But of course, any inappropriate*

behavior on my part would alert the administration. I motioned him towards the archway that led to hospital kitchen, away from the prying eyes of the staff. I was incredibly happy to see Aidan. He held my face in his hands and kissed both cheeks and my forehead. He called me his darling and admitted he was unable to stay away from me any longer. We talked for a brief time, knowing that his presence would lead to my immediate expulsion if we were found. Before he left, he put a small box in my pocket and told me to open it when it was safe. 'It's a wee Wren Day present,' he said. 'In Ireland we celebrate St. Stephen, and I have given you a gift to commemorate the occasion.' And with that he gave me another quick hug and was gone.

I waited for him to leave and then opened the little box. It held a small gold coin, a bird's feather, and, wrapped in a small piece of cotton batting, a beautiful silver locket. An intricate design of woven knots adorned the outside. The small clasp opened to reveal space inside to store a photograph, or perhaps a curl of hair. Under all this was a note, which I put away to read later.

A silver locket with intricate knots?

Kate pulled a black velvet bag out of the dresser drawer. Loosening the drawstring, she angled it until the contents fell into her hand. As she opened the locket, she could hear Mom saying, "This belonged to your grandmother who gave it to me on my sixteenth birthday, and now it's yours."

The picture inside captured the sparkle of Mom's personality as she nuzzled the chubby cheek of the little pale-haired girl with a crooked smile. Kate touched the likeness of her mother. She didn't try to hold back the tear that trickled its way down her face, as she unclasped the chain and looped it around her neck. She crawled back onto the bed and picked up the diary.

The next few months' writings were brief. Kate was down to the last couple of entries before the distraught June message.

> *May 20 – Today my joy is unspeakable. Aidan has asked me to marry him, and I have accepted.*
>
> *In June, we are taking a trip to visit his Aunt and Uncle in St. Louis. I am very excited about it. Aidan gave me a posh steamer trunk as an engagement present. He said it came from a famous French designer, Louis Vuitton. He told me he'd met Louis at an international exhibition in Paris in 1857. I laughed out loud and reminded him that he would have to be at least 66 years old now to remember such an event. He grinned and slapped his knee, probably amused that I caught onto his joke. He must come from a delightful family. It will be wonderful to meet Aidan's relatives. I want to get to know them as well as he knows mine.*

It didn't make sense.

What had happened between May and June that caused her grandmother to change her mind about marrying Aidan?

Kate hung Mike's shirt on the bedpost and opened the French doors. The rain had stopped, and the air held an earthy, clean smell. For the second time, Kate had to scoop rainwater out of the hollows before she could sit on the stone. It dribbled down her wrists and forearms and dotted her shirt with splotchy patches, but she didn't care. It made her feel better to be outside on her rock, slumped against the tree; a silent observer as the mockingbird and blue jay overhead battled for possession of the willow. A warm breeze rippled its leaves and blew loose tendrils of hair away from her face.

She studied her wristwatch. Mike asked her to call him after six. How long after six?

Social ineptitude was such a curse.

She was heading to the house when the phone rang.

"Hey." Mike's voice sounded warm. Smiley. "I have to work late tonight. Mr. Clarke wanted to do an inventory check and said it may be midnight or later before we finish. But the good news is he gave me tomorrow off, so I wondered if maybe I could swing by and pick you up? We could go to the state park and go swimming, grill some burgers or hot dogs. Think you might be interested?"

"Well, I was gonna… "

Kate paused. She didn't have a reason to say no. Wasn't sure she wanted to. She peeked out the kitchen window and saw her excuse.

"I was gonna mow the yard tomorrow."

"Mowing?" Mike chuckled. "You would rather mow the yard than go to the lake?"

It did sound pretty lame.

"How about this?" he countered. "How about if I help you mow, then we go for a swim?"

No way she could argue around that.

"Make *you* a deal," she said. "If you mow the yard, I'll buy the stuff for our cookout."

At least that way it didn't feel so much like a date.

See? She mollified her subconscious; *I'm trying to protect us.*

"I'll be there around ten tomorrow morning," he said.

She wrapped the kinked phone cord around her finger. "Okay, I better let you get back to work."

Hesitation from Mike's end. Kate got the idea he wasn't quite ready to end the conversation. Finally, he spoke up. "Yeah, okay, see you tomorrow."

It had been one of those nights. She was bone-tired but unable to stop the thoughts that tossed around in her head like a feather in a hurricane. Last time she'd checked, it was after two a.m.

Now barely sunrise, she was already wide awake.

She groaned out loud.

I probably look great. Dark circles from lack of sleep...

Remembered her brush with the mayor.

... plus these ugly bruises where Darcy grabbed me...

She brought her wrist up to her face.

Her rambling mental soliloquy ceased.

The bruises. Just like the cut on her cheek.

Gone.

Chapter 6

This was getting bizarre.

Why did her injuries keep healing so fast?

Possible theories ranged from 'I'm losing my mind' to 'aliens visited during the night', but Kate didn't have an answer. Not one that made sense anyway. She chose the Scarlett O'Hara approach. One she adopted fairly soon after her mother's accident.

I can't think about that right now. If I do, I'll go crazy. I'll think about it tomorrow.

Besides she didn't have time to dwell on it. She still had to shower, dry her hair, put on makeup, get dressed, run to the grocery store to get the food for the cookout, pack her bathing suit–

"Oh my gosh," she moaned, "I didn't bring my suit with me."

So now, to top it all off, she was going to have to stop in at Callie's Closet. Otherwise, it would be cutoffs and a halter top. Callie's didn't open until nine. She'd be cutting it close to get back to the house and gather all her stuff together before Mike got there.

She arrived at the grocery store with list in hand, checking it off as she tossed the items into the basket. Buns, hot dogs, mustard, mayo. No onions. Didn't want bad breath. Dill and sweet relish, because people can be real picky about what kind of relish they like on their hot dog. Potato chips? Corn chips? She had no idea what

Mike liked, so she grabbed a bag of both. Charcoal, lighter fluid, paper plates and napkins, what else? Oh yeah, drinks. Kate chose a carton of Cokes. Didn't everyone like Cokes?

She deposited the sack of groceries onto the back seat of her car and crossed the street, checking her watch. Five minutes until nine. As luck would have it, when she arrived the lights were on, the door unlocked.

Callie herself was at the checkout counter, threading receipt tape.

"Hi there sweetie! Anything I can help you with?"

"Yes, ma'am. I need a bathing suit. If you can just tell me where they are..."

Apparently, Kate did not know how Callie and her Closet worked.

"Let's see," she calculated. "You're slender. But kinda tall. Maybe 130 pounds? And I'm guessing what --- size 11? Come take a look at these."

Callie personally escorted her to the small rack of swimwear.

Right away Kate skipped past the string bikinis. The one-piece suits all resembled something her grandmother would wear. She decided on a compromise, a pale yellow baby-doll style with an apron of crocheted lace.

Bikini with a touch of modesty, Kate laughed to herself. Until she picked up the price tag. Then she cringed.

But Callie nodded in approval.

"That'll look good with your dark hair and complexion."

Kate viewed her reflection in the dressing room mirror and agreed. She selected a large beach towel and a striped beach bag and thanked Callie for her help. Happy that it had taken as little time as it did. Not so happy that she had used up almost all the money in her wallet. She hurried to the car and reached for the door handle.

Oh dear god, not again.

Mayor MacMurray walked down the sidewalk towards her.

Kate deposited her bundle onto the passenger seat and slipped behind the wheel.

Wasn't quite fast enough.

He grabbed the top of the car door to prevent her from shutting it.

"Miss McKenna, I need a minute of your time."

After the confrontation at the library, Kate assumed that any further dealings with the mayor were not going to be pleasant. She braced herself for this new attack.

Summoning a feeble smile, she replied, "Yes, sir?"

"There seems to be an issue regarding some of the items you sold at the flea market last Saturday. I need you to come by my office tomorrow morning at eleven. It appears you might have a serious problem on your hands. In Ardee, we frown upon lawbreakers such as you."

She stared after his receding figure. What could she have possibly done for him to accuse her of breaking the law? She slammed her hand on the steering wheel. Threw the gearshift into reverse, doing her best to bridle the urge to burn rubber as she took off toward home.

By the time she finished packing the supplies for their outing, Kate had calmed down considerably. But when tires crunched across the gravel driveway, she parted the living room curtains, just to be sure.

Mike's El Camino.

She heaved an exaggerated 'whew' and stepped onto the front porch. The look on Mike's face replaced her jitters with giddy elation.

"You look great," he said.

Kate wore a pair of cutoff denim shorts and her favorite striped 'popcorn' shirt. Stretchy knit. Hugged her body in all the right places.

"So," Mike rubbed his hands together. "Let's get started." He peeled off his t-shirt and laid it on the hood of the truck. "I don't want to get this all sweaty."

Kate tugged idly at some shriveled vines that curled around the porch column. It was a lame stall tactic, but it had been a while since she'd seen a man shirtless. His biceps hardened as he grabbed the cord to start the motor; his shoulders rippled when he gave it a hard yank. It nearly took her breath away.

As the engine roared to life, Mike looked up. His gaze caught hers, and he smiled. Her face reddened. She shrugged and gave him an 'okay you caught me' look and retreated inside to ice down the drinks.

He finished with the front yard in no time. Kate met him in back with an icy glass of sweet tea, which he consumed in three huge swigs.

"Do you want more?" she laughed.

"Nah, I'm fine. Just about done."

Mike finished the job in half the time it would have taken Kate.

An hour later they exited FM 271 and wound their way through the eastern red cedar-lined road that opened to a parking area. Growing up in Michigan, Kate thought of lakes as enormous bodies of water. She'd been swimming in Lake Huron and Lake Michigan. Even Island Lake, where Mom taught her how to swim, was ten times the size of this one. It was small but in an intimate sort of way. Several picnic tables dotted the landscape, each with a metal grill for barbecuing. Downhill from Mike and Kate, a husband and wife were setting up a tent while their three children splashed around in the shallow water. A long wooden dock extended into the lake, ending in a rectangular fishing pier. Near the dock, a covered pavilion shaded several more picnic tables and a jukebox. A handful of teenage girls in string bikinis were gathered around the jukebox, singing along to a popular tune. Their male counterparts ogled them with lust, punched each other in the arm.

"We can set up at one of these tables, or we can go to another beach, a little further away from here," Mike said. "It's your choice."

An outburst of giggles and squeals reverberated their way from the pavilion to the El Camino.

Kate's choice?

They continued down a narrow dirt road that ended at a clearing adjacent to a smaller beach. Kate spotted the picnic table and grill. No one else in sight. Much better.

They unloaded the basket and ice chest, and Mike grabbed the charcoal.

"I'm starved, how about you?"

He dumped briquettes into the grill, dousing them with way too much lighter fluid. Kate stepped back as Mike tossed in a lighted match. Rolled her eyes when he laughed at the burst of flames that shot up into the air.

"What is it about men and fire?"

She spread the checkered tablecloth and began unloading the basket. Mike poked at the hot coals.

"I think it's in our DNA." He pounded his chest, Tarzan style. "A throwback to our caveman days."

He opened the package of wieners and placed several on the grill. Soon, the smell of roasted hot dogs permeated the air. Mike speared one with the grilling fork, proclaimed "done," and piled the rest onto the platter Kate held out to him.

After they had filled their plates, Mike reached into the ice chest and grabbed a couple cokes.

"Let's eat down there," he suggested.

They sat cross-legged on the brown-sugar sand. Mike was so close; his knee touched Kate's. She started to move away then changed her mind. Decided it was more aloof if she acted like his touch *didn't* make her chest thump a little harder than normal.

"Do you come here a lot?" Kate asked, and took a bite of her hot dog.

"I've been here a few times. A guy that used to work at Clarke's brought me and some of his other buddies here to show off his new boat. It's a great place to chill when you want some alone time."

Kate started drawing swirls in the sand beside her.

"It's a pretty lake. So do you bring all the girls you know out here to impress them?"

"All the girls I know," he repeated with a slight chuckle. "That's a good one. Ardee's a small town. Not a lot of girls my age around." He shrugged a shoulder. "I've endured flirting from a few."

Kate shot him a look and scoffed. "Endured."

"But, they didn't interest me," Mike continued, searching her eyes for the answer to an unspoken question. "Not like you."

Kate's scalp prickled, and her face started to warm, and it wasn't from the sun that shimmered through the heat haze overhead. She finished her chips and brushed the sand off her legs.

"Do we have to wait an hour now to swim?"

They gathered up the picnic leftovers.

"You know that's an old wives tale, right?" Mike said. "The basic premise was that food digestion requires greater blood flow to the stomach, and exercise requires greater blood flow to the lungs and heart, which would deprive the stomach of oxygen resulting in a muscle cramp."

Kate laughed, "Geez, who needs an encyclopedia when you're around?"

"Just call me World Book," he retorted.

She reached into the truck to pull out her beach bag when it dawned on her that she'd made a bad wardrobe decision. Instead of wearing her suit under her clothes, she'd assumed there would be an outdoor restroom nearby where she could change. No such luck.

"Uhm...you know. I'm gonna have to find someplace to change into my bathing suit."

"No problem." Mike stripped down to his swim trunks. "I'll head out into the water, and you can change behind the truck."

He waited for her at the water's edge. Let out a low wolf-whistle when she came into view.

Yeah, that made it worth the price.

She kept to the shallow part of the lake, not submerging in it like Mike. He emerged after a couple of standing dives, shook his head and smoothed his hair with his hands. Water traced its way down his chest, a rivulet or two veering off to follow the indentations that defined his muscled abdomen.

Kate exhaled slowly. Was it her, or had the temperature of the lake just risen a couple of degrees?

"Hey, come on out here with me," he called.

Kate shook her head, splashed a handful of water in his direction. Mike paddled to her, threatened to pull her in. He playfully caught her arm then let go with an apology.

"I'm sorry, I forgot about your wrist. I hope I didn't–"

He picked up her arm to examine it.

"Wasn't this the wrist you hurt yesterday?"

She pulled away and hid her arm behind her back, a childish maneuver maybe, but she was stalling for time.

How was she going to answer that question?

Why did he have to be so darned observant?

Kate slogged back to the beach and sat down hard.

Mike followed. Dropped onto the towel beside her.

"Kate?"

She closed her eyes. Squeezed her temples with the palms of her hands and expelled a frustrated breath.

"I don't know. I mean, first the cut on my cheek and now my arm. It's like, every time I get hurt, my body seems to heal itself within a few hours. I didn't use any extraordinary antibiotics or do anything different than I have my whole life, but now... And I haven't got an answer. I wish I did... you don't know how much I want to know what's going on. But I don't."

Mike put his arm around her. "Hey, at least it's not a bad thing. I've heard stories about spontaneous healers. So, maybe it's an aleatory gift."

She glanced over at him and gave him a dubious look.

"Okay, look, I have a confession to make," he said. "I don't tell this to a lot of people, but my Aunt Cass. She can see things or know stuff about people just by touching them. Some people call it second sight. Or clairvoyance or ESP. Whatever you want to call it, the point is that you're not freaking me out. I've been around weird my whole life."

Kate raised an eyebrow.

"No, I...I mean," he laughed softly and shook his head. "That didn't come out right. I didn't mean you're weird." He pulled her in closer; his lips brushed her temple. "What I mean is, this isn't a bad thing. Just a mystery to figure out. And I'm sure Aunt Cass will be able to get a read on whatever's going on once she meets you."

Mike stood up, took Kate's hand and lifted her to her feet.

"Come on, forget about that for now and have some fun."

They went into deeper water this time. Kate dog paddled around. She wasn't a skilled swimmer, but she could hold her own. Mike swam even further out, disappearing under the water. He surfaced behind her, circled her waist with his arms and pulled her along to the shallow area. When their feet could touch bottom, Mike turned her around to face him.

"I'm glad you came out here with me today."

He lowered his mouth to hers. His hands slipped beneath the crocheted apron of her bathing suit. She shivered as they slid across her bare skin. The pressure of his kiss intensified. She reached up and laced her fingers through his hair, pulling him closer. Her lips parted under the gentle probing of his tongue. Cocooned in the gentle swaying of the water surrounding them, Kate surrendered herself to Mike's kiss and the upheaval of emotions created by his touch.

Was it only a minute, or had ten minutes passed before he released his tight hold around her waist and slid down into the water.

"I need to cool off," he joked and splashed water at her.

You and me both, she thought and flicked a little water towards him in retaliation. She returned to the beach to sit on her towel. She wrapped her arms around her legs and hugged them tightly to her chest. *This was crazy.* Mike was tearing down walls faster than she could build them.

He was all smiles as he came to sit beside her.

"You are something else. Don't take what I'm about to say the wrong way, but I've kissed women before. None of them has ever affected me like you do." Mike propped back on one elbow to look at her. "Maybe you do have a little magic in you."

Kate pushed against him. He lost his balance and fell back in the sand with a laugh. She grabbed her towel and wrapped it around her waist. "Wait here while I go change. I'll be right back. Seriously, don't move," she commanded.

She hurried to dry off and dress as fast as possible. Mike had already changed and was lying on his back in the sand, hands behind his head, waiting. He frowned when she came into view.

"We need to get you inside. Your face is sunburned."

Kate lifted the collar of her shirt, grimaced at her fiery shoulders.

"That settles it. You're coming back to my place. I'm sure between my medicine cabinet and the pharmacy we can keep that from becoming too painful."

A short while later, they pulled into the parking lot behind the pharmacy. Kate followed Mike up the outside stairs that led to his apartment.

"This is a novel idea. Much more creative than 'come up to my place and I'll show you my record collection'."

"Tell you the truth," Mike said, "I have a pretty cool record collection. The Beatles, of course, got the White Album, Jim Croce,

Crosby Stills and Nash, James Taylor, a little Eric Clapton. If you're into it, I have Sabbath Bloody Sabbath, Aqualung, there's even a Chopin and Beethoven mixed in somewhere."

Pretty cool was an understatement, Kate thought, as she shuffled through the dozens of albums on his bookshelf. The rest of his apartment was about as she had imagined it would be. A large leather sofa and matching chair took up most of the room. Edmund Scientific books, 'The Picture History of Astronomy' and newspapers littered the coffee table. On the wall hung two maps sketched, Mike told her, by the same cartographer who drew the one in his office at work.

He excused himself. Returned with a tube of ointment and an aerosol can shaped like a fire hydrant.

Kate had to laugh.

"You are nothing, if not prepared."

She pulled aside a shoulder of her shirt to reveal the angry red skin. Mike winced.

"I could kick myself for not making sure you had lotion or sunscreen on. We need to slather this on your shoulders and back."

He gave her shirt a doubtful look and disappeared into his bedroom. Kate heard the scrape of a drawer opening and closing. Mike came back with a clean, V-neck t-shirt, which he handed to her.

"What you need to do," he directed, "is go into the bedroom, and change into this. That way this ointment won't mess up your shirt."

Kate obeyed without hesitation.

Mike was on the couch when she came out of the bedroom. She sat on the floor in front of him. He lifted the shirt up, careful to preserve her modesty. His touch was gentle as he rubbed the soothing lotion on her shoulder.

She shivered.

"Am I hurting you?" Mike withdrew his hand.

"No, it's sorta cold," she said. She was not about to explain the other reason for her reaction.

Before he smoothed on the next application, Mike rubbed his hands together to warm up the creamy substance. When he had finished coating her shoulders and back, he lowered the t-shirt and handed her the tube.

"I'll let you do the rest."

"Thanks, it feels better already. Man, this would be a great time for spontaneous healing, wouldn't it?"

She applied the salve to her legs.

"Are you hungry?" he asked.

She glanced at her wrist. It was after six.

"Sure, what did you have in mind?"

"Something quick and easy. Spaghetti. That sound okay?"

"Fabulous, I love spaghetti."

Mike went into the kitchen, emerged with a bottle of Cabernet Sauvignon.

"You know who my favorite chef is?"

He poured the dark purple liquid into a wine glass and handed it to her.

"The Galloping Gourmet?"

"No," he laughed, "Julia Child. Grew up watching The French Chef."

She took a sip of wine.

"Good. Then I'm gonna sit on the couch and let you amaze me with your culinary skills."

She stopped at the bookshelf of albums and after sorting through them selected one.

"Do you mind?"

"Not at all," Mike called over his shoulder as he threw chopped garlic into the butter already melting in the skillet. "Let me know if you need any help."

She put on James Taylor's "Gorilla" and began singing the words to "Mexico." The leather couch felt cool against her skin.

Kate laid her head back, closed her eyes, and relaxed into the cushions. The aroma drifting in from the kitchen intoxicated her as much as the wine.

Kate began to sing "How Sweet It Is To Be Loved by You" under her breath. Moments later, she felt leather cushion sink under his weight, as Mike slid onto the sofa next to her. His warm breath tickled as his lips caressed the nape of her neck, then moved forward, following her jawline across her cheek to hungrily find her lips.

Kate felt the delicious ache of desire. She arched her back and pressed into him. His hand slid under her shirt. A soft, involuntary moan escaped her lips.

Mike abruptly pulled away.

"I'm sorry, I'm sorry," he muttered. "God, Kate, do you even know…"

His voice turned cold.

"Supper's ready, let's eat."

She stared at him, eyes wide, dumbstruck by the reversal in his demeanor. Both of them were enjoying the pleasure of the moment. Or at least she'd thought so. Why was he suddenly so… aloof, offended?

Kate took a seat at the table. Mike placed a plate piled high with spaghetti in front of her. Without a word, he picked up his fork and began to attack his food with a vengeance, wouldn't raise his head to look at her. Kate twirled her fork through the strands of noodles. What had she done wrong?

The tense silence grew stronger with each passing minute.

She laid her fork down and lowered her eyes to her plate. Unbidden tears made their way down her cheeks. She depleted her glass of wine. As she reached towards the bottle for a refill, Mike covered her hand with his. His voice was tender.

"Kate, I'm sorry. It's not your fault. I'm not mad at you. I'm mad at myself. You are so beautiful, and you were sitting there with this look on your face, and I…" He hesitated. There was a slight catch in his voice as he continued, "I never want to hurt you. I don't think you know how you affect me. I don't want to do anything out of line."

Kate sniffed a couple of times and took a swallow of air before she spoke.

"I thought I'd done something to offend you. And the last thing in the world I want to do is offend you. You don't know how you make me feel. I miss you when you aren't around and..."

She stopped when she realized how vulnerable that sounded. The wine had obviously gone to her head.

Mike pulled her to her feet. His arms surrounded her.

"Don't worry about it," he murmured, burying his head in her hair. "You didn't do anything wrong. I need to learn to rein in my impulses when I'm with you."

He led her to the couch, sat down beside her, and gently wrapped his arm around her shoulder.

"Truthfully, I've never felt this way before either. I've always prided myself on being the level-headed pharmacist. Never rattled. Always in control. But you," he shook his head, "you have this effect on me and frankly..." He left the thought unfinished.

Okay, so it's not a bad thing.

She gave a gentle sigh of relief. Her eyelids felt suddenly heavy. She folded her feet up under her. With a slight yawn, she closed her eyes and leaned against him, draping one arm across his chest. Her head dipped slightly. There it was. The soothing beat of his heart. The last thing she remembered before nodding off to sleep.

The aroma of sizzling bacon, combined with the smell of brewing coffee, wafted into the bedroom. Kate burrowed her head deeper into the pillow. An indolent smile crept across her face, until the moment she was awake enough to realize it was morning and this was not her bed.

She peered through her lashes. She was alone, still dressed in her shorts and Mike's t-shirt from last night.

Last night.

How did she get to bed?

It had to be Mike's doing. She sat up and rubbed her temples. On the nightstand beside her were an alarm clock, a glass of water, and two small white tablets.

Aspirin.

That's a pharmacist for you.

Didn't stop her from taking them, though. She eased out of the bed, straightened the blanket and pillow, and hurried to the bathroom to take care of personal business and splash some water on her face.

Kate tiptoed through the living room and paused in the kitchen doorway. Mike was extracting two pieces of perfectly browned bread from the toaster. His face broke into a dimpled grin when he saw her.

"Good morning," he greeted and handed her a cup of freshly poured coffee.

Kate took the cup in both hands and stammered, "I am *so* sorry. I was tired. Didn't sleep much the night before. Then the combination of the sun and the wine…"

Mike swept her apology aside with a brush of his hand. "You had a long day yesterday. Don't worry about it. Oh, come here," he waved her towards him, "let me see your sunburn." He raised the back of the shirt slightly. "Well, no miracle healings, but at least it isn't quite as bad as yesterday."

"Thanks to you."

Mike handed her a small plate that held a slice of buttered toast, two strips of crisp bacon and a mound of scrambled eggs.

"Uhm…" Kate munched on a bacon strip and asked as nonchalant as possible, "So where did you sleep?"

His mouth twitched at the corners. She could tell he was stifling his amusement.

He nodded toward the couch. A pillow and a fluffy blue and green plaid blanket balanced on the arm.

Kate formed a silent "oh."

"You don't mind if I drop you off at your house soon, do you?" Mike asked, washing down a forkful of eggs with a mouthful of coffee. "I have to be at the pharmacy by ten this morning."

"Oh my gosh, of course." Kate finished her last bite of toast and slurped one more sip from her mug. "I hope I didn't cause a problem passing out like that."

Mike kissed her forehead. "Don't think another thing about it. It was kind of nice, to see you sleeping so peaceful in my bed. Almost like you belonged there."

It took her a split-second to realize his comment wasn't about hormones and physical desires. It implied a sense of permanency.

Belonging.

Her emotions struggled with the idea. Part of her yearned for that, but the cost –

Her old fear resurrected its familiar barrier, and she let the remark go without a response.

When they arrived at her grandmother's house, Kate decided to tell Mike about her encounter with the mayor.

"He made an obscure comment about me being a lawbreaker. I'm supposed to go by his office today to try and clear it up. The man is so antagonistic. It's like he has some vendetta against me. You know how Peg mentioned that falling out my mom and Darcy had? When I visited her the other day, she said that they had been best friends in college." Kate shook her head. "Mom and Darcy? Best friends? I can't imagine how that came about, but if they did have some blow-up, surely he can't hold that against me?"

"That would be one heck of a grudge," he said.

He carried the picnic hamper and cooler and set them down at her front door.

"I'll talk to Aunt Cass today. Find out when we can come by and visit."

Kate rubbed the back of her neck and responded with an absentminded nod. Her thoughts had already shifted to the appointment with Darcy. Mike must have sensed her mood.

"Try not to worry too much about your meeting." He dropped a light kiss on her cheek. "Why don't you come by Clarke's afterward? I'll buy you a cup of coffee and you can tell me how it went."

She stopped by the hospital first. Seated in the chair beside her grandmother's bed, Kate massaged lanolin cream into her grandmother's hands. Her insides squirmed at the idea of facing the mayor, not knowing what he would accuse her of.

"I wish I could talk to you, Grandma. I have this meeting today with Darcy MacMurray, and I sure could use your advice…"

She stopped midsentence when a slight squeeze pressed against her palm.

"Grandma?" Kate leaned over the rail. Searched her grandmother's face. "Grandma, can you hear me?"

The door pushed open, and an ICU nurse entered the room to let Kate know her fifteen minutes were up. Kate told her what had happened. The RN, who introduced herself as Patty, offered an explanation.

"Sometimes when a person is in a coma, they have reflex actions in their hands or their legs, little twitches or jerks, which might feel like a hand squeeze. But in this case, it doesn't mean anything, especially since she's still oblivious to stimulation."

To prove her point, Patty lifted the sheet and ran her fingernail along the instep of her grandmother's foot. She didn't even flinch.

"I'm sorry." Patty bobbed her head in sympathy.

Kate didn't care what that nurse said; convinced her grandmother was trying to speak. She bent forward and gave her grandmother a peck on the cheek.

"I know you heard me, Grandma. Keep trying. You can make it back. I know you can."

Kate trudged up the stairs to the second floor of the courthouse. Her watch read five minutes until eleven. She'd avoided arriving too early, fearful that the knot twisting in her stomach would escalate to something worse if she had to wait.

A gold-plated plaque proudly displayed the name, Ashling Walters, but there was no one manning the front desk.

What is the protocol here?

Should she wait for this Ashling to return, or just enter, unannounced?

One minute before eleven.

If someone didn't come soon, she'd be late to her meeting.

Not a good idea considering she was already on the mayor's bad side.

As if on cue, a side door opened, and Darcy's secretary entered the room.

Kate had imagined her as a prim, gray-haired, schoolmarm type.

There was nothing prim about Ashling Walters.

Chestnut ringlets of silken hair hung almost to her waist. Her makeup was impeccable. Bright red lips matched her manicured fingernails. A short, straight skirt showcased her long legs. Very professional, Kate thought, except for the top button of her navy jacket. It was unfastened, exposing ample mounds of creamy flesh.

Intentional? Kate wondered as she introduced herself.

When Ashling answered, Kate recognized the vocal inflection. Like Robert Kavanagh's.

"Ah yes." Her lavender eyes swept over Kate. "Pearl McKenna's granddaughter. I heard you were back in town. Such a pleasure to finally meet you. I've heard so much about you."

Really? Because I've never heard anything about you, was Kate's first thought.

"All good, I hope," she said out loud, with a nervous chuckle.

Ashling answered with a pinched smile and picked up the phone.

After a brief conversation, she nodded towards the door. "Mayor MacMurray will see you now."

A massive mahogany desk occupied a prominent position in the middle of the Mayor's office. Bookshelves that reached from floor to ceiling covered two of the walls. The third wall was a bank of windows, cloaked by burgundy curtains so dense, not even a sliver of sunlight made it through the folds. That meant the room's only source of light was the Tiffany floor lamp, positioned to highlight the mayor. He was sitting in an oversized burgundy leather chair, shuffling through a stack of papers. Didn't bother to look up as she entered the room.

"Be seated. I'll be with you momentarily."

Kate perched on the edge of the wooden chair. She ran her tongue across her lips and wove her trembling fingers together. Tried to regulate the tempo of her heart by focusing on the vase of flowers that sat on his desk. Out of character, she thought, with the room's austere decor.

Darcy let several minutes pass before he removed his glasses, folded the earpieces in and set them in their leather case.

Slow, deliberate actions. Intimidation was his game, Kate surmised, attempting to swallow the lump that threatened to close her windpipe. Apparently, it was working.

Using the back of his pale fist to rub his eye, he exhaled heavily.

"It has come to my attention that, at the market last Saturday, you sold fresh produce." He picked up a piece of paper and read, "Bundles of basil, thyme, and lemon balm, to be exact."

Laying the sheet back down, he rose and pressed his knuckles into the desk.

"Miss McKenna, are you aware that it is against the law to sell fresh vegetables or fruit without a vendor's license in this county?"

Kate realized she'd been holding her breath. She exhaled a quiet, "No."

"I'm sorry. You will have to speak up."

Darcy walked around the desk and towered above her, his upper lip curled in derision.

"I repeat. Did you know that it is against the law to sell fresh vegetables without a permit in this county?"

She wiped her clammy hands down the skirt of her dress and cleared her throat.

"No, sir, I…I did not."

"Miss McKenna." His words dripped with false concern. "If you are going to be an active member of our community, it would be in your best interest to understand and be mindful of the laws concerning these types of activities."

Kate's eyes darted past his desk, towards the wall of books to her right, as she searched for a response. It came to her in a flash.

"Sir, if I may, my grandmother has been selling herbs at the flea market for years. I'm sure she has a permit and if so, wouldn't I fall under its umbrella, since I'm selling goods on her behalf?"

"The devil is in the details, is it not, Miss McKenna? Your grandmother sells only dried herbs, which are not classified under the term "fresh." You, on the other hand, were selling fresh herbs in," he snatched the paper off his desk and read, "in glass containers filled with water."

He picked up the phone.

"Ashling, will you please send in Chief Collins."

Chapter 7

Kate clasped her hands in her lap and tried to maintain her composure as the uniformed officer entered the room.

His face was puffy; eyes red-rimmed, like he'd imbibed just a little too much last night. Gray streaks faded his dark hair. Deep creases lined the corners of his mouth.

He'd aged a lot in three years.

But Kate still recognized him.

Andy Collins.

The deputy who'd spoken to her at the hospital about her mother's accident.

Chief of Police now?

"Miss McKenna, Chief Collins and I have discussed your case. Since this is your first offense, and because you are the granddaughter of one of our most honored long-time residents," he gave her a charitable smile, "I have asked that you be given leniency in the matter."

Andy Collins approached Kate and handed her a piece of paper.

"This is a ticket for a Class C misdemeanor, violation of Ordinance 2902.2 regarding the selling of fresh vegetables or fruit at a public market without a permit. It requires a cessation of activity for a probationary period of one month and a fine of $500. If you will sign here, please." He handed her a pen and a clipboard. "You have fourteen days in which to pay the fine or you will be incarcerated until such time as the judgment is deemed satisfied."

This was leniency?

Warmth spread across her cheeks. Her hand shook as she signed the page. The Chief took the clipboard. His voice lowered, and he gave her shoulder a slight squeeze.

"Real sorry to hear about your grandmother's condition. Sure hope she recovers soon."

When Kate and the mayor were alone again, he spoke.

"I'm almost glad your grandmother is not awake to see the family name tarnished by her flesh and blood. She's also spared the knowledge that her granddaughter is blatantly sleeping around with a virtual stranger. I saw you leave his apartment this morning wearing the same clothes you had on yesterday." He clucked his teeth, making a 'tsk' sound.

Kate jumped to her feet. Her hands coiled into fists at her side.

"I most certainly am not sleeping with anyone! And if you are referring to Mike Sheehan, I'll have you know he is a perfect gentleman. Who are you to be spying on me, anyway?"

Darcy took two long steps and was in front of her. He grasped her chin in his hand. It was all she could do to meet his glacial stare without flinching.

"Who am I, indeed? You do not know who you are dealing with, Miss McKenna." His clasp tightened. "Your mother underestimated me. You'd be a fool to do the same. Oh, I know more about you than you think. I know all about…"

His eyebrows arched.

"Now I understand," he said under his breath. "No one ever told you." Darcy seemed almost gleeful as he continued talking to himself. "Oh, this is priceless…"

His words.

His tone.

They ridiculed her.

The walls of the room began to tilt towards Kate. Her stomach tensed and her heart thumped hard against her ribs.

"Are we through now?" she asked, desperate to escape.

His release was abrupt. Kate wobbled and reached out to the chair to steady herself. As she turned to leave, Darcy put his arm out to stop her.

"Wait."

He reached down. Picked up the pendant dangling from the chain around her neck.

"This was Kathleen's."

Using his long, yellowed fingernail, Darcy opened the locket to reveal the picture inside. Kate caught a flicker of surprise, quickly veiled.

"Your mother and you?"

She nodded and watched as his pupils shrank to hard pinpoints. He snapped the locket shut.

"You may go," he murmured curtly.

She walked past the reception desk, fixated on the buffed tile floor to avoid eye contact. Ignoring Ashling's, "Something wrong, cailín?" Kate rushed down the stairs and out onto the sidewalk. The sunlight suddenly seemed too bright. The sky too blue. Their intensity burned her retinas. She quickened her pace.

Home.

She just needed to get home.

A bell tinkled as she passed the pharmacy.

"Kate, wait," Mike called after her.

She paused and turned. Gave him a blank look.

"What the heck happened?" Alarm reflected in his voice. "What did he say to you?"

Her lip quivered. "I can't talk about it right now. Please. Let's just talk later."

"Sure, okay," his voice was conciliatory, "but can I come by after I get off work?"

Kate didn't want to alienate the only friend she had.

"That's fine. I'll see you later."

Back home, she pulled the Nova under the carport and walked around back to the willow tree. Dropping to the ground, she laid her head on the cool stone slab.

It had never occurred to her that she could sell dried herbs and not fresh ones. She was so caught up in her grand plans. Now they had come crashing down around her. Not only had she managed to lose a month's worth of revenue for Grandma, but she also had no idea how she was going to come up with the money to pay the fine. She'd socked away enough of her inheritance to pay for college tuition and apartment rent each month. And the money she made from her part-time job at the shoe store kept her fed and bought gas. But she certainly hadn't amassed any money for emergencies like this. And she wasn't authorized to sign checks on Grandma's account. Then there was Darcy's cynical comment about her mother...

Grief and confusion exploded, splattering large drops of salty tears onto her dress. Kate wept for the loss of her mother, for her grandmother laying in the hospital unconscious, for her foolhardiness, and for the dilemma she now faced. Most of all, she wept because she was alone and helpless and scared. Unequipped to handle the enormity of life and its complexities. The seemingly insurmountable roadblocks thrown her way. She pictured the Barrett coat-of-arms.

Unbowed?

Unbroken?

Its mockery opened a fresh wound in her heart.

The shadows had begun to angle towards the east when Kate choked down her last sob. She wiped away the remaining tears and rose to her feet, brushing away the leaves that clung to her dress. Her loud sniffs almost drowned out the melodic sound drifting faintly across the fields through the summer heat.

What was that?

Whistling?

Someone was walking down the dirt road that ran alongside the farm, whistling a tune.

Who had the nerve to be so happy on what could easily qualify as one of the worst days of her life?

She stepped from under the tree, shading her face with her hand.

Robert wore a red shirt; sleeves rolled up to his elbows, sporting a plaid vest and an old fashioned driving cap pulled low over his forehead. He must have spotted her at the same moment because the whistling stopped. He waved.

"I was just coming to see you," he shouted across the distance. "Is it all right if I come over and chat with you a bit?"

The last thing she wanted right now was company. Cursing her well-mannered upbringing, she hollered back, "Sure, come on around."

"Fine then, be right there."

It would take him a few minutes to circle past the barbed-wire fence and come up the driveway. She used the opportunity to splash cold water on her face, hoping to lessen the puffiness around her eyes and the red blotches on her cheeks.

"Let's sit under the willow," she said, awkwardly balancing a plastic pitcher of sweet tea, a couple of tumblers and the two folding aluminum chairs she'd retrieved from the carport.

"Please, let me carry those for you."

With a shrug, she relinquished her hold on the chairs.

"Would you like a drink? I've got iced tea."

"That would be delightful, thank you."

Robert took a seat. Kate handed him a glass.

Okay, the niceties were finished. If this was more bad news, might as well get it over.

"I haven't been on your property again if that's why you're here," she stated, hands on her hips.

He laughed, unruffled, and took a sip of tea.

"That wasn't the exact reason I stopped by, but it will do as an icebreaker since I did come to talk about the greenhouse."

He nodded towards the other lawn chair.

"Please."

Kate lowered herself, guarded, to sit on its edge.

Robert pulled a leather pouch from the pocket of his vest.

"Do you mind?" he asked.

Kate squirmed in her seat. She just wanted him to get to the reason for this impromptu visit, but manners superseded anxiety. She gave him a concessionary nod.

He unzipped the pouch and pulled out a pipe.

"Peterson of Dublin," he remarked. "Charles Peterson himself made this one. Excellent craftsmanship. This one is Briarwood."

Kate had to admit, it was a beautiful pipe. Its dark red stain emphasized the swirling grain, polished to a mirror shine. A band of silver circled the stem. She squinted to get a better look at the symbol etched into it.

"A clàrsach. An Irish harp," Robert clarified and filled the bowl, one pinch of tobacco at a time, compressing it until it was full. He ran the matchhead across the sole of his shoe, sparking it into the golden flame which lit the pipe's surface. He drew in long, deliberate puffs until smoke curled up and around his head, a fragrant halo of bourbon and caramel.

"I received a call today from a colleague regarding a matter that requires me to fly back to Leinster for several weeks. Perhaps even a couple of months. I came to see if you might be interested in taking care of the greenhouse in my absence. I've made such a splendid start. I'd hate to see it all go to rubbish."

Kate searched Robert's face. He seemed sincere.

Her shrug and "Okay" were meant to sound doubtful but in actuality, she was intrigued.

"It is my proposition that you come to the greenhouse on Sunday. I will show you where I keep the tools, fertilizer and explain to you what's necessary for you to do. You can work whatever days and times suit your schedule, as long as everything is taken care of. I know you have your grandmother's garden to tend, so I want to make it worth your while to work my property as well. I'm prepared to pay you one hundred dollars a week."

Robert relaxed back into his chair and took another draw on his pipe.

"You want to pay me a hundred a week to take care of your greenhouse," Kate echoed in disbelief.

"Yes, you see I put a high premium on its contents and take great pride in the plants I've grown there. I've observed how well you have done, caring for your grandmother's garden. I feel you could do the same for mine."

Kate did a quick calculation.

"I'll do it on one condition. I need to get an advance before you leave town."

Robert's brows drew together as he concentrated on tamping the tobacco and relighting his pipe. Kate felt her bravado slipping. She sucked in a breath, prepared to explain her predicament when Robert began to nod his head.

"Since I'm not exactly sure how long I'm going to be gone, it would make perfect business sense for me to pay a portion in advance."

He stood and offered his hand.

"Miss Katherine, we have a deal. Can you come by the greenhouse on Sunday afternoon, say around two? I'll be sure and clear a path to the greenhouse."

The tension melted from her shoulders. The knot in her stomach was gone. Kate nearly upended her lawn chair when she jumped forward to give his hand a hearty shake.

"Mr. Kavanagh, we sure do have a deal, and I'll see you Sunday."

"Please call me Robert," he chuckled.

"Robert it is, and you can call me Kate. You have no idea how much this means to me."

His voice softened. "I believe I do."

She gave him a questioning look.

"Your expression. Much happier now than when I first arrived."

"Oh...yeah...that," Kate shrugged. "This has been a rough day."

"Then I appreciate that you took the time to talk to me and look forward to doing business with you."

He doffed his cap in a grand gesture. As he fit it back on his head, his eyes connected with hers. Funny how the first time she met him, Kate thought of them as aggressive, intimidating. Now she realized they weren't that at all. Their deep blue color reminded her of Lake Huron in winter, and their twinkle was the sunlight glinting off the ice floes that moved along the shore of Thunder Bay. He gave her a wink and, with one more drag on his pipe, started toward the driveway, whistling "When Irish Eyes Are Smiling."

Kate unconsciously began to hum the tune herself as she opened the door to her bedroom.

Robert's advance. Mike's cash. The money she'd made at market. Maybe it would be enough to pay the fine and buy a few groceries. She dug the envelope out of the dresser drawer. Twenty, forty, sixty, eighty, one hundred, one-twenty, one hundred and forty dollars. Depending on how much Robert advanced her, this might work out after all. She breathed a sigh of relief for the second time that day.

Things were looking up.

They improved even more when Kate heard the gravel crunch in the driveway. She glanced over at the grandfather clock. It had been a wedding gift to her grandmother from Granddaddy Mac;

German-made out of ornate, hand-carved wood, with specially weighted pendulums and a gold-plated face. Grandma used to say you could set your heart by the tick of that clock.

Think I'm beginning to understand what that means now.

Kate greeted Mike with a smile.

"Well, this is a surprise. After your reaction to the meeting with the mayor, a smile was the last thing I expected."

He pulled his arm from behind his back and produced a little bouquet of pink carnations and baby's breath.

"My favorite. How did you know?"

His dimples deepened with his smile. "Just a lucky guess."

"Well, they're beautiful. I need to get them into some water."

He eyed her sleeveless sundress.

"No mystical healing today," he said and followed her into the house.

She pulled down one of her grandmother's cut-glass vases from the top shelf of the étagère.

"Not that fortunate this time, I guess."

"So, what happened today at the mayor's office?"

Kate centered the flowers on the kitchen table.

"I have a lot to tell you."

She led him around to the willow tree and poured him a tall glass of tea. He took a huge sip and settled onto one of the lawn chairs.

"Obviously I'm not the first person who sat here today."

He picked up Robert's abandoned glass, his brows raised.

"Yeah, like I said, I have a *lot* to tell you."

She described her appointment with the mayor.

"That sounds a bit extreme," Mike commented when she told him about the fine.

"I thought so too. But that's where Robert Kavanagh comes in."

"Who's Robert Kavanagh?"

Kate told him about the greenhouse and how Robert had offered her a job tending it while he was gone.

"I'm hoping the advance is enough to pay the fine so I won't go to jail. I still need to find a way to make up for the lost revenue," she frowned as she bit the cuticle around her thumbnail. "Right now, I'm just trying to overcome one hurdle at a time."

"You've been placed in a difficult situation, and you're doing your best. And you know I'd never let you go to jail. I can loan you money if you need some." He leaned in towards her and teased, "I'm sure we could think of ways for you to repay me."

Kate snickered. Rolling her eyes towards the sky, she replied, "I can only imagine."

"Oh, that reminds me," Mike's mood became serious. "I called Aunt Cass today. She was heading out of town but wants us to come by on Monday evening. She's very interested in meeting you. Asked if your grandmother had told you about some gift or present or something. I didn't quite get what she was talking about. Figured she could tell you more about it on Monday."

"But you told her about the cuts and bruises that heal so quickly?"

"Yep. Said she has an idea, and that she'll explain it all when we see her. See? I knew she'd have an answer."

Kate's stomach interrupted with a loud rumble.

"And that," Mike laughed, "is why I am concerned about your eating habits. Up for a burger?"

Chapter 8

They scooted into a booth near the back of the diner. Kimmie, the blonde who'd waited on them last time, brought over two frosty mugs of root beer. Kimmie was a nonstop talker. In a matter of minutes, they learned that she was born and raised in Texas, and proud of it. She was the same age as Kate. Regularly attended the First Baptist Church in Bonham, where she and her high school sweetheart, Larry Don, had tied the knot when they were sixteen because the bible said it was better to marry than to burn with lust.

In the middle of all that, she took their order. Returned a short time later with two cheeseburgers and a basket of Texas fries.

"Anything else I can get for y'all?"

They reassured her everything was fine. Kate picked up her burger to take a bite then stopped and laid it back on the plate. The mayor's comment was haunting her. Maybe talking about it would help her figure out his insinuation.

"You know, right before I left his office, Darcy told me not to underestimate him as my mother did. Then he said the weirdest thing. His exact words were 'now I understand, no one ever told you.' Then he laughed. Like it was some private joke." She shuddered. "What can Darcy know about me that I don't know? There just isn't anything remarkable about my life. My father left us when I was only a few months old. My mother never dated or married again, so no complicated ex-husband craziness. Then there was the car wreck. That's it. That's all I know."

"There has to be something you've overlooked. Tell me what you know about your dad."

"All Mom would ever say about him was that he was a good man who was there in a time of need. Everybody else called him a rat or a deserter, but that wasn't the way she portrayed him at all."

"But you don't know anything about his family? Where he was from or how she met him?"

Kate stared at her plate, lost in thought, wracking her brain to dig up any comment her mother might have made. Anything she might have blown past as unimportant at the time. Couldn't come up with a thing.

She shrugged. "Mom was real private about her life. I respected that. Didn't question her about the why's and why not's of not having a dad around. We had each other, and that was fine," her voice dropped, "until the accident. And now with Grandma in the hospital, it's just me."

"Hey," Mike said gently, "it's not just you. I'm here now. And I'm not going anywhere. There's something different about you. And I don't mean the mystical healings or the drama with MacMurray. It's not even those green eyes that melt me faster than a snowman in South Padre."

She smiled briefly at his corny humor but didn't look up, too afraid of losing her balance on the emotional tight-wire she was walking.

He reached across the table for her hand.

"Kate, look at me."

She raised her head slowly.

"It's what's inside," he said with a voice so full of emotion, it made her heart bounce out of rhythm for several beats. "It's the Kate that even *you* don't see."

Their moment was cut short by Kimmie standing over them, check in hand.

"Can I get y'all anything else? We got fresh baked apple pie today. Tastes awfully good with a scoop of homemade ice cream on top," she winked at Mike.

"Uh, no thanks we're good."

Mike dug a bill out of his pocket.

"Keep the change."

Kimmie gawked at him. Her smile widened.

Kate watched her kiss Lincoln's face as she sashayed towards the counter.

"You just made her day," she chuckled. Then she sobered. "And you made mine too."

Morning came too soon. She groaned and punched the alarm button, silencing its incessant beep, and pulled a pillow over her head. Kate wasn't ready to get out of bed, but she needed to get out and work the garden before it got too hot. She peeled back the sleeve of her t-shirt to look at her shoulder. The blistered red skin had faded to a light pink. She pressed her finger against it to see if it was still tender, muttered an "ouch" and laughed to herself. *Why do I do that?* It's like pressing on a bruise the second day to see if it still hurts. Of course it hurts. She grabbed the sunscreen, gently slathering it over her arms and legs. She also filled her plastic glass with ice and sweet tea to set it in the hollow of her limestone bench for later.

As Kate chopped at the dandelions and chickweed, she recalled Mike's parting words from last night.

"We'll figure it out. The best defense is a good offense. Know what he knows. And stay out of his way as much as possible."

Know what he knows.

How was she going to figure out what Darcy knew about her?

The June sun beat down in full force, adding to her frustration. Even frequent breaks for a swallow or two of iced tea couldn't keep it from being miserable. When she reached the end of the last row, Kate stopped to wipe her forehead with the back of her hand. One of these days she was going to remember to wear a hat.

She stretched backward to ease her cramped muscles. As she straightened, a deep purple-blue splash of color growing up through the lavender bushes caught her attention.

Where did that come from?

The flower's delicate petals overlapped the stamens to form a sort of hood that grew from its long, slender stems. She couldn't tell if it had a fragrance or not, but thought it would look lovely in a vase with a few rosebuds mingled in.

She reached to break off a stalk.

"You don't want to do that, Kate."

She whirled around to face Robert. His eyes were troubled, but his voice was calm.

"This is Aconitum napellus, commonly known as monkshood. Have you heard of it?"

Kate's pulse thrummed in her ears. She shook her head.

"Monkshood is one of the most lethal plants known to man. Its toxins are absorbed through the skin. Some people call it an assassin's weapon of choice. It's untraceable in a toxicology report, and in an autopsy, it appears as though the person died from asphyxia." He rubbed his chin with his hand. "Who would have planted it here?"

Kate swayed.

Blood flow to the head, that's what you're supposed to do when you feel faint, right?

She bent at the waist and grasped her knees for support.

"Kate, are you okay?" Robert's voice raised an octave. "You didn't touch it, did you?"

"I think… I think it's the heat, and you startled me…"

Her vision narrowed, and her body felt light, floaty – like she was falling onto a bed of clouds.

The next few moments were a blur of strong arms, long strides, and cool limestone as Robert caught Kate and carried her to sit on the grass beneath the willow tree.

I'm pretty sure I didn't touch it, she tried to reassure herself. But her head was swimming, and her chest felt constricted.

She massaged her temples and willed her eyes open.

Robert had removed her glass of tea from the hollow and was dipping his handkerchief into the condensation puddled at the bottom.

"It's not much." His tone was skeptical, but he folded the handkerchief in half and brushed it across her forehead. The water felt soothing to her flushed face. Her heart began to slow to its normal rhythm.

"I don't know what brought that on," she apologized.

"But you didn't touch it? You're quite sure?"

"Pretty sure."

"I'm going to remove the plant immediately. Unless you want me to stay with you for a while," he volunteered.

"No, I think I'm okay now."

Robert held the handkerchief briefly again to her temple. Kate still felt a bit light-headed. Even imagined that his hand radiated a faint luminosity. But when she blinked, it was gone.

"Maybe I do need to lie down," she confessed.

A touch of apprehension remained in Robert's voice when he asked, "May I check on you later?"

"I don't think it's necessary" – Kate hesitated – "but sure, if you want to, yeah."

"It would be my pleasure. Now go get some rest."

She closed the doors and lay down on the bed, draping the handkerchief across her forehead. A peaceful calm started at her head, gradually flowing down to her toes, sending her into a state of deep relaxation. A smile tugged at the edge of her lips as she slipped into dreamy unconsciousness.

Why was that stupid woodpecker tapping on the door?

"Cut it out," Kate groaned aloud, not ready to emerge from the languid bliss that engulfed her. But the tapping persisted. She rotated onto her side. A silhouette blocked the outside light from coming into the room. Someone was knocking lightly on the wood doorframe.

"It's me, Robert. May I come in?"

Still drowsy from her deep sleep, Kate yawned. "Oh yeah, sure."

He peeked around the door.

"I don't want to disturb you, but I did promise to come by and see how you were doing. And I brought you something."

Kate swung her feet over the side of the bed.

"Oh no." She stretched her arms wide and rotated her shoulders. "You're not disturbing me. What time is it?"

Robert pulled out a pocket watch. "It's almost five-thirty."

"You're kidding me, right? I slept away half the day?"

"Don't be too hard on yourself. Your body needed the rest to mend. Now, I hope you don't mind, but I brought you a few items."

He set a brown shopping bag on the bed beside her.

"This book is about plants." He laid it in her lap. "Both good and bad so that you can learn the difference."

She grimaced.

"I'm sure I deserved that."

"Kate, I don't mean any offense. I'm merely trying to help." He pulled out another book. "This is about Irish history, folklore, and mythology. All still quite important, even today. I see that you display your Barrett coat-of-arms. The meaning of Irish names and surnames is not a small thing. Names carry a great deal of importance. Much more than most people give them credit for."

He pointed to the tapestry.

"Did you know the Barrett name was first recorded in Lincolnshire? But after they joined Strongbow in his invasion of

Ireland in 1172, he gave them land in County Mayo and County Galway, and they became staunchly Irish. And your last name, McKenna, has a noble meaning. Loosely translated, it means born of fire."

He sure seemed to know a lot about her family. More than just a casual neighbor. She couldn't quite decide if that was disturbing or flattering.

"Now these last two items I made myself."

He pulled out a small, covered baking dish. "This is shepherd's pie."

He removed the lid. The savory aroma made Kate's mouth water.

"It's a traditional Irish dish. This recipe has been in our family for centuries."

He set it on the nightstand beside her.

"And this," Robert produced an ornate silver flask, "this is called mead. It's a drink similar to your wine, only made with honey and herbs. Drink it with care," he warned with a grin. "The alcohol content in this batch is a wee bit higher than regular wine."

"I," she stammered, glancing at the pile in her lap. "I don't know what to say."

"A simple thank you will suffice." His words were solemn, but his eyes crinkled with humor.

"Oh, of course, thanks. It's just that when you asked if you could check on me, I had no idea you would bring all this. It's way too much. I don't think I can accept it."

"I can't imagine why not. Besides, the topic is not up for debate."

Kate could tell from his tone that he meant it. She lifted the lid off the shepherd's pie again to inhale the savory smell.

"I'll leave you, then, to enjoy the rest of your evening. Take care, Kate. I will see you on Sunday afternoon."

After he left, she gathered up the items, depositing the baking dish and flask on the kitchen counter. She understood the reason for the book about plants, but the one about Irish history and mythology… She shrugged and laid them on the table.

Moments later the phone rang. Five minutes after six.

"Hi," she answered with an unexpected level of enthusiasm.

"Well, don't you sound happy? You must have had a good day. Are you up for company this evening?"

"I would love some company. And come prepared to eat dinner, because Robert Kavanagh, you know the guy who hired me to take care of his greenhouse? He made me homemade shepherd's pie that I thought we could eat together. Brought some books too, and a flask of this stuff called mead. It's an Irish drink. Have you ever had it before?"

Silence.

"Mike? You still there?"

"I'm here."

"Is something wrong?"

Another pause, then he answered, "No, nothing's wrong. I'll be there in a little bit."

"Okay, see you soon."

What caused *that* shift in attitude? Surely he didn't view Robert as competition. The idea would have been funny, except the thought of hurting Mike's feelings wasn't amusing.

Kate met him on the porch.

"I could tell from your voice that something wasn't right. After we hung up, I got to thinking that you might consider Robert as someone I like. I mean, don't get me wrong, I do like him, but not," she emphasized 'not,' "the way I like you. The way I feel about you is, well, it's…" she struggled for the right words but wound up with a feeble, "it's just not the same."

"You don't have to explain," Mike said. "I guess I've never felt jealous before. It was a bit of a punch in the gut."

Jealous? That was a new one for Kate, too. She was absolutely positive she'd never prompted *that* reaction from anyone.

It was a little disconcerting. Eager to change the topic, she grabbed his hand and pulled him towards the door.

"I know you're *starving*," she exaggerated the word. "Let's dig into that shepherds' pie."

Mike offered to set the table. He picked up the books.

"These are very nice. High quality. What made him bring all this by?"

Kate relayed the story, concerned that the "how did he happen to be there at that exact moment" question might come up. Even *she* didn't have an answer for that one.

"He asked if he could come back to check on me." Kate placed the warmed pie on the table. "I didn't see any reason to say no. He showed up with a bag of stuff. I'm sure the book about plants was inspired by today's scare. But this..."

She picked up the other book.

"I don't know what to think. He's the second person who has encouraged me to read up on Irish history. Peg told me the same thing last week, even spent a lot of time talking about folklore and myths. Advised me to pay more attention to my Irish heritage and—"

She stopped talking when the idea that popped into her head blurred her concentration.

Mike eyed her quizzically. "What's wrong?"

The time for denial was over.

"Nothing that you'd call wrong." Kate slunk into the chair next to his. "I was just thinking. About an explanation for the cuts and bruises that healed overnight. With all this talk about Irish folklore and banshees and faeries. What if I do have some magical power, and it has to do with being Irish?"

That sounded about as weird coming out of her mouth as it did in her head.

She looked to Mike for his reaction.

"Okay."

"That's it? 'Okay' is your response to me saying I might have magical powers? You're not freaked out or anything?"

Mike shrugged. "I've seen the cuts and bruises disappear, so we know something's going on. And you know about my Aunt Cass. So yeah, I absolutely believe there are things beyond explanation. But I don't think we should be afraid of them." Mike reached out to take Kate's hand. "It's gonna take more than a little magic to run me off. I'm not going anywhere. I love you for you, and if magical powers are a part of that, then I accept them along with everything else."

The blood rushed to Kate's cheeks.

Did he just say love?

Mike must have read her mind.

"Yeah, I said it. I love you, Kate McKenna. I love that after I spend the day with you, my clothes smell like basil and lavender. I love how you do that lip-biting thing when you're thinking." Kate stopped biting her lip as he continued, "I love the way you fall asleep on my chest, clutching at my shirt like I'm your security blanket. Which is great. Let me be your security blanket, Kate. Let me be someone you can hold on to when you need me. And hold onto even more when you don't need me. When you just want me to be around."

He pulled her over to sit on his lap. Starting with her forehead, Mike kissed his way down Kate's face. Her eyelids, the tip of her nose, her chin, finishing with a gentle press to her lips.

"You are a beautiful, courageous, talented woman. I don't care what this unconventional thing is that you've got going on, but we'll figure it out together. And we'll figure out this mysterious past of yours. Find out what Darcy MacMurray knows. Everything will be okay."

His lips sought hers, sealing his promise.

"Now let's eat that shepherd's pie," Mike said. "I'm starving."

The next morning, Kate was up as soon as sunlight began to filter into the bedroom. The uncertainty of Grandma's condition presented a financial dilemma, and she'd stayed awake half the night worrying about it. It didn't make sense to keep paying rent and utilities on her apartment when funds were so tight, and she wasn't sure how long it would take her grandmother to recover. She'd made up her mind; today's task was to make a trip to pack up her belongings and bring them back here.

She'd just poured a cup of coffee and was sitting at the kitchen table, busy with her mental walkthrough of everything that had to be done when the phone rang.

She jumped to answer it, relieved when she heard Mike's voice on the other end.

Kate leaned against the kitchen wall, twisting the phone cord around her fingers. A nervous habit she'd developed over the past few weeks. Mostly connected with calls from Mike. She was sure there was some psychological implication but didn't feel like delving into self-analysis at the moment.

"Are you sure you can't wait until Sunday?" he said. "I'm off work, and we could take the trip together. I just hate for you to make that four-hour drive up there and back in the rain."

Kate hated it too. But she couldn't cancel her Sunday meeting with Robert. She needed the money, and he hadn't given her a way to contact him.

"I can make it there by noon. With any luck, I'll be back before dark."

Mike sighed. "Okay, well please call so I know you got there okay."

The windshield wipers kept a steady beat, so hypnotic Kate had to stop at a 7-Eleven in Sweetwater to get coffee. As she pulled back onto the highway, the force of the rain intensified, coming down in sheets so dense she could hardly see the road in front of her. She slowed the Ranger to a crawl and thought to herself, *if this rain keeps up it'll be a long trip to the University and back to Grandma's house.*

Driving in torrential rain. The University. Her grandmother's house.

The string of words became a trigger. Scenes exploded through her mind; a panoramic reminder of that night. She was standing in Grandma's kitchen. Answering the phone. Talking to the doctor. Riding in the car through the hammering rain to the hospital. Holding Mom's hand as her life slipped away...

Kate's airway tightened. Her eyes brimmed with tears.

Give me something. Anything to drown out the memory.

"Philadelphia Freedom" blasted through the truck's speakers. Kate and Elton belted out the tune. Kate sang her portion at the top of her lungs. And she did the same with every subsequent song until her vocal chords were raw. But it worked. By the time she reached Hawkins, she'd released her stranglehold on the steering wheel. The gray maze of buildings and sidewalks that made up the sprawling university campus slipped past as she took the Washington Street exit and pulled into the parking space beside her apartment. Heavy humidity had replaced the cool, rain-infused air. Sweat began to trace its way down her temples. She grabbed the cardboard boxes and climbed the stairs.

The moment she stepped into the tiled entryway, Kate realized how little she'd invested in this place. Mike's office, his apartment – they reflected his personality, his interests, things that were important to him.

Nothing like that existed here.

No pictures graced the walls or cluttered the bookshelves that stood empty except for a lone crushed Coke can she neglected to throw away. Stark-white blinds shut out all but the faintest light. The couch sat like a big, beige mushroom, devoid of colorful throws or pillows that would have added warmth. The wood floors were dull and bare. Text books, stacks of paper, and notebooks scattered across the coffee table. Everything was covered by a layer of dust.

The epiphany punched the breath out of her, and she dropped the stack of cardboard boxes and leaned against the doorframe, closing her eyes. The room. A reflection of her life the past three years. Bare. Empty. Because what right did she have to enjoy life when Mom had given up hers so that Kate could be here—

She squeezed her eyelids tighter. Beads of sweat trickled their way down the small of her back. She unfastened another button on her shirt and wiped the nape of her neck.

Just get this over with.

Kate turned the knob of the window unit, but the stale air would take forever to cool the room. She propped the door open, prayed for a breeze, and grabbed a cardboard box. She sorted. She threw away. Packing was time-consuming, even if she didn't have a lot of stuff.

Several hours and a stack of boxes later, and Kate was almost finished. Which was good, because this place was suffocating. Not just from the humidity, but from the revelation her life had been at a virtual standstill since her mother's death. She crumpled onto the sofa, cradling her head in her hands. *Grow up, Kate.* Time to face the past and deal with it. No more avoiding or running away. As much as she'd dreaded it, returning to Ardee had been cathartic. Even with Grandma in the hospital and her bizarre dealings with the mayor, Kate felt more alive the past week than she had in the past three years. Especially since she'd met Mike.

Oh my gosh, Mike.

She'd forgotten to call. She dialed the number of the drugstore, recognized the voice that answered. It was that kid, Jake. He told her Mike wasn't available. Wanted to know if he could take a message. What choice did she have? Using her sweetest voice, she asked him to tell Mike she was at the apartment and would call him the minute she got back into town.

Then she threw herself into packing overdrive.

It was the second load to the truck when the thought hit her. Her calves didn't twinge, and her arms didn't shake as she carried the boxes down the stairs. Kate smiled to herself, playfully flexing her arm upward.

Not so much of a 'city- gal' anymore, huh Peg?

To prove it, she took the stairs two at a time back up to the apartment.

The furniture and the ancient black-and-white television had been included in the furnished part of her rental agreement. That left one more item.

Mom's cedar chest.

When she moved in, the landlady's son helped carry it up the stairs, but now... Kate gave it a dubious look. She might have gained some body strength, but the chest was extremely heavy. Only one way to get it down the stairs – remove the contents and haul it down empty.

She rummaged through her tool kit and found a screwdriver and a hammer. With a 'wish me luck' prayer, she began to pound away at the rusted lock until the outer case gave way. The strength of her blows increased and the inner case shattered sending the remaining parts to the floor in a loud clatter, signaling the lock's defeat.

Kate slid to the floor beside the chest. A light sweat dotted her upper lip as she hesitantly raised the lid, braced for the stabbing pain that always accompanied memories of her mother.

This time it was different.

An unexplainable peace blanketed her as she began lifting out items to transfer to the cardboard box. A clear plastic bag contained a poodle skirt, an angora sweater with its mother-of-pearl buttons, and a varsity sweater with AHS embroidered across the front. Kate remembered pictures of her mother posing with her fellow cheerleaders. Maybe those were in here too. She removed a pile of newspapers, an old Bible, Mom's college and high school yearbooks.

Her heart melted when she uncovered the bundle secured by a pink and white striped ribbon. There was a baby book surrounded by handmade baby blankets and tiny gowns sprinkled with flowers and lace. She picked up the little pair of pink booties and held them to her nose. Was it her imagination or was there a hint of baby powder still clinging to them? She retied the bundle and placed it atop the growing pile of memorabilia.

Inside a shoe box, Kate found stacks of old photographs. Something to go through later. She riffled through the other odds and ends crammed into the chest. Playbills from college theater productions. Birthday cards. A mound of letters. As she grabbed a handful to transfer over, an envelope slipped out of the pile and spiraled to the floor, spilling its contents. Kate picked up the yellowed newspaper clipping.

College student missing
Friends questioned for clues to her disappearance

"The Hawkins University Police Department is seeking everyone's help in locating a 21-year-old student who has been missing since Friday, May 14th. According to police, Kathleen McKenna was last seen on the Hawkins campus late Friday afternoon. She has dark brown hair, green eyes, is 5'7" tall and weighs approximately 130 lbs. Anyone with information leading to her whereabouts should contact the University Police Department."

She dropped her hand to her side. The paper slipped from her fingers. Her eyes felt scratchy, her throat suddenly dry.
Mom? Missing?

Chapter 9

A slamming door jarred Kate from her stupor. She pulled aside the blinds. Shuffling across the yard towards the apartment was her landlady, and she didn't look happy.

Kate snatched up the article and stuck it in her purse. The remaining items she dumped into the box that she carried down the stairs and set on the tailgate of the truck.

"Mrs. Moore, good to see you." She rubbed her hands on the thighs of her jeans, wiped the sleeve of her shirt across her forehead. "I'm going to be at my grandmother's house longer than I expected and wondered if it would be okay to turn in my keys so you can find another tenant?"

Mrs. Moore's frown deepened. She answered with a rheumy cough and in a voice that could only have come from decades of nicotine use. "I s'ppose that's okay since your grandmamma is sick and all." Then she glared at Kate through a hazy, gray cloud and wagged the two fingers that sandwiched her half-smoked cigarette. "Of course, you won't get your deposit back, because you didn't give me a month's notice. You know that right?"

"Oh, of course, I wouldn't ask for it."

Kate had paid rent for the whole month, and this was the eleventh. A pro-rata refund would've helped. But she wasn't going to stand here and quibble.

"Give me an hour to finish up and I'll be out."

Mrs. Moore grunted and lumbered back towards her house, flicking ashes and mumbling something about ungrateful college kids.

In half the time she'd promised, Kate locked the door and slid the key under the doormat. Cranking up the Ranger's motor, she put her foot on the clutch, threw it into first gear, and turned onto the street that led out of town.

Never once looked back.

It was already five. Packing had taken longer than she anticipated. She stopped at a little gas station on the outskirts of town. While the tank filled, she went inside to get a coke. In the back corner, she spotted a payphone. Kate pulled Mike's business card out of her purse, dropped in the coins for the long distance call. She was rewarded with the high-pitched, beep of a busy signal. *Figures!* She banged the receiver onto its cradle, cursing her lousy luck. After the crappy day she was having, she'd secretly looked forward to hearing Mike's voice.

Kate took a long swig of her drink. Tired, sweaty, dirty. She just wanted to get back home.

The clouds had blown past and stars dotted the sky by the time she turned into the driveway. Even exhaustion and a killer headache didn't keep her from smiling when her headlights spotted Mike's truck, parked near the house. He was leaning against the El Camino, arms crossed. She pulled under the hackberry tree and climbed out, anxious to thank him for this surprise welcome, until the greenish glow from the utility pole overhead illuminated a different emotion etched into his face. Her stomach clenched as he removed the space between them in three long, deliberate strides and anchored himself inches from her. His jaw tightened, and his gaze seared her expanding pupils.

"I've been sitting here for two hours. I thought you were going to call," his words accused.

This was not the greeting Kate expected.

"I did call," she retorted with a lift of her chin. "I asked that fountain clerk, Jake, to give you a message. Then I called you again as I was leaving town, but all I got was a busy signal."

She slammed the truck door and pushed past him.

"Thanks for the nice welcome home."

She jerked the tailgate open, grabbed a box and stomped her way to the front porch. Dropped it with a thud. Her chest ached with disappointment. She'd been looking forward to coming home, seeing Mike.

But now.

Her jaw clamped, and she stared straight ahead, ignoring him as she stalked back to the truck. She reached for one of the heavier boxes; her ear tuned for the crunching steps that would signal his goodbye.

So this is how it ends, huh? A miserable end to a miserable day.

Tears stung at her eyes and she sucked in a sharp breath.

"Kate, I'm sorry. I was worried because I hadn't heard from you."

He moved in beside her and turned her to face him, pulling her against his chest.

"I let my imagination run crazy, not knowing if you were okay or if something awful had happened. Look," he cupped her face in his hands. "I just found you. I can't stand the idea of losing you." His kiss was tentative. "Am I forgiven?"

Her emotions were a chaotic mess, but that was no reason to take it out on Mike. He was still here. He was apologizing. Besides, how could she stay mad at those chocolate-brown eyes begging for absolution?

"Fine," Kate pouted. But she let Mike kiss her again before she pulled away. "I just want to get this stuff in the house."

When they finished unloading, Kate stared at the boxes piled in the middle of the living room floor. Where was she going to put all this? It was too much to deal with tonight. She collapsed onto the couch, exhausted.

Mike kneaded her shoulders. "Why don't you go take a bath, and I'll fix you a sandwich. It'll make you feel better."

He was right. After a bath, a change of clothes and a couple of aspirins, she felt more like herself. When she walked into the kitchen, the table was set with silver flatware and a cloth napkin. A china plate held a thick ham sandwich, chips, and a pickle spear. Honey-colored liquid shimmered in a crystal goblet.

"Mead," Mike answered before she could ask.

He poured some for himself.

"This is tasty, but I can see how it could go to your head quickly."

Kate took a big gulp. She sure hoped so. That newspaper article about her mom's disappearance was unsettling. She was desperate for something to take her mind off it. At least until morning.

Mike finished his drink and pulled his keys out of his pocket.

"Do you have go now?" she asked. "Couldn't you stay a little while longer?"

They relocated to Kate's bedroom. She crawled under the blanket wearing shorts and a tank top. Mike lay on top of the chenille bedspread, his pillow propped against the headboard. Kate rested her head on his chest. Over his heart. So she could hear its steady thump. Mike wrapped his arms around her.

"Will you go to sleep now?" he whispered into her hair.

"Mm hum," was Kate's drowsy reply.

She was talking on the phone to mom, elated to hear her voice. Kate told her how much she missed her. They talked about Grandma. About Mike. As long as she had Mom on the phone, maybe this was a good opportunity to ask about yesterday's discovery.

"Mom, you know, I was going through your cedar chest and found this old newspaper article. And," she stumbled on awkwardly, "well, I don't understand. It said you had disappeared, but I've never heard anything about that. So...what happened?"

The voice on the other end of the phone grew cold.

"You shouldn't be asking these questions."

Kate's heart rate ratcheted a notch. Something was wrong. It wasn't Mom at all. The voice deepened. With a growl it repeated, "You shouldn't be asking these questions."

Terror rose in Kate's chest.

"Mom, why are you talking like that, please stop," she cried out.

"YOU SHOULDN'T BE ASKING THESE QUESTIONS."

A black mist oozed through the receiver and formed twin tendrils that reached out and encircled her head. One split in half and crawled into her nostrils; the other forced its way into her mouth, past her clenched teeth, worming its way down her throat.

Kate clawed at her neck.

Can't...breathe...

"Kate."

A disembodied voice called her name.

"Kate, wake up."

She convulsed back into reality.

"I think you were having a nightmare," Mike said. "You were moaning."

She sat up and ran her fingers through her hair, taking deep, uniform breaths to subdue the pounding in her chest.

"It was horrible."

She gave a shudder, scrubbed her face with her hands. Then she glanced over at Mike and gave him a questioning look.

"You stayed?"

"It felt nice laying here beside you. I fell asleep." He rose up on his elbow. Reached to tuck a strand of hair behind her ear. "Are you gonna be okay?"

She gave a halfhearted nod.

He glanced at the alarm clock beside the bed.

"It's almost six. I should go home and get ready for work."

Kate still straddled the dimension between her nightmare and the real world. Mike's presence kept her tethered to this side of her personal twilight zone.

"Can't you stay and let me fix you some breakfast?"

They sat at the kitchen table. Mike attacked his food while Kate explained to him about the newspaper clipping.

"And you had no idea that ever happened?"

"None whatsoever," she said, refilled his coffee mug.

"I wish I had more time to talk about this," he said. "I figured you wouldn't venture into town today, after MacMurray's restriction from the market. But do you want to meet someplace for lunch?"

"What about that park just south of the square? We can have a picnic. Afterward, I can go to the library. This clipping only mentions a date. I can't tell what year it's from. Thought I'd drop in and see if the Ardee Informer ever published anything about it. And I want to check out a theory."

"And that theory is?"

"I want to see if it coincides with Peg's story about Mom quitting college to move up north."

Mike collected the breakfast dishes, kissed the top of Kate's head as he passed her on his way to the sink.

"You're a regular Miss Marple."

She wrinkled her nose.

"I hope not. She was an elderly spinster."

Kate followed Mike to his truck. She trailed her fingers along its side, still reluctant to see him leave.

"Thanks for staying with me last night," she said.

He caressed her face and gave her a gentle kiss.

"No other place I'd rather be."

Two things were at the forefront of her mind right now – the newspaper article and the books Robert had given her. After Mike left, Kate poured another cup of coffee and picked up the horticulture book. It had the antique smell of rich, hand-tooled leather and fine parchment. She opened it and skimmed the title page – 'The Complete Hothouse Gardner,' John Stockton, 1789, First Edition. *First Edition?* She turned several pages. Kate had seen these types of illustrations before in older manuscripts. They were copper-engraved etchings. She propped her right elbow on the table and rested her temple against her palm. This was an expensive book. Why had Robert given her something so valuable? She massaged her head as she ran her left index finger down the list of topics until she found it. Poisonous plants.

"Beautiful but deadly, these plants can cause mild to severe symptoms, even death," she read aloud. Hemlock she recognized as a long-time favorite for poisoning kings. She'd heard of castor oil but didn't know that the castor bean plant was toxic. And the oleander was one of the most toxic of the flowering plants. This was a revelation, because they grew everywhere in the area. Even Peg had several pink oleander bushes growing in her front yard.

The next page was devoted to the flower Robert had saved her from. Monkshood. John Stockton advised that the plant be handled with care; gloves worn because even a slight dose of its poison could cause an allergic reaction and render the victim in need of medical attention. She went on to read that it was very easy to extract poison from the plant. One had only to crush it in a suitable amount of water and then give the monkshood imbibed water to the intended victim.

Someone with knowledge like this would be able to do significant damage, and nobody would even know.

No wonder Robert had been so concerned about whether she'd had contact with the plant. And something else troubled her. She had the notion that she'd seen monkshood somewhere besides the clump in the middle of the lavender bush.

Kate reached for her coffee, but it had gone cold. That was okay. She had things to do before her lunch with Mike. She closed the book and grabbed the roasting pan from the kitchen cabinet.

It was a beautiful day. Puffs of feathery clouds moved in unison across the sky, and the slight breeze was just enough to keep the midday temperature from being too oppressive. Kate was careful to avoid the streets close to the flea market, although she did feel a stab of remorse. If not for her ignorance, she'd be there again today.

A large oak provided the ideal spot, shady and away from the playground. She spread a quilt and unpacked the picnic basket. It was a feast – chicken salad sandwiches, potato salad, a container of bread-and-butter pickles and some pickled okra she'd found in Grandma's canning pantry. She'd even thrown together a half dozen deviled eggs.

Kate waited for Mike, gnawing on what was left of her fingernails.

Know what he knows.

A disturbing idea was beginning to form from the dark cloud swirling around in her head.

Mom's disappearance. Did it have something to do with Darcy?

The park was only a short walk from the pharmacy. Kate saw Mike cross the parking lot. She waved to get his attention.

"So, how's it goin'?" Mike plopped onto the blanket beside her, eyed the picnic spread.

"I know, don't tell me," Kate said and rolled her eyes. "You're starving."

She piled food onto a paper plate. Stabbed a fork into the middle of the heap of potato salad and handed it to him.

"Here," she said. "Eat."

She pulled the old newspaper clipping from its envelope and read it to him. Her shoulders slouched as she exhaled a discouraged sigh. "It's like, each day I uncover another secret from my family's hidden past."

"You'd never think such a sweet, beautiful girl would come with such a huge closet of skeletons."

"It's not funny." She punched him in the arm. "It's troubling, and all I seem to find are more questions and no answers."

"Ouch." He rubbed his bicep. "Somebody doesn't know her own strength."

"Be serious," Kate implored. "I feel like I'm on the right track of 'know what he knows.' That dream I had still bothers the heck out of me. And Darcy's comment about not asking the question unless I'm prepared for the answer. You don't think that the dream was, you know, some warning, do you?"

She hoped Mike would laugh at the idea. Instead, he shrugged.

"I don't know how to answer that. Lots of people think the subconscious mind gives us dreams to protect us or inform us about things going on in the conscious world. I wouldn't worry about it. Then again, I wouldn't necessarily discount it either."

He offered Kate his hand, helped her to her feet. "I have to go back to work now, but I'll be over later and we can talk about what we know so far, see if we can make sense of it." He pulled her close, kissed her forehead. "I love you, and I'm in this with you. We'll figure it out."

Mike loped across the park towards the town square while Kate packed the leftovers back into her Nova. It was a short drive to the library. She produced her library card and asked Mrs. Stewart for the newspaper slides from early spring to summer of 1954. She was skimming the pages from the May twentieth edition when the words 'Hawkins University' caught her attention. As she began to read, a familiar tension squeezed the oxygen from her lungs.

Local girl missing - Police question evidence

The Hawkins University Police Department has reported that there is no new information regarding missing local girl, Kathleen McKenna. Miss McKenna was last seen on the Hawkins campus around 3:00 p.m. on Friday, May 14th. Police are reluctant to label the disappearance as an abduction, but sources say evidence found in Miss McKenna's dorm room suggests a possible struggle took place. As always, anyone knowing the whereabouts of the missing student should contact the University Police Department.

Disappearance an abduction?
Possible struggle?
She looked up at the ceiling.
Mom, what the heck happened?

Back at the house, Kate opened her journal to the notes she'd taken and laid the newspaper article on the table beside it. Remembering Darcy's reaction when he first saw it, she removed the pendant from around her neck and set it on the journal. She stood back, crossed her arms, and hugged herself tightly.
There has to be some connection. There just has to be.
Her stomach became a knot of nerves as Darcy MacMurray's warning to not underestimate him replayed in her head.
Okay, I've got to quit obsessing over this for now.

She pulled out the cutting board and began shredding lettuce, slicing tomatoes, cucumbers, zucchini, green onions, red peppers, mushrooms and celery into a big wooden salad bowl. She added green and black olives and pepperoncini. Threw in chunks of roasted chicken and fresh herbs she'd cut from the garden. It was her favorite 'everything but the kitchen sink' salad.

At the sound of the El Camino pulling into the driveway, she stepped out onto the porch. Mike was already out of the car and headed toward her. He carried a bottle of wine in one hand, a carton of ice cream in the other.

Kate laughed. "I thought it was wine and flowers."

"Aha," Mike countered, "under most circumstances, you'd be correct. But this is not most circumstances. And this," he emphasized, "is no ordinary ice cream. This is the best store-bought ice cream you will ever put in your mouth. No, seriously," he said as he stuck it in the freezer, "this is from a creamery south of here in Brenham that only sells to grocery stores in Texas. I was lucky to get a container before it sold out. It tastes like home-made vanilla ice cream, and it is a-mazing."

"Maybe we should skip dinner and go straight for dessert."

"Oh no, I have plans for this ice cream. I envision eating it out under the stars."

He scooped a mountain of salad onto his plate. Drowned it in Green Goddess dressing.

"What's this?" he asked, thumbing towards the objects on the table.

"It's silly, I guess. I had the idea that if I laid it all out where I could concentrate, I might get some clue as to what happened." She shrugged and gave a frustrated huff. "I just don't have enough information."

Mike picked up her journal and read the entry she'd copied from the Ardee Informer.

"So Peg said your mom's falling out with Darcy took place in the spring after she turned twenty-one. And this newspaper article you found, it's from May of '54?"

"Yeah. And that part about a possible struggle and abduction." Kate shuddered. "I have to keep reminding myself that it all turned out okay. I mean, whatever happened, she survived, right? I just wish I knew how long she was missing, or when she turned up again. It could have been weeks. Months. Who knows?" She took a deep breath to try and calm the queasiness that churned in her stomach.

Mike's brows gathered together, and he picked up the pendant, concentrating on the picture inside.

"You were born on…?"

"May 30, 1955."

"So you were born a little over a year after she went missing."

What exactly was he implying?

Kate's eyes narrowed.

Mike must have read her expression. He stumbled on, apologetic. "I'm trying to get a grasp on this. I'm not trying to insinuate anything."

She covered her face with her hands. Shook her head slowly.

"You don't have to. The evidence is right here. I should have done the math calculations myself. Three months after my mom disappeared, she got pregnant. Was it a shotgun wedding? Is that why they got divorced so soon afterward?" The words were bitter on her tongue. "Was she even married at all?"

Everything Kate thought she knew.

Everything she'd always believed.

It was all beginning to feel like one massive lie.

She grabbed the wine bottle. Filled her glass to the brim and took a long drink.

This is what happens when you face the past. You get kicked in the teeth.

"Come on, let's go outside and see if we can spot some falling stars. Never got to make my wish the last time," Mike said, in an undisguised attempt to change her mood.

Kate let him take her hand and lead her outside. He grabbed a colorful Indian blanket out of the front seat of the El Camino. Spread it out near the old concrete storm shelter in the backyard, the telescope positioned at its edge.

"You wait here," he instructed. "See if you can locate the North Star. I'll be back in a minute."

She did as she was told, mostly because she was still in shock. For as long as she could remember, Kate had idolized her mother. Beautiful, funny, smart, hardworking. And she was the most upstanding person Kate had ever known. What happened that spring of 1954 and the ensuing months? Questions swirled through her mind like a tornado. Why did her mother disappear? Who did she meet in those three months? Who *was* her father?

Mike's footsteps crunched across the driveway. He balanced two bowls, filled with ice cream. The melting contents had already begun to dribble down the sides. Kate rescued the tottering bowl just before it spilled all over the blanket.

"That's more ice cream than I could eat in a month," she said.

"Too bad... guess I'll have to finish off what you don't eat."

Mike dug into his bowl. Kate took a few bites, set hers aside, and lay back on the blanket.

"I was thinking about what you said. How the planets and stars we can see are the equivalent to a handful of sand. Who am I and what are my problems compared to the universe? Just thinking about it makes me feel small and insignificant."

Mike lay down beside her, propping up on his elbow. He smiled and brushed a wisp of stray hair from her cheek.

"You're not insignificant. You're important. To a lot of people. Particularly me."

Running his hand along her jawline, Mike tilted her head. He traced her neck with his lips. The warmth of his breath made her pulse accelerate. A slight turn of her head and her lips found his. Lingered. Then she pushed him away.

"Your ice cream is melting."

Mike laughed. "If it wasn't before, it sure is now."

They lay watching the stars. Mike sat up and adjusted the telescope to show her a closer view of Venus.

"Look," he grabbed her arm. "Did you see that? Our shooting star. Quick, make a wish."

"But I didn't see it."

"That's okay. I'll use my wish for something good for both of us."

Kate sighed. "I guess I better put these ice cream bowls away before we attract unwanted ant visitors."

She started to the house. Mike followed her inside.

"Mr. Clarke asked me to open a little earlier tomorrow. So I probably need to head home."

Kate retrieved her pendant from the table and fastened it around her neck, unable to hide her disappointment.

"Awww....don't look at me with those sad, puppy-dog eyes. You know I can't leave when you look at me like that."

Lying on the bed as they had the night before, her face nuzzled against Mike's chest, they talked in hushed tones. Warm. Intimate.

"As soon as I get more experience, I want to leave Ardee," Mike said. "Maybe try Dallas or Houston. I want to live in a bigger city after this. Not that I'm in any hurry to leave here, but I'd like to find a place where the whole town doesn't know every move you make. The pay would be better too. Give me more options to do the things I want to do. Like settle down. Get married and start a family."

He pulled her closer. Buried his face in her neck.

"What do you want Kate?"

He dozed off before she could answer. But it was something she'd asked herself a hundred times lately.

What *did* she want?

The question troubled her.

Maybe that was the reason for the vision.

Afterward, she lay awake most of the night, unable to get past the sight of Darcy MacMurray's face imprinted on the velvet backdrop of her closed eyelids. His lips curved in a sneer as he asked in Robert Kavanagh's melodic dialect, "You didn't seriously think you were in control of your destiny. Did you?"

Chapter 10

Two o'clock on the nose.

Excitement fluttered in Kate's stomach. Up until now she hadn't realized how much she anticipated seeing Robert again. She rapped on the greenhouse door and gave it a yank. It swung open easily. Maybe he was already inside. She called out. No answer.

She walked the length of the greenhouse. Still no sign of Robert, but on the potting table was propped an envelope with her name written across the front in florid script. Might as well open it.

She raised the flap and extracted the contents. Her fingers shook as she counted the bills. Four hundred dollars. Almost enough to pay the fine. She held the envelope to her chest, looked up at the skylight and uttered 'thank you.' Then she opened the note that accompanied the cash.

> *Dear Kate,*
>
> *I greatly apologize for my hasty departure and for not being able to meet with you in person. I am disappointed because I was looking forward to discussing the care of my plants, but handwritten instructions will have to suffice. You will find a notebook on this table that will likely answer all your questions about what needs to be done.*

I am unsure how long I will be absent, so I gave you an advance that should cover several weeks' worth of your time and labor. I hope you find this acceptable.

I also wanted to speak on another very important subject, but it appears this conversation will have to wait until my return. I don't know if you had a chance to look at the books I gave you, but please pay close attention to the passage marked in the book on Irish history and folklore. You see the gift, for those who know how to use it, can be of great value. Guard it carefully.

> *Your faithful friend,*
> *Robert*

She picked up the notebook and flipped through several pages. He had organized the instructions like a schematic and had drawn pencil sketches that depicted each bed and below that, a legend that named each plant and its position in the flower bed. He'd also included specifics on how to care for the more delicate African violets and the orchids.

Robert could cook, he was an expert horticulturist, and these drawings were astonishingly detailed. Kate shook her head. It would have taken her three lifetimes to acquire that kind of talent, and this guy had accomplished it in, what, thirty years?

She stuffed the cash and the message back into the envelope, stuck it between the notebook's pages and looked around one more time. If Robert wasn't going to show up, she might as well take the notebook back home with her to read, right?

Who was she kidding?

She wanted to go pull out the book on Irish history and find the section he'd marked.

It lay on the kitchen table where she'd left it the night before. How had she missed the green tassel that poked its way out of the top? She slid her forefinger between the pages. The tassel attached to a woven silk bookmark. There was a verse stitched into the cloth.

'May the sun shine brightly on your windowpane, may the rainbow be certain to follow each rain.'

Coming from Robert, she assumed it was an Irish blessing.

Her eyes tracked the page, down to the bracket penciled around several paragraphs. The first passage was about Brighid the 'Exalted One,' daughter of the Dagda.

"Known as the Goddess of healers, poets, Goddess of fire and hearth, folklore and customs regarding Brighid have carried down over the centuries more than all the other Gaelic deities combined. Brighid, or Brigit, as she was sometimes known, would perform miracles that included blessing and cursing elements. Legend says that Brigit had cursed a woman for her stingy nature so that her apple trees would no longer bear fruit. Then later blessed a generous nun so that her garden would yield twice the ordinary amount of fruit."

Kate paused. Where had she heard this before? Maybe it was one of the bedtime stories her mother had read to her when she was young. She shook her head and continued reading.

"The belief in blessings and curses is a Celtic tradition that has survived long into Christian times. One such artifact associated with this belief is the bullaun stone, or cursing stone, a large, rectangular block of weathered rock, often limestone. 'Bullaun,' pronounced bullán, refers to the deep bowl-shaped depressions hollowed out of its upper side. Naturally rounded stones sit in the hollows. One can administer blessings or curses whilst turning the stone clockwise in the hollow. Folklore often attaches magical significance to the bullaun stone, such as the belief that rainwater collected in a stone's hollow has healing properties. These stones have an indisputable association with water, and with the worship of the Celtic fire goddess Brighid. Few of these stones still exist. Most are found in remote areas of Ireland and Scotland."

Kate closed the book and tilted back in her chair.

Blessings? Curses? Magic?

Her emotions were fighting a civil war; a battle between disbelief and what she'd seen with her own eyes the past few days. There was no denying something unusual was going on and this bullaun stone story if it were true, would sure explain a lot.

And what about Robert? He must have known. Why else would he have given her the book and marked that specific paragraph?

She walked down the hallway to her room and flung open the French doors. In the past, the stone bench had been her oasis, a place of comfort. Now, she approached it with a blend of exhilaration and caution.

It was impossible to determine how old the slab was. The book said that some stones from Ireland dated as far back as 500 B.C. She ran her fingers across the surface, tracing the bullauns. No wonder the smaller stone fit into the hollow so perfectly.

The hot, southerly wind blew through the willow's draping branches and made them dance as wildly as her thoughts.

Did Grandma know this was a bullaun stone?

Was that why she was never sick?

Had she used the stone to keep herself healthy?

But that didn't make sense. If that were the case, she wouldn't be lying in a coma up at Memorial right now.

Something was still missing. Some bit of information that would help explain it all.

Kate huffed with exasperation.

I wish Robert were here. I know he'd be able to answer my questions.

And she was impatient to talk to Mike. As soon as the El Camino pulled into the drive, Kate rushed out to meet him.

A grin spread across his face. "You found out something and you can't wait to tell me."

"Oh I'm not going to tell you," she teased, "I'm going to let you discover it yourself."

She handed him the book, opened to the marked paragraph. Watched his expression. Saw exactly when the revelation hit him the same way it had her.

"So, the cut on your face and your bruises, the healing had to do with this...this bullaun stone?"

Kate nodded, told him about accidently splashing rainwater on herself both times.

Mike's brow furrowed. "But how is Robert Kavanagh involved in this? He must know something since he highlighted that particular section for you to read."

"Yeah, I wondered the same thing." She showed him the note Robert left, then read the last sentence aloud. "Do you think, being from Ireland, maybe he recognized what the stone was as soon as he saw it? But why didn't he say anything? In his message, he said he might be gone for several weeks. I'm sure he'll contact me as soon as he gets back into town, but in the meantime, more unanswered questions."

Her shoulders drooped as she closed the book and laid it on the table.

"Let's go get something to eat," Mike said. "I always think better on a full stomach and right now I'm–"

"Don't say it," Kate cupped her hand over his mouth, laughing.

He drew her into his arms and held her close. "I've missed you today. I thought about you the whole time."

"I sure hope not." Kate wriggled from his grasp. "I wouldn't want to think I was responsible if you didn't fill those prescriptions right."

"I'm serious," Mike protested. "I miss you when you aren't around and I look forward to the next time we can be together."

"That's what you say. I just can't imagine anyone wanting to be with me that much."

"Try harder," he whispered into her ear as he grabbed her hand and led her towards his truck.

After they had placed their order, Kate settled back into the booth and glanced around the room. Black and white tiled floors. A row of vinyl topped stools at the counter. Menu board that never changed.

She liked the cozy feel of the place.

You always knew you were going to get a delicious burger, a frosty mug of root beer, a friendly smile, and warmhearted chatter from Kimmie.

No variables.

No surprises.

Why can't life be like the Dairyette?

"I guess it's fairly obvious about the healings," Kate said, dredging her cheesy fries through a river of ketchup. "But what do you think of the part about blessings and curses? Do you believe that works too?"

"I don't know why it wouldn't. You could test it. Start small, like wishing that your grandmother's garden would prosper. Or maybe that Peg's cows produce richer milk or more calves. It might be one of those things where you can only bless others and not yourself. Too bad it didn't come with instructions."

Kate had just picked up her burger to take another bite when she inhaled sharply and dropped it back onto the plate. Her eyes widened as she met Mike's.

"Know what he knows," she said. "What if this is what he knows? What if Darcy knows about the stone and, you know, everything it can do."

"You think your mom knew about it and told him?"

"If Mom did know, and she and Darcy were as close as Peg said they were, I would almost guarantee she did."

Mike let out a slow breath.

"Well, certainly an unsavory person would have a lot to gain with knowledge like that. Doesn't make sense, though. If he knows about it, why didn't he do something a long time ago? There's still a piece of the puzzle we're missing."

He polished off the last bite of his burger and eyed Kate's abandoned half. "Uh, if you're not gonna finish that..."

She pushed the plate towards him. She wouldn't have been able to swallow past the lump in her throat anyway. Kate absentmindedly watched while Mike consumed the remains of her burger. What would a man like Darcy do if he got hold of that kind of power? Curse his enemies? Use blessings to obtain wealth for influential friends? Become a 'god' benevolently healing whomever he wished? The idea made cold chills race down her spine.

Mike walked Kate to the front door; fingers laced through hers. She started to untangle them and reach for her keys, but Mike wouldn't release her. He pulled her closer and leaned his head to hers, searching for her lips.

"Would you like to stay a while?" she interrupted his kiss with her question. "Have a coke or a glass of tea?"

They sat on the front porch, serenaded by crickets, cicadas, and frogs, with an occasional interrupting hoot from a barn owl. Kate liked that they didn't have to always talk. It was enough just to be together, shoulders touching, fingers entwined.

Mike broke the silence.

"Wouldn't it be great to lay out a couple of sleeping bags and spend the night under the stars? We should do that. We should go on a camping trip. They have some campsites at the state park. Or better yet" – his excitement seemed to grow at the prospect – "there's this campground up in Oklahoma that I heard the guys talking about. It's in the Kiamichi Mountains. Really nice place, and you can set up close to the river. You haven't lived until you've eaten bacon and eggs cooked over a campfire."

"You're serious about this," she said.

"Sure. There's tons of stuff to do there. You can rent boats, there are hiking trails. We can fish, swim. Heck, we can just lie around in the sun all day if we want. You know, I'm due some vacation time. I can talk to Mr. Clarke and take a long weekend. That is if you're interested."

Mike's mood was contagious. A few days away might be just the thing to get her mind off all the craziness of the past couple of weeks. As they discussed their plans, the moon rose higher and brighter in the sky. It was getting late, but Kate had already made up her mind. She was *not* going to ask Mike to stay again tonight. Her insecurity might make her weak, but her pride stood its ground, braced for his departure.

She needn't have wasted the energy.

"You know, I could come in for a while…hang out. That is if you want me to."

Mike sat on the bed with the mythology book while Kate brushed her teeth. When she re-entered the room, he commented, "You know, this is interesting," and began to read aloud, "On rare occasions, someone will leave the mortal world to live in the Faerie realm by choice. They don't usually stay in the Faerie realm for long before returning to their home. None of them returns the same, however. They will have changed in some way. Traditionally, one who returns will possess a gift and may be a master of herbal or magical knowledge."

Kate took the book out of his hands and laid it on the nightstand.

"If you had told me two weeks ago that I would be having a serious discussion about Faeries and magical stones, I'd have said you were crazy. This might be legends and myths for some, but I guess it's my reality now."

"Our reality now," Mike corrected.

Kate turned off the lamp and crawled under the covers to lie on her side. Mike snuggled against her back, his arm draped over her, hugging her tightly to him. She dropped off to sleep, his reassurance echoing in her head.

"Whatever happens Kate, it will be okay."

Before he left for work, Mike promised Kate he'd call his great-aunt and find out an exact time for their visit. In the meantime, she decided to act on Mike's suggestion about testing the powers of the bullaun stone. Now was as good a time as any to give it a try.

She eyed the limestone slab. Bit her lower lip.

If this was her new reality, better get used to it.

Besides, she needed something substantial to prove to herself once and for all that it was true. She reached for the smaller stone. Rotating it to the right, she closed her eyes and imagined lots of calves frolicking around in Peg's fields. Visualized thick, rich milk from her cows poured into tall glasses from a blue ceramic pitcher. Envisioned Peg's cotton crop with fluffy, white fiber bursting from their bolls. Concentrating hard on what she should do next, Kate took a deep breath.

"Peg Flanagan – may every good seed you planted bear fruit. May your cattle multiply with abundance and produce the richest milk in the county and may all your poultry yield two-fold. May everything you put your hand to, prosper."

She made the sign of the cross, opened her eyes and shrugged her right shoulder.

"Amen?"

Kate carried the smaller stone into the house with her and set it on the dresser. She was still a little unclear as to whether it was this particular stone, or just any stone that would make the blessing come true. But she wasn't going to take any chances by leaving it outside anymore.

After a quick shower and change of clothes, Kate retrieved the envelope with the money Robert advanced her. She counted out four hundred dollars and added the twenties she'd made from the market. That fine would be paid today. One more weight off her shoulders.

Thirty minutes later she was in the courthouse lobby, staring at the receipt stamped '*Paid in full.*'

On an impulse, Kate walked up the stairs to the mayor's office. A little voice questioned her lucidity, but she was determined to face him.

Honor and Courage.

No more intimidation.

Unbowed. Unbroken.

She'd show him that the Barrett name still meant something.

Ashling eyed Kate, her perfectly penciled eyebrows raised.

"Miss McKenna. I didn't expect to see you back so soon."

"I know I don't have an appointment, but is the mayor busy? I just need a moment of his time. And please," she gave Ashling a sunny smile, hoping to thaw the icy look she'd received, "call me Kate."

Ashling picked up the phone. Her formal announcement rejected Kate's overture of friendship.

"Miss McKenna is here to see you."

Ashling dropped the receiver onto the cradle and crossed the lobby to the large, ornate doors. With an elaborate sweep of her hand, she opened them. The doors closed heavily behind Kate.

The thick curtains were parted enough to let in a slice of sunlight. The mayor was seated, his back to Kate. He let several minutes pass before rotating to face her, elbows resting on the chair arms, forefingers pressed together, tapping restlessly against his lips.

He heaved an annoyed sigh.

"Miss McKenna, how may I help you today?"

Kate held out the stamped receipt.

"I came by to show you that the fine has been paid."

"And I'm supposed to react...how? Be impressed? Praise you for taking care of your obligation in a timely manner? Please, I have more important..."

His words were drowned by the drumming pulse in her ears. The hair on Kate's arms raised as Robert's words rocketed their way back into her head. Exploded into comprehension.

An assassin's weapon of choice.

Darcy stood abruptly. Broke her concentration. Kate's gaze shifted slowly from the nearby vase of flowers to his face. His eyes became narrow slits and his lips crooked into a smirk.

Or was it an actual smile?

His tone dismissed her.

"Do I need to show you to the door or can you find it yourself?"

By the time she arrived at the hospital, her hands were no longer shaking. Kate took the elevator to the floor where her grandmother had first been assigned.

"Hi, how're you doing today?" Kate asked in her cheeriest voice.

The nurse looked up from her paperwork.

"Can I help you?"

"I'm Pearl McKenna's granddaughter, Kate. She's in the ICU now, but before that she was a patient on this floor."

"Right, I know Mrs. McKenna."

"Great! So when I visited my grandmother before she was moved, I noticed she had some floral arrangements on the window sill. I wanted to get the cards off them so I could send thank-you notes. I know that's what Grandma would want." Kate allowed her bottom lip to tremble slightly. "But since flowers aren't allowed in the intensive care unit, I wondered if maybe someone had collected the cards before they were thrown away."

The nurse nodded and crossed the speckled linoleum to a tall, green filing cabinet where she extracted a manila envelope.

"Sorry, we didn't get these to you sooner. One of our candy stripers, Rebekah, was here the day they moved your grandmother to the ICU. She was the one who gathered these, then took the wilted flowers out to the dumpster. The day got a little crazy after that, so it slipped my mind."

Kate had opened the flap to peer down into the envelope. Something inside nudged her to stop what she was doing and pay attention. She frowned and inclined her head toward the nurse.

"Really? What happened?"

"Well, she didn't come back right away, so we sent an orderly to locate her." The nurse clucked her teeth. "Poor thing. He found her by the dumpster, violently ill, clutching her neck like she couldn't breathe. Scared the living daylights out of us, for sure. She spent a night in the hospital for observation, but we never did figure out what brought it on. Haven't seen hide nor hair of her since." She shrugged. "Can hardly blame the girl, though."

Kate forced herself to remain calm as she stuffed the envelope into her bag. She gave the nurse another grateful smile.

"Thanks again, I sure do appreciate this."

"No problem. Hope everything turns out okay with your grandmother."

Kate rode the elevator up to the ICU.

She took her grandmother's hand. Spoke quietly into her ear.

"It's okay. I think I understand now, and I know what needs to happen. You hang in there." She brushed aside the lock of silver that curled across her grandmother's forehead. "You hang in there until I figure out exactly what to do."

Chapter 11

Mike got to the house a couple of minutes before seven. He opened the door to the El Camino, and Kate started to climb in, but before she could, he grabbed her around the waist and pulled her to face him.

"Oh, no you don't. Not until I get a kiss."

His kiss articulated how much he'd missed her.

"Huh, uh. We have stuff to do first." Kate pushed firmly away from his chest. "Plenty of time for that later."

Mike's aunt lived east of town. He exited the highway onto a strip of asphalt road, which wound between field after field of cotton and hay until a sharp left landed them on a narrow, dirt lane. Kate swore if you didn't know it was there, you'd miss it completely.

"She likes the privacy," Mike responded. "I've tried to get her to move closer to town so I can keep an eye on her and make sure she's okay. But she's bullheaded. Once she gets her mind set…" He grinned across the bench seat at Kate. "Think maybe that trait runs in the family."

The further they drove, the thicker the pecan, and live oak trees became. They reached across the road and entwined their branches together, forming a thick canopy overhead. Kate got the distinct impression it wasn't a random design, but that the trees were deliberately creating an archway to honor something or someone dear to them.

At the end of the road, the trees parted to reveal a large lot where a white, wood-frame house stood, surrounded by more pecan and live oak trees. Wild roses in various shades of pink and red climbed its sides, and amethyst plumes of salvia lined the walkway. The front porch held a small metal table, brightened by a colorful square of fabric. Two wicker chairs sat nearby, their deep cushioned seats inviting company to come on up, relax, and sit a while.

"It's a pretty little house," Kate said.

"The old homestead. She and my grandmother grew up here."

The front door was open.

"Aunt Cass?" he called through the screen door. "It's Mike. I'm here with my friend, Kate. You know, Mrs. Pearl's granddaughter."

They stepped inside.

Cassidy Quinn rose from her rocking chair; ninety pounds of pink porcelain, with a rope of braided silver hair that circled her head like a halo. Her steps were slow but graceful as she came forward to greet them.

"Come in, come in. So delighted to meet you."

She reached for Kate's hand and gave it a slight squeeze. Her hazel eyes brightened.

"Michael said you were special. He was right. Come sit down, my dear. I have so much to tell you."

Kate glanced at Mike, but he just shrugged and mouthed 'don't look at me.'

A teapot began to whistle on the kitchen stove.

"Please, make yourself at home. Would you like a cup of tea, dear?"

Cassidy poured hot water over the leaves in the Blue Willow-patterned cup.

"Oh, no thanks, Miss Quinn," Kate answered.

"Let me get that for you." Mike reached for the saucer and held it while his aunt pulled the rocking chair closer to Kate, who had taken a seat on the edge of the couch.

"Dear me," she patted Kate's hand. "Please call me Aunt Cass. I'll be offended if you don't."

She took a sip of tea.

"You are here today to find the missing pieces to a puzzle that has been laid out before you."

More a statement than a question, Kate decided. She gave a nod.

"Oh, where to start," Aunt Cass muttered to herself. "Well, they always say to start at the beginning."

She began a gentle rock, back and forth, as she proceeded to tell her story.

"Back in the early nineteen-hundreds Ardee was a small town with a proud Irish heritage. Many of the families were descendants of the first settlers who had come straight from Ireland. Michael tells me that you have been reading up on Irish history and folklore, so you understand that our beliefs are strong, even to this day. Tradition is of great importance to us. The founding fathers of Ardee loved tradition as much as anyone, so they established July 10th as Founder's Day and held a festival each year to commemorate the occasion. This particular story revolves around that very celebration. I remember the year like it was yesterday. Nineteen hundred and twenty-three. My little sister, Caireanne and I..."

"I'm sorry, I mean, excuse me please," Kate tried to interrupt politely. "You said your sister's name was... How do you say it?"

"The English pronunciation is more like Karen, but it's spelled C-a-i-r-e-a-n-n-e."

"Was she the best friend my grandmother wrote about in her diary?"

Aunt Cass smiled broadly.

"One and the same. Pearl was an only child, but Caireanne was like a sister to her. They were working the concession booth at the Founder's Day Festival that year Pearl met Aidan. A more handsome man you'd never find. Tall, dark hair, deep blue eyes. All the girls were aflutter about him, but it was Pearl he wanted. Courted her from day one. Always bringing her flowers, scarves, little trinkets. I remember her birthday that year she turned twenty. Aidan had given her a beautiful Claddagh ring. She showed it to Caire and me privately. She wasn't sure how her parents would take it, a man giving her a ring after such a short period. She needn't have been concerned, though. That Aidan, he could win anyone with his smile and irresistible personality. Had her parents eating out of his hand in no time.

Aidan continued to woo Pearl, even when she was off at nursing school. And I see," she reached out to touch Kate's silver pendant, "that you wear the gift he gave her for Christmas that year. Those two. They spent every minute they could together. As soon as Pearl returned from school the next spring, Mr. and Mrs. Barrett put their engagement announcement in the newspaper. Everyone was excited about the upcoming nuptials.

Pearl told Caire that they were going to St. Louis to meet some of Aidan's family. They left, oh, I guess it was early June, for what was supposed to be a two or three-month visit. What happened next, none of us anticipated.

I remember the evening Mrs. Barrett came to the house, as distraught as I've ever seen anyone in my life. Her eyes were red-rimmed and puffy like she'd been crying for hours. I answered the door. She begged me to find Caireanne. They went into the parlor and closed the doors, but I could still hear them. Mrs. Barrett was pleading with Caire to come talk to Pearl. She said that Pearl had broken off her engagement and wouldn't tell anyone why and that she refused to eat anything and would hardly drink enough water to stay alive. Mrs. Barrett though she might confide in her best friend.

Caire did try to talk to her, but Pearl stayed silent. It was many years later before she told Caireanne the whole story."

Aunt Cass stopped to take another sip of her tea.

"I know you are impatient to have your questions answered, but I wanted to lay the groundwork. Michael," she set her teacup aside, "could you please fetch that bible off the mantle and bring it to me?"

To Kate she said, "Your grandmother gave these to Caireanne many years ago. When my dear sister lay on her deathbed, she entrusted me with the story. I think she knew maybe someday, someone would need this information. And here you sit."

Aunt Cass stopped rocking. Took Kate's hand.

"You are aware that something unusual is taking place in your life right now. I think you will understand when you read these. My question to you is – do you honestly want to know the truth?"

Kate's mouth was drier than a Permian Basin dust storm. She croaked out, "I do."

Aunt Cass held out the sheets of parchment.

Kate's fingers trembled as she took them.

She recognized her grandmother's writing and knew exactly what they were. The pages missing from the diary.

"It is hard to know where to begin. I suppose I should start with the trip to St. Louis, which turned out to be the pivotal point in our relationship, indeed, of my entire life.

Our journey began on a beautiful, sunny summer day in early June. We left Ardee in Aidan's butter-colored Duesenberg. He and I were both in excellent spirits. Aidan was humming a lovely Irish tune, and we laughed about all the fun we would have when we could be together forever. After a bit, he became quiet, pensive. I asked him if anything was wrong.

He found a solid stretch of land beside the road and pulled over. He took both my hands and admitted that he must tell me about himself, something about which he had been less than forthcoming. My heart dropped. Had he been married before? Was he a gambler? Is that how he was able to give me such lavish gifts?

He pulled me closer and lifted my face to his. His lips were soft as he pressed them against mine and professed his love. Then he revealed his secret.

At first I chuckled, then laughed aloud. This was another of his pranks like he used to pull with his brothers, Niall, and Robert. But when I saw the gravity of his countenance, I was convinced he was telling the truth.

Aidan said that he was a descendant of the goddess, Danu, driven into exile to live in the Otherworld. A place called The Land of the Young. His kind could exist in perfect happiness, never wanting for food or drink or any material comforts, and they would not grow old, not as long as they stayed there.

I know you have doubts, he said, because humans have been led to believe that Faeries are tiny little creatures with wings that fly like twinkly lights in the woods. But you can see that is not true.

Aidan begged me to come with him, to see where and how he lived. I was not afraid to go with him, but I love my world – even nursing school. I know it was hard, but I truly loved it. I believe I have a gift of caring for others, of helping heal their wounds, giving them strength to carry on with their lives. Those were things I would have to think about, but I made up my mind to visit Tir na nÓg."

Kate raised her head. Aunt Cass rocked back and forth with her eyes closed, an angelic smile on her face. Mike, on the other hand, sat on the edge of the couch, bouncing his knee. When Kate's eyes met his, he rubbed his hand down the leg of his jeans and raised a brow. She gave him the pages she'd finished reading then concentrated on the last few entries.

> *"My visit was like a dream come true. All the Faeries were strong and beautiful. We spent our days lounging on emerald green lawns, strolling by lakes that sparkled like liquid sapphires. We dined on the most decadent foods. It was a wondrous world, and anyone else would have gladly traded places with me, I'm sure. But it didn't feel right. What about Mother and Father, my friends, my life? More important – what about my dreams of being a nurse? There was no need for nurses where everything was perfect. Maybe too perfect for a human like me.*
>
> *My unhappiness was quickly evident. I would burst into tears with no apparent reason, and I lost my appetite for food. Finally, I convinced Aidan to take me home. I explained that I could not marry him. That I cannot walk away from what I know is a special calling – the desire to care for the sick and infirm. I know I am making the right decision, but it is the hardest thing I have ever done in my entire life. Because the truth is, I love Aidan with all my heart. I hope he will never forget me, as I will never, ever forget him."*

The print became a blur.

To walk away from that kind of love. All because her conviction to become a nurse was also a call from the heart. Kate wiped the wetness from the corners of her eyes and read the remaining pages.

"This I must tell you, Dear Diary because it is going to impact, as I see it, many things, including my future—and that of my descendants.

Today I made a trip into town with Mother and Father, my first trip outside the house in several weeks. It is July 10th – one year from the day I met Aidan. The Founder's Day celebration takes place today, but I could not bring myself to go. I wanted to avoid any possibility of seeing Aidan. The pain is still too fresh.

Mother wanted to attend, so she and Father settled on a compromise. She went off to buy a cake from the Women's Auxiliary booth. Father waited in the car with me. He knew I was miserable and understood my refusal to attend.

We were away from the house perhaps an hour or more. When we arrived home, I went to my room as usual and closed the door, locking it behind me. I tried to shut out the maddening voices in my head, still arguing about whether or not I had made the right decision. It was suffocating. I needed some fresh air.

I stepped out into the backyard. Right away I saw the large, stone block under the willow tree. A piece of paper fluttered beneath a fist-size rock. It was a note from Aidan. He asked me to meet him at the bridge. He wanted to explain to me about a gift he left me under the willow. I searched but found nothing. I suppose my curiosity got the better of me.

Was I doing the right thing by meeting him? Would I change my mind at the sight of his adoring face? My hands shook as I entered the wooded area near the stream and made my way to the wooden bridge.

Aidan appeared from out of the woods, handsome as ever in his shirtsleeves, wearing a plaid vest, his dark brown Ivy cap in one hand. With the other, he took my hand and led me to sit on a flat tree stump nearby, where he crouched on one knee beside me.

Dearest Pearl, he said, I love you with all my heart, and will love you always. I know you are tormented right now, and I do not want to cause you further grief, so I have left you a gift. I replied that I didn't see a gift, only a large slab of limestone and a smaller round rock. At this, he grinned, his indigo eyes sparkling. Aye, but that IS the gift, he said to me.

It's called a bullaun stone. He told me how to use it for blessing and curses. And about the healing rainwater. But the best part, he said, was the unique power it held. If I change my mind and want to be with him, all I need do is turn the stone clockwise and speak his name. He would for me, and we could be together – forever young and forever in love.

The power of the bullaun stone will only last one year, he said. But the second, more important part is this – any female offspring from the Barrett bloodline will be entitled to the same power in the year of her twenty-first birthday. If I ever changed my mind, she too could fetch him so he could return and take me away to be with him.

If I had not been to Tir na nÓg myself, I would have found his story quite implausible. But I know what he said is true. The Faeries have magic we mortals cannot fathom. I begged him not to bestow so great a power on a mere human, but his love is so strong, and he trusts me implicitly. I could not dissuade him.

He took my hand and escorted me back to the bridge. I was shaking as he scooped me into his arms and held me close one last time. Then he released me. I could not stop the flow of tears, knowing it was the last time I would ever see my beloved Aidan."

Kate handed the last of the pages to Mike.

"Is it true?"

"It is," Aunt Cass nodded solemnly. "If you have questions, I think I can answer most of them. But first, Michael," she inclined her head, observing him as he read the diary entries. "You are part of this since you have befriended Kate. What do you think? Are you in, or are you out? You can walk away this moment, call it all rubbish and return to your life as if it never happened. I can draught a potion that will make it seem like it was only a dream. It's your decision."

Mike looked up from reading the page clutched in his hand.

"Are you kidding me?" His face broke into the familiar dimpled grin. "I wouldn't miss this for the world!"

Many of Kate's questions had been answered by reading the pages torn from Grandma's journal.

Except one.

The story of the bullaun stone. It was a big deal. A life-changer. So why hadn't Mom ever told her about it? Or Grandma?

"Child, what's wrong?" Aunt Cass asked.

Kate's face had betrayed her feelings.

"I don't understand," she said evenly, attempting to restrain the anger that burned up her windpipe. "This is something that affects my life. And somehow nobody thought it was important that I know? Nobody thought it might be a good idea to tell the girl with the power what..." The rest of the sentence lodged in her throat.

Aunt Cass's response was gentle.

"Perhaps they were waiting for the right time. But things happen that are out of our control. Your mother's accident. Your grandmother's coma. That's why I wanted to talk to you. When Michael came to me about the healings, I realized at once that you didn't know about the stone. It must have been very strange for you. I'm truly sorry."

She reached out and touched Kate's shoulder. A soft gasp escaped her lips, and she drew her hand back quickly. Kate looked down to see why.

Aunt Cass's fingertips were bright red.

Scorched by the intensity of Kate's outrage.

Kate's eyes widened. She looked up at Aunt Cass, but there was no accusation. Just hazel eyes brimming with compassion.

"I–" Kate started to apologize, but Aunt Cass held her finger up to her lips and nodded towards Mike, who was still engrossed in the diary pages. She shook her head, implying that what just happened was between the two of them.

"We should probably go now," Kate announced abruptly.

"Before you do," Aunt Cass rose from her chair, "I need to tell you something, dear. About the stone; be careful. It's been my experience that the more powerful the magic, the greater its cost." She smiled once more at both of them. "Now give me a kiss."

Mike gave her a fond peck on the cheek. When Kate did the same, a shadow crossed Cassidy Quinn's face.

"Find a way to work through your pain, Kate. Anger, at its core, is hurt lashing outward instead of inward. And try to forgive yourself the same way you forgive others."

Kate hung her head.

"Thank you, Aunt Cass." She picked up the journal pages from where Mike laid them on the coffee table. "Can I have these?"

"Of course you can, my dear, just keep them safe. Mustn't fall into the wrong hands."

Kate was quiet on the way home. This information was a lot to digest. And no matter what Aunt Cass said, hurt sliced razor-like through her heart to think that Mom had never seen fit to tell her about the stone and its history.

Mike must have sensed her mood because he didn't try to initiate a conversation. He did make a quick a detour to the Dairyette to run in and grab something for them to eat. After they had demolished their supper, Kate took Mike's hand.

"Let's go sit outside. I have something I need to tell you."

They sat, side by side, legs dangling over the edge of the tall porch. Kate turned to face Mike.

"You know last week when I found the monkshood? I've been wracking my brain trying to figure out where I'd seen similar flowers. Today I stopped in at the mayor's office to show him I'd paid the fine..."

Mike's left eyebrow lifted.

"I know, I know, probably a stupid thing to do. But while I was standing there waiting for him to acknowledge me, I noticed the floral arrangement on his desk. Do you know what was mixed in with all the other flowers?"

"Monkshood," they said simultaneously.

"Yes, and the weird part is when he saw me staring at them, he smiled. Seriously, he smiled."

Her words trailed off as the realization hit her.

"He knows that I know." Her voice fell to a whisper, "He *wanted* me to know."

"Wanted you to know..." Mike prompted.

"That he's poisoning Grandma." Kate shook her head slowly as she considered this new revelation. She started ticking off the points. "He knows about monkshood. He knows how dangerous it is. The symptoms of exposure – they match Grandma's. And he's the mayor; no one's going to think to trace it back to him. After I left his office, I stopped by the hospital. I wanted to find out what they did with the floral arrangements in Grandma's room before she went into the ICU. I was looking for the cards they put on florist's deliveries to show who sent them. To see if anything had been sent to her from the mayor. His name wasn't on any of the cards, but I found enough proof."

She told him about the candy-striper who became inexplicably ill.

" She must have had contact with the monkshood when she tried to dispose of them. And the day Grandma went into a coma, I saw Darcy coming out of the hospital as I was going in. I know it all seems circumstantial, but it makes sense."

"And if MacMurray knows that on your twenty-first birthday you inherit the power from the bullaun stone, he'd have to get your grandmother out of the way in order to coerce you to use it on his behalf."

"But he hasn't done anything so far. He hasn't made a move to force me to use the stone for his purposes. Just keeps making those obscure threats."

Kate grabbed Mike's hand.

"You know that camping trip you talked about? How quickly could that come together?"

"I think if I had a day or two, I could arrange it. Why? What are you thinking?"

"I need some time away. Time to think. We have to try and figure out his next move. And right now, I don't feel very safe."

Mike put his arm around her and pulled her closer. "You're safe with me. I'll talk to Mr. Clarke tomorrow about time off. And there's no way I'm leaving you here alone."

They spent the rest of the evening lying on the bed, making plans for their camping trip, drawing up a list of items they'd need. It would've been fun if it was more of a vacation and less a hideout. Still the idea of getting away for a few days was appealing.

Mike nodded off to sleep, chin resting on his chest. Kate tucked a quilted throw around him and reached into her pocket to retrieve the journal pages Aunt Cass had given her. She stuck them in the back of the diary, along with the picture and Aidan's note. After burying the diary under a pile of shorts in the dresser, she crossed the room; drew aside the lace curtains.

Moonlight bathed the patio. Kate watched the willow's branches stroke, like gentle fingers, across the bullaun stone.

Possessive?

Foreboding?

Maybe it only seemed that way, as Aunt Cass's warning repeated in Kate's head.

"The more powerful the magic, the greater its cost."

She was going to need powerful magic to pull off her plan.

Exactly what was it going to cost her to succeed?

Chapter 12

Kate stood at the kitchen sink, washing dishes. Daydreaming about the trip to Oklahoma. Tonight, Mike was bringing his camping gear. Together they'd sort through it and pack what they needed in his truck. It was about a three hour trip to the foothills of the Kiamichi Mountains. If they left as soon as he got off work tomorrow, there'd still be enough daylight to pitch the tent. Her heart smiled with anticipation. She'd never been camping before. Not real camping. There was the time in the fifth grade when her class went on an 'end of school' camping trip. But they had stayed in cabins, not tents, and there was a cafeteria. Mike sure made it sound like a lot of fun…

She plunged her hand into the soapy water. The sharp bite of the knife brought her back to reality.

A slice across her palm.

Bled like a stuck pig.

Hurt like the devil.

She pressed a clean dishtowel against it and managed a weak smile. Not a problem anymore. Not with the bullaun stone in her backyard.

"Kate, hey, Kate."

Peg rapped on the screen door and, without waiting for an invitation, bulldozed her way into the kitchen.

"I heard about the mayor heaving a fine on you. Shutting you down at market and all. Danged hateful thing to do, if you ask me. Man's got a mean streak a mile wide; that's for sure. I figured I'd come by and check on you, see how things was going. And I brought this."

She set a large wicker basket on the breakfast table.

A rivulet of sweat traversed its way down Peg's cheek. She wiped it with her shirtsleeve and asked, "What'd you do to your hand?"

Kate shrugged.

"Cut it washing dishes. Nothing bad."

Peg wagged her head.

"You sure have a knack for getting hurt. Maybe this'll cheer your day."

She pulled a handful of Mason jars, a ceramic crock, and a cardboard egg crate out of the basket.

"I don't know what's going on, but my animals are producing like nothing I ever seen. I got more honey than I know what to do with. And eggs. Look at them eggs."

She opened the lid, displaying the large, brown orbs.

"Chickens are laying faster'n I can pick 'em up. Lord have mercy; I may have to hire me some extra hands to keep up with the milking, and that's a fact. Never seen anything like it. So I brung over this basket, thinking maybe y'all could use some fresh produce. I threw in a couple jars of homemade jam, and that there fresh butter is the creamiest ever. Oh, and my cotton is growing like crazy, too. Don't know what's going on, but it sure is a blessing."

Blessing?

Kate's heart did a little dance.

It was all she could do to keep from telling Peg the reason for her sudden prosperity.

"I'm real happy for you," Kate said, "and thanks for sharing. Oh, by the way, I'm going out of town tomorrow. Should be back by Sunday afternoon, latest."

"Okay, hon, thanks for letting me know. I'll keep an eye out. Now you go see to that cut."

Right. Time to visit the bullaun stone.

She made her way outside, allowing the scenario to play through her head again as it had at least a hundred times since she learned of the power of the stone. She would use the healing rainwater on Grandma, who would get well and come home. Then she and Kate could spend the next few months together – catching up on old times, working in the garden during the week and at the market on the weekends. They could sit at the kitchen table and eat lemon sherbet and homemade ginger snaps, just like they used to when she was a kid. Kate smiled, maybe she could even go fishing again on Boyd Creek.

She reached the stone, prepared to dip her hand into the hollow, but her daydreams shattered and the pain that stabbed through her chest made her forget about the throbbing in her hand.

The summer heat had evaporated every drop of rainwater.

She collapsed in a heap beside the rock slab.

When Mike arrived later that afternoon, she was still under the willow tree, head buried in her arms. Kate felt his touch on her shoulder. She looked up at him with a tearstained face.

"What's wrong?" Mike asked gently. "And how did you hurt your hand?"

"It's hopeless. There's no water in the bullauns. No way to heal."

"That's not hopeless." He examined the cut. "We can always fix this the old-fashioned way. Be right back."

He thinks the tears are for me.

She opened her mouth to tell him the truth, then stopped. She couldn't share the real cause for her despair. Not yet.

Mike returned with the first-aid kit. "This is why we need to get away," he said, covering the cut with antiseptic cream and a swatch of gauze and tape. "A lot has happened, and we need to clear our heads. Come up with a solution for your grandmother and this Darcy situation. There," Mike kissed her palm lightly, "all fixed. Now come see what I brought for our camping trip and tell me what else you think we might need."

Kate followed him to the El Camino.

"I've got a tent, sleeping bags, lantern, folding table and chairs. Figured we could use your ice chest. Picked up a couple of mess kits from the Army Navy store. I have an iron skillet left over from my Boy Scout days. If we think of anything else, we can always pick it up at Gibson's in Broken Bow. It's just a stone's throw away."

Kate showed Mike what she'd packed.

He picked up the jar of honey.

"This looks good. Where'd it come from?"

"Peg dropped it off. Seems like all of a sudden her livestock, hens and bees are producing a lot more than in the past. Her cotton is growing thicker and faster than usual, too. Wonder what could have caused such a thing?"

Mike's grin mirrored Kate's.

"You didn't... Did you?"

"I did. Just yesterday. And already things are improving. Seriously, what else could it be?"

"That's great. Now we know the blessings work. But what about curses?"

"I can't bring myself to do that. It's like, I can't get around the notion that if I do, it will come back on me somehow. I know it's not part of the legend, but I want to be careful. Don't want to bring any condemnation down in retaliation for my foolishness."

"Smart move." Mike put the honey jar back in the picnic basket. "You don't strike me as the kind of person who would want to put a curse on someone anyway. Except maybe Darcy MacMurray."

"Yeah, and he probably deserves one. I can't shake the thought that somehow he's tied to Mom's disappearance. I thought I'd unload that cardboard box. Put her things back in the cedar chest. Maybe I'll run across something that'll shed some light. Want to help?"

Mike sat down on the couch and pulled the packing box in front of him. Kate sat on the floor at his feet. He picked up a playbill for the college production of "Dark of the Moon." Kathleen McKenna was billed as the 'Conjure Woman.'

"That's not type-casting, is it?" Mike said.

Kate punched him lightly in the leg.

"Not funny."

She removed more items until she came across the pastel bundle tied up with its striped ribbon. She opened the baby book. There were black and white baby pictures. A lock of pale hair was stuck to a page by a strip of yellowed scotch tape. A small, velvet envelope contained what was probably her first lost tooth. Several report cards rested between the other pages. The rest of the book was empty.

Kate snapped the book shut.

"What's wrong?" Mike asked.

"Did your mom keep a baby book for you and your brother?"

"Yeah, why?"

"You've seen it? Looked through it?"

"Yeah…" Mike gave her a quizzical look.

She reopened hers to the first page.

"See anything unusual about this one?"

Mike shrugged, "It's got pictures and stuff. Typical memorabilia."

"I mean this." She pointed to the empty lines. "Baby was born at – nothing. Mother's name – nothing. Father's name – nothing. No birth certificate. No baby bracelet. Why is everyone determined to keep me in the dark about who I am? Who my father was?"

Mike took the baby book from Kate and closed it.

"I think it just feels that way because of all the stress you've been going through. Your mother sounds like a wonderful person. It was probably just a chapter in her life that was finished, and she chose to move on. I'm sure the lack of information wasn't intentional."

Kate mumbled "there seems to be a lot of that lately," and continued to transfer items to the chest.

"This your mother's college yearbook?" Mike held it up.

"Yeah. I doubt you'll find anything important in there."

"I'm curious to see what old Darcy MacMurray looked like when he was younger."

Mike flipped the pages until he came to the junior year pictures.

"Kate, look."

Kathleen McKenna. Mahogany tresses hung in waves around her slender young face. Long, thick eyelashes framed big, expressive eyes. Her full, sensuous lips curved up in a smile.

"You adored her," he said quietly.

Kate nodded. "If you could have met her... She was the most amazing person I've ever known. She drew people in like a magnet and could make complete strangers fall in love with her. I think it was this gift she had for making people feel important. And it didn't matter how old they were, or their skin color, or their social status, she respected everyone, was truly interested in who they were, their thoughts, their ideas, their feelings. And I think they sensed that. I guess that's what always puzzled me about us moving around so much. If she was that good with people, why couldn't we stay in one place and become part of a community? I began to think of her as a butterfly – so beautiful, doesn't stay too long in one place, always flitting about. I told her once that she was like a butterfly. Know what she said? That I might be right. That a butterfly goes into hiding as one type of insect and emerges a different creature. Funny, I hadn't thought about that in a long time." She shook the images from her head, "Anyway, I always thought she was just wonderful."

Mike kissed the top of Kate's head. "Like her daughter."

He turned to the next page.

"There he is."

Darcy was not an unattractive young man. The absence of color in his skin and hair accounted for his unusual appearance, but that's not what troubled Kate. It was his eyes. Already cold and dull. Made the hair on the back of her neck stand up.

If the eyes were the windows to the soul, it was clear Darcy MacMurray's was already gone.

"How could my mom have taken up with a guy like that? Anyone can see he's aloof and unfeeling. Mom was a cheerleader, for Pete's sake. Complete opposites. What did she see in him?" She shook her head, bewildered.

They continued to search through the remaining items. Postcards and letters mostly. Several were postmarked from Ardee. Kate picked up an envelope dated January 5, 1954.

"This was sent a few months before Mom went missing."

Opening it, she skimmed the first few lines, then read aloud:

> *Kathleen, I know when you left here it wasn't on the best of terms. You were angry with me for 'interfering' as you called it. Darling, you know I have deep concerns about your friendship with Darcy MacMurray, mainly this year, which marks your twenty-first birthday. We both know what an important year it is. I have tried hard to impress upon you the necessity of being discreet about certain matters. You must be careful with whom you align yourself. I am only telling you this for your good. Darcy is not the person you believe him to be. Perhaps it is your*

constant desire to see the best in everyone that has put blinders over your eyes. I hope and pray this does not become your downfall. Father sends his love. We would like to come and visit on your birthday weekend. Please tell Professor Willis I said hello. Love, Mother

Kate slumped against the couch. "So Grandma had concerns about Mom's relationship with Darcy and tried to warn her about him."

Mike was thumbing through the pictures in the shoebox.

"These photos," he splayed a handful, like playing cards, "they're pictures of you?"

"Yeah," she took them from him, examining each one separately. "This was me when I was about six months old. This one," she pointed to the photo of a young girl with long, pale hair, "I'm about three years old in it. And look." She jumped up and grabbed the picture of her mother off the mantle. "See this?" She pointed to her mother's hair, then to her picture. "When my mom was about fourteen, her hair went from platinum-blond to reddish-brown. Mine did the same thing. Some odd genetic trait, I guess."

Mike frowned.

"What?" Kate asked, slightly alarmed by the look on his face.

"Didn't you say MacMurray opened the pendant that first time you visited his office?"

"Yes, he recognized it was Mom's, but when he saw the photo, he dropped it like it was on fire. Why?"

Mike hesitated before answering, "Maybe that's why Darcy hasn't done anything yet."

"What do you mean?"

He sucked in a deep breath and ran his fingers through his hair.

"Maybe he thinks you're his daughter."

She stared at him in wide-eyed disbelief.

"Why would you even say such a thing?"

It crossed her mind to punch him again. Harder this time. To inflict some real pain for that suggestion.

"Your mom and Darcy were very close. Everyone knew it. Your grandmother even knew it. Something happened. Your mother disappeared. She comes back with a baby. A baby with white hair. And no one said exactly how old that baby was when your mom came back to visit, right?"

Her cheeks flushed hot. She could feel the vein pounding in her temple.

"Listen," Mike pleaded. "We both know the white hair that turns brown as you get older is a family trait. I'm not saying Darcy *is* your father. I'm saying maybe he *thinks* he's your father. That could be to your advantage. Maybe he'd be less likely to do something harmful if he believes you're his daughter."

Kate stewed in silence. Considered his words.

Darcy McMurray.

Her father?

An involuntary shudder accompanied the thought.

She absentmindedly played with the locket that hung around her neck, sliding it back and forth along its chain. As much as she hated to admit it, Mike might be right. Darcy's reaction was very peculiar when he opened it and saw the picture. And that would explain why, if he was aware of the gift and the stone, he hadn't done anything about it yet.

"I wish we were leaving tonight."

Mike drew her down beside him and leaned over to kiss her. Kate wrapped her hands around his head and threaded her fingers through his hair, pulling him in. Mike melted back into the couch and, arms encircling her, slid Kate onto his lap. Her long hair fell around their faces like a curtain, shutting out the world. They continued the gentle exploration of tongues. Primitive. Sensual. She lost herself in the intensity of the moment. Mike's hand slid languidly across the bare skin of her leg sending waves of heat through her body and igniting an ache she'd never felt before. She gasped and broke away, resting her head against Mike's neck while she tried to calm her irregular heartbeat. His lips grazed her temple, and he pulled her tighter against his chest.

"I hate to see you upset," he mumbled into her hair.

Upset was not the emotion she was fighting at the moment. His kiss was like a fine wine, relaxing her from the inside out, easing her from fear into bliss. The feeling was addictive. All she could think about was another sip of his lips. She started nuzzling his neck, from the small indention below his Adam's apple up to his earlobe, which she nibbled gently, flicking her tongue at the inside. She'd seen it in a movie once, and it had elicited a positive response from the male lead, so she thought maybe...

She felt the tremor that shook his body, heard him mutter a soft curse.

"If you don't stop that," he threatened but didn't finish his sentence. Instead, he unceremoniously picked her up and placed her on the couch beside him. "I'm going to make a sandwich, who's with me?"

That wasn't exactly the response she expected, so she pushed him back against the cushion and bounded towards the kitchen. "Loser has to wash the dishes."

Mike reached her as she opened the refrigerator door. He wrapped his arms around her and kissed the top of her head. "Do you know how crazy I am about you?"

"Show me," Kate responded with a devilish gleam in her eyes. Leaning back against him, she offered Mike her lips, like an alcoholic hoping for one more buzz.

"Oh, no," Mike laughed, put his hands up and backed away. Kate stumbled to gain her balance. "You...you are a brat. Do you even know what you do to me when you act like this? It's all I can do to maintain a sense of decorum."

"Fine then," Kate feigned offense, "at least you can make yourself useful."

She reached into the refrigerator and started tossing him packages of ham and cheese.

I'm not a brat; she told herself.

Was she a brat?

She handed him a container of mustard.

"I'm not a brat," she said out loud and reached back into the refrigerator for the pickles.

Mike grabbed her by the waist and turned her around to face him.

"You are a brat," he tilted his head to the side, "when you flash those 'come hither' eyes and do things like that... like that ear thing. Holy cow, where did you learn..." He shook his head. "Never mind, go sit down," he ordered, but his eyes crinkled around the edges and tiny creases dimpled his cheeks.

They sat at the table eating thick ham and cheese sandwiches and mountains of potato chips, planning their getaway.

"So I was thinking. Why don't you take me to work tomorrow? I'll leave the truck with you, and you can come by my apartment and pick me up. We'll leave from there. I feel safe leaving the camping gear in the truck out here. Keeps it away from prying eyes."

Later, as they lay next to each other on the bed with the lamp out, the curtains parted to let in the moonlight, Kate remembered Darcy's accusations about her sleeping with Mike.

"Do you worry about gossip? Ardee is such a small town. I mean, you and I know we aren't doing anything immoral here. But some people seem to thrive on casting doubts about the reputation of their neighbors."

"Doesn't bother me." Mike buried his head in her hair. "We know the truth, and that's enough. I love you, Kate. Let me be here for you."

"Oh, so you don't care that my reputation might be ruined?" She playfully pushed her elbow into his ribs.

"Why do you do that?" Mike sat up abruptly, his voice full of exasperation. "Why is it when I try to tell you I love you, or that I care about you, you turn it into a joke or brush it off?"

Kate sat up too and pulled her legs up to her chest, wrapping her arms tightly around them. "I'm sorry, I never thought about it before." She tried to organize her thoughts. "It's... complicated." She bit her lip. "After I lost Mom... I," she faltered. *Vulnerable. If you tell him the truth, you'll be vulnerable,* came the warning, but she stumbled on. "I never wanted to feel that kind of pain again. So I kept telling myself, don't get too connected. Maybe then it won't hurt so much when they're gone."

"I already told you. I'm not going anywhere," was his gentle response. "You're gonna have to learn to trust me. I'm going to be here as long as you'll let me." He took her hand and kissed her palm. "Kate, I can't begin to imagine how it must have felt to lose your mom like that. I'm not even going to try. I think you're doing a great job getting your life back together. I'm sure your mom would be real proud..."

"Proud?" She cut him off and jerked her hand free. Her words came out with a choking cough. "How could she be proud of me? You have no idea." She bowed her head. "You don't understand anything. Nobody does. Not you, not Grandma. Not anybody."

She began to rock back and forth as she waged war against the truth that had been locked in her heart for three years, now trying to escape.

Tell him then, her mind taunted, *tell him and let him see what a horrible person you truly are.*

The words were exhausting to move from her head to her mouth; it made her lightheaded.

"It was my fault," she whispered. "The night my mother died," her pitch rose, and hot tears scalded her cheeks as she continued, "*it was my fault.* I was staying here with Grandma when I got a phone call. The scholarship committee at the University had received an unexpected endowment and wanted to meet with Mom and me the next morning. It was a godsend. We were poor, there was no way I was going to get to college without help, so I called Mom, begged her to come get me." Kate drew an uneven breath. "She promised to be at Grandma's house that night. But… the drive from San Augustine… and the weather. They said it was one of the worst storms of the season and the road was slick." Kate struggled to continue through the chokehold of pain that was crushing the air from her lungs. "She was almost here. The deputy said they found two sets of tire tracks. Said another vehicle might have been involved. All I know is that her car left the road and crashed into a tree. They don't even know how long…" She squeezed her eyes together, and the moan that managed to escape through the fist that covered her mouth sounded more animal than human. "They don't even know how long she suffered out there. Alone. Before someone found her and contacted the police."

Her lungs constricted. The pain that daggered her heart thrust deeper. It was hard to breathe. Even harder to concentrate, but she forged on.

"They rushed her to the hospital. Kept her alive long enough for Grandma and me to get there. She was wrapped in bandages. Hooked up to all these monitors. I took Mom's hand. It was so – Cold. I… I told her I loved her, but I think she was already gone. I didn't even get to tell her goodbye. It was my fault." She finished with a small, plaintive sob, "it was my fault, and I didn't even get to tell her I was sorry."

Mike wrapped his arms around her. "My god, Kate, is that what you think? That it's your fault your mother died?"

Kate nodded against his chest.

"Nobody in their right mind would blame you for your mother's accident. She wanted to come back. Wanted you to get that scholarship. You didn't *make* her come back. You had no control over the weather. It was an accident."

Kate was too distraught to respond. Mike settled against the pillows and pulled her to him, stroked her hair and kept repeating, "It wasn't your fault."

Eventually, her tears subsided, but Kate's mind insisted, *He doesn't understand. She wouldn't have been on the road that night if it wasn't for me. It WAS my fault that Mom died. How can I ever make up for that?*

The answer came to her, so sudden and bright it almost took her breath away.

The next morning, she sat on the side of the hospital bed, holding her grandmother's hand.

"I talked to Cassidy Quinn yesterday, Grandma. I know everything now," she confided. "I know all about how Aidan gave you the bullaun stone. I promise to take care of this precious gift. Most of all, though," she leaned in and put her mouth close to her grandmother's ear, "I promise I'm going to find a way. Whatever it takes, I will find a way to get you out of here and back to Aidan where you belong."

Chapter 13

Try to contain your paranoia.

Kate pulled into the parking space behind Mike's apartment. Fought the urge to look up at the mayor's window; convinced he was keeping tabs on her somehow. Nothing she could put her finger on. Just a gut feeling.

A short time later, Mike emerged carrying a duffle bag, fishing rods, and tackle box. She scooted to the passenger side.

"You don't have to move that far away."

He patted the bench seat beside him. With Mike's arm around her shoulder, they headed up to Oklahoma.

The next couple of days were filled with activity. They explored hiking trails, took a canoe ride, went horseback riding. At night, Mike would make a fire, and they would cook fresh catfish over the open flame. Sip coffee from tin cups. Talk late into the night until they crawled into their sleeping bags, exhausted. The trip was a welcome respite from the tension back home. But it was getting harder to ignore the fear that bullied its way into her imaginings. If Darcy had gone so far as to poison her grandmother, what else was he capable of? Kate made Mike put his sleeping bag next to hers. It was the only way she could fall asleep. She needed to be able to reach out and touch him.

Maybe Mike was right. Maybe he was her security blanket after all.

"I had a good time," Mike told Kate as he pulled into the driveway and put the El Camino in park. "And I want you to know that you're the greatest thing that's ever happened to me. I'm not going to let anything change that."

After promising to be back in time for supper, Mike left for his apartment. Kate walked out to the garden and sat down on the swing. The vines that twined over the arch had become so closely-knit they almost blocked out the sun. Honey bees zoomed past her in a mad dash to see who could collect the most nectar from the orange trumpets that had blossomed practically overnight.

Kate stared across the garden at the rows of plants that appeared to have grown three or four inches in the few days she'd been gone.

She wiggled her eyebrows in a Groucho Marx sort of way and smiled.

What if it did work that way?

What if the more you blessed others, the more it came back to you?

Instant Karma.

Just like Lennon said.

To pass the afternoon, Kate pulled the shoebox full of pictures out of the cedar chest and began sorting through them. There were typical photos of her grandmother and grandfather holding her mother as a baby. School pictures. Birthday pictures. A small beige envelope contained photos that were taken when Mom was in high school. Tons of snapshots of her cheerleading team. Prints of tight-lipped teachers that looked twice their actual age. Group pictures of fresh-faced girls in full skirts and net petticoats. Boys in jeans with rolled up cuffs, wearing varsity sweaters. The next group of prints appeared to be of Mom's high school graduation. Several were of her mother standing between Grandma and Granddaddy Mac, pride evident by their broad smiles and adoring looks. Several were fun pictures – Mom cutting up with her classmates; mugging for the camera with goofy grins and facial distortions. One showed a row of girls in their caps and gowns; arms laced together doing high-kicks. In another, her mom and a fellow student stood shoulder to shoulder, attempting to look serious, but Kate imagined from the glimmer in their eyes, they were on the verge of busting out into a hail of giggles. She smiled and started to file it away when a pale figure in the background caught her eye. She squinted to get a better look, but the quality was grainy. Kate retrieved the small, handheld magnifying glass from her grandmother's cherry-wood secretary and plopped back onto the couch to examine the image.

The camera had captured another student celebrating graduation day. Darcy MacMurray stood several feet away dressed in his cap and gown, clutching his diploma. A short, plump girl with frizzled hair stood beside him; arms wrapped possessively around his waist. Even the blurry snapshot couldn't hide that unmistakable toothy grin.

Kate sank back into the cushions. Peg and Darcy were friends? She said he didn't have any friends. She sure didn't act like one, judging from the way she talked about him. And why would she conceal her friendship with him, while eagerly disclosing information about Darcy and her mom? The thought left an unsettled feeling in the pit of her stomach.

As she placed the shoebox back in the chest, Kate's eye caught her baby book and baby clothes and blankets, stacked neatly together in the far corner. Something wasn't right. She sorted through the items, but it didn't seem like anything was missing. She shrugged. Nothing to fret over. Right now she had to finish making supper.

Meatloaf was in the oven. The clock said ten minutes until six. She filled a pot with water and put the potatoes on to boil and dumped a can of green beans into a pan to heat up later.

Kate met Mike in the driveway. He sprang out of the El Camino. Picked her up and swung her around before letting her body slide down the length of his.

"Why are you so happy today?" Kate asked.

Mike took her hand and led her to sit on the porch.

"Okay, when I got to my apartment this morning, there was a note on the door from Mr. Clarke asking me to come see him as soon as I got back into town. I gotta admit, I was worried – that's like the equivalent of being called to the principal's office. I knocked on his door, and he yelled at me to come in. He was sitting at his desk. Told me to have a seat. He took this envelope and shoved it across the desk at me. I've never been fired before, but I was pretty sure that was how it felt. 'Open it' he says. So, I opened it. Guess what?" Mike pulled an envelope from the pocket of his jeans.

"Seems while I was gone, Mr. Clarke realized how valuable my services are to the drugstore. Look. Can you believe it? He gave me this bonus and said I was gonna get a ten-cent an hour raise. Ten cents an hour!"

"That's great Mike. I'm so proud of you. If Mr. Clarke's impressed, you must be doing a good job."

"Yeah," he agreed, but sounded distracted. He sniffed the air. "What's that smell?"

"The meatloaf!" Kate yelped and ran into the house.

She rescued it right before the top charred. Salvaged most of the potatoes, although they did have a slightly scorched taste. She hadn't lit the fire under the beans yet. At least those were edible.

"This is really good," Mike commented, as he loaded another helping of potatoes onto his plate. Kate crinkled her nose, silently questioning his taste buds. He polished off the remainder of the green beans too.

"How in the world do you keep from gaining weight?"

She lifted his tee-shirt, poked at his tight abdomen.

"You think I stand around all day and count out pills and put them in bottles?" Mike said. "You should come see me at work. I have to offload huge crates of merchandise and spend the day sorting through containers, bending, lifting, and organizing products on the shelves and —"

"Okay, okay," Kate interrupted laughing. "I get it. You burn it off at work."

She was relieved that something positive had happened and for once the conversation wasn't about her problems. Later, as they lay wrapped in each other's arms, the words to a song danced through her head.

"If I could make days last forever, if words could make wishes come true, I'd save every day like a treasure and then, again, I would spend them with you."

A sigh of contentment escaped her lips.

"What was that for?" asked Mike, stroking her hair.

"I feel at peace. And believe me, it's been a long time since I felt at peace about much of anything."

"Good," he nuzzled against her neck. "I want you to feel peaceful with me."

Hang onto this. Hang onto it, her drowsy mind repeated, *as long as you can.*

Gray clouds dominated the skies the following week, but no rain came. Kate visited Grandma every day. Holding her hand. Searching for pleasant things to talk about even as her personal despair increased. The doctors had warned Kate that her grandmother could not sustain this state much longer without suffering permanent damage.

Time was running out.

So were the options for getting Grandma home.

Mike commented, in his kind but concerned way, that Kate wasn't eating right. She was losing weight and the dark circles under her eyes had returned. He tried to entice her with frequent trips to the Dairyette for juicy burgers and her favorite Texas fries, but she didn't have an appetite. Even the ice cream sundae he made couldn't raise her spirits.

After Mike left for work on Friday, she crawled back into bed and buried her head in the pillows. She wasn't sleepy. She just couldn't bring herself to face another day of seeing Grandma lying comatose in the hospital bed when recovery was just a cloudburst away.

Was there nothing that could be done to save her?

It came to her in an instant.

The doctors were unable to treat her grandmother because they didn't know the cause. But if Darcy was using the monkshood to poison her, maybe he had an antidote. Some way to reverse the effects. She punched the pillow with her fist. Even if he did, how could she convince him to make her grandmother better?

As soon as the question formed, so did the answer.

Kate took a shower and put on her favorite sundress, the turquoise one that fit so well and deepened the color of her eyes. She arranged her hair in soft waves and applied her makeup carefully. Dusted on extra blush to make her complexion appear healthier. She wanted the mayor to believe she was unperturbed by the situation. Not desperate like she truly felt. She reached down to slide on her sandals. As she straightened, her eye caught the Barrett coat-of-arms and its reminder.

Unbowed and Unbroken, Honor and Courage.

Kate gave a mirthless laugh. Darcy was right after all. Nonsense to think she could ever live up to that maxim.

Still time to turn back, a voice inside her warned as she approached the front desk. Kate dismissed the thought with a toss of her head. Despite the previous chilly reception by Darcy's secretary, Kate flashed her sweetest smile.

"May I speak to Mayor MacMurray?"

Ashling tilted her head, her eyes narrowed.

There was something cat-like about her expression, Kate thought.

And I'd hate to be the mouse.

"Always a pleasure to see you, Miss McKenna," she said and announced Kate's arrival into the phone.

The mayor stood planted behind his desk, arms crossed.

"Miss McKenna," he gestured toward the hard wooden chair. "Please be seated and tell me what I can do for you today." He emphasized the word 'today' as a look of annoyance crossed his face.

"No thank you, I'd rather stand if it's all the same to you."

"Your choice," was his curt reply.

"I'll be brief. I've come to make a bargain with you."

Darcy's eyebrows rose, but he remained silent.

"You have something I want. And I have something you want. I'm here to make a deal."

Darcy sat down slowly and motioned for Kate to do the same. This time she took a seat.

She met his eyes, unflinching.

"I know you are poisoning my grandmother with some derivative of monkshood. They were in her hospital room the first time I went to see her. And you had them in the flower arrangement on your desk."

She paused to gauge his response. His eyes didn't flicker, but a slight upward twitch at the corner of his mouth told Kate what she needed to know.

"I believe you can reverse whatever it is you're doing to make my grandmother ill. In return, I'm prepared to give you what you want from me."

She moved to the edge of the chair, lowered her voice.

"You know about the bullaun stone. And you know I'm the one with the ability to use it."

She continued, seductively, "Imagine you have the power to bless your friends. Curse your enemies. What price would you pay for that?"

She let the idea marinate for a minute and then rose, standing as tall and straight as she could.

"Let me know when you have an answer."

She started for the door.

Darcy's quick strides cut her off. Her heart skipped a beat at the uncensored lust on his face.

"You have – you have thought this through, have you?"

Kate held her chin up. "My grandmother's life in exchange for the powers of the stone. It's that simple. You make her well enough to come home, and my abilities will be at your disposal."

His gloating chuckle made her stomach churn.

"Fair enough," he answered and stepped aside. "You should see a significant improvement in your grandmother's condition within the week."

As she pushed the door open, he called after her, "I'll be in touch with you soon to initiate *your* end of the bargain."

She fled the reception area. Ashling's lilting voice trailed after her, "Come back again soon, Miss McKenna…"

Her hollow laugh followed Kate down the stairs and out the front door.

She made it as far as the outskirts of town before the waves of nausea overcame her. She barely had time to pull off the road and open the car door before the contents of her stomach spilled to the ground.

Now I know how it feels to make a pact with the devil.

And the cost of saving her grandmother?

Kate's soul.

When Mike arrived after work, Kate was sitting on the porch, leaning against the ivy-covered column. She managed a feeble smile that didn't alter his look of concern.

"What's wrong?"

"I don't feel good. Must be something I ate."

Mike convinced Kate to at least sip on some lemon balm tea, but she resisted his offer to fix her a bowl of soup. She was sick alright. Sick over the deal she'd made with Darcy. But what other option did she have?

That night she lay down with Mike, but as soon as he was asleep, she crept outside to sit on the bullaun stone. No wonder Grandma transferred to a nursing school out of town and Mom disappeared into oblivion the year they celebrated their twenty-first birthday.

If I were smart, I'd have disappeared too. Instead, I get to be a pawn in an unscrupulous miscreant's power game.

At least she could keep her promise to Grandma. That brought her enough peace to be able to catch a few hours of sleep before facing the questionable future.

She dragged herself out of bed around noon, stirred into action by the only motivation she had left.

Grandma's garden and Robert's greenhouse.

The sweet-scented herbs had a consolatory effect as she hoed her way through the garden, chopping up weeds. She didn't even mind the sweat that trickled past her brows and stung her eyes. At least it made her skin feel alive.

Something she couldn't say about her heart lately.

Robert's greenhouse was next. As she pulled clumps of henbit and watered the hothouse beds, Kate's shoulders bowed. She found it hard to swallow past the lump in her throat. How had everything gone so wrong so fast...

"Miss McKenna." The familiar voice interrupted her thoughts. "So nice to see you again."

Chapter 14

Kate gave a startled jump.

The dirt floor had muffled Darcy's footsteps.

"What are you doing here?" she asked through clenched teeth.

"Now, is that the kind of greeting I deserve?" he said, "Especially since I've come to tell you such important news."

"What news?" Her voice dripped venom.

"Oh, come now there's no need for such a tone. I only came to tell you that your grandmother has miraculously awakened from her coma. I'm sure the hospital will call to inform you shortly. But," his voice quavered with mock jubilance, "I couldn't wait to tell you myself."

Kate hoped the hatred in her eyes showed. Her ragged nails bit into the flesh of her palms.

"How do you know about this place? How did you know I was here?"

Darcy laughed.

"Oh my dear, I told you. I know a good many things about you. You didn't think I was going to let a treasure like you out of my sight, now, did you? My old friend, Peg, has been extraordinarily helpful in letting me know your whereabouts ever since you arrived here and–"

Darcy stopped midsentence.

Mimicked Kate's wide-eyed look.

"Oh. Didn't you know? Peg has been a faithful friend for a long time. I'm sure she filled you in on what good pals your mother and I were in college. After my dear friend, Kathleen, confided to me about her extraordinary gift, I was sure she and I would use her abilities together. To ensure a comfortable future for us both. But unlike you, Kathleen developed a conscience. Shame about that," he paused to sigh and flick a piece of lint off the label of his jacket. "Wasting her entire twenty-first year and all that wonderful magic."

He moved towards the door, halted, then turned back towards her, his mouth angled into a derisive smile.

"If only I had known sooner how easily her daughter could be bought."

It was all she could do to finish up in the greenhouse and stumble her way back home. She threw herself across the bed, indifferent to the caked dirt her sneakers ground into the grain of the wood floor or the dark streaks her grimy hands left on the chenille bedspread.

Kate lay frozen.

Not asleep.

Not awake either.

Trance-like.

She didn't want to think anymore.

Didn't want to move.

Didn't want to be.

She had no idea how long she'd laid there until the grating door hinges announced Mike's arrival. He called to her, but she couldn't will herself to answer. She heard each footstep as he made his way down the hallway. Felt him kneel beside the bed. He stroked her hair and spoke her name quietly.

"Kate. Kate honey, are you okay?"

She just couldn't face anything or anyone tonight.

Especially Mike.

He tried once more to rouse her before easing off her sneakers. He retrieved a throw from the couch and draped it across her legs.

Still, she lay motionless; her eyes pinched shut. But her ears were tuned to Mike's every move. The refrigerator door opened and closed. Utensils clanked against china. Water pipes shook when he turned on the hot water. The room darkened as the sun faded, and nightfall approached. She strained to hear any noise that might indicate his leaving.

There it was. The front door opened and closed.

That's it then.

He's gone.

A dull ache crushed her chest. She waited for the rumble of the El Camino's engine, making his departure official. Instead, the front door opened and closed again. Footsteps echoed through the house, approached the bedroom door. Kate felt him slide onto the bed beside her. Wrapping one arm around her waist, Mike snuggled as close as possible. His voice was tender when he spoke.

"I love you, Katie-bug. It's gonna be okay."

Katie-bug? That was Mom's nickname for her.

A flood of tears coursed silently onto the pillow as Kate's heart grasped the truth. Mike wasn't going to leave. He was here to stay. She moved closer to him so she could feel his warmth and allowed her fears to slip into blissful abeyance.

The next week passed without incident. Kate visited Grandma in the hospital daily and each time she seemed more cognizant, stronger. The doctors were amazed by Pearl McKenna's miraculous recovery. Congratulated themselves for their excellent care.

Only Kate knew the truth.

She never asked Darcy what he did to make her grandmother better. Didn't want to know. It was hard enough living with the knowledge that sooner or later she was going to have to make good on her end of the bargain.

Once, she had allowed herself to wonder about Darcy's intentions. Exactly what was he after? Did he want to become a millionaire? Or were his sights set on something more powerful, such as Governor, or even President? And how bad would the curses be? Did they only affect things like crops and livestock? Or did it extend to people's businesses or maybe their health? Or worse yet – what if he made her curse his enemies' families? Their children? Her imagination careened so out of control, she became physically ill. After that, she willed herself not to think about what kinds of favors he might require her to make on his behalf. But the anxiety haunted her every waking hour.

As for Peg, Kate hadn't seen nor heard from her.

Not that she wanted to.

She never imagined Peg was consorting with Darcy, using friendship as a ploy to gain her confidence. A way to keep track. Just thinking about Peg's betrayal caused tiny shockwaves of heartache to rebound off her ribs and shoot through the center of her chest.

Kate avoided going into town as much as possible, only visiting Donovan's when she absolutely had to. Mike tried to get her to come see him, just to get her away from the farm. A change of scenery might be good, he said. But the pharmacy was adjacent to the mayor's office. The thought of another encounter with Darcy made her stomach churn, so she refused as politely as possible.

Her life became an endless succession of empty days and sleepless nights. She started dropping pounds she couldn't afford to lose. Did her best to camouflage, though. Took to wearing baggy jeans and oversized shirts, even on the warmest days. And she always wore makeup in an attempt to hide the purplish-black hollows under her eyes.

But honestly, who was she fooling?

She saw the pained look in Mike's eyes as he stood by helpless, watching her decline without a clue as to what was wrong. In her heart of hearts, she knew it was unfair. But she just couldn't bring herself to tell him. What if he hated her for it? What would she do?

On Sunday, Mike told Kate that he had to go to work for a few hours. Before he left, he kissed her cheek.

"You know what today is, right?"

She gave him a blank look.

"It's the Fourth of July, silly head. The bicentennial. Would you like to go swimming at the state park, maybe cook out again like last time? I hear they're putting on a great fireworks show tonight."

He was trying hard to pull Kate out of her funk. She understood that. She just couldn't get into celebration mode. Not with her decision weighing heavily on her heart.

"I'd rather stay here."

Probably sounded sulky, but in her state of mind, she couldn't drum up a plausible excuse.

"Sure, we can do that." Mike put his arms around her and held her close. "Baby, I don't know what's wrong, but I know I love you, and if there's anything I can do, please tell me." He raised her chin. His eyes searched hers. "You know I'm here for you. I'm not going anywhere." The grandfather clock chose that moment to announce the quarter-hour. Mike glanced over at it and gave a short chuckle, "Except to work."

Kate forced a weak smile and pushed him away.

"Go," she commanded, "before you're late. I'll see you after lunch."

Kate sat on the bullaun stone and leaned against the willow tree, her mood as dark as the coffee she sipped. She'd resolved not to dredge up any memories that would compound the misery she already felt.

It wasn't working.

Mike's comment about the date was the catalyst. Reminded her that this month was the anniversary of her mother's death.

God, she'd give anything to be numb. To make her mind quit reliving the night of Mom's accident over and over…

She ground her fist into her temple.

Happy thoughts. Think of something happy.

Fourth of July.

Island Lake.

Island Lake was where Mom would take her in the summertime for picnics.

She remembered one July fourth when she was about eight. It played like a movie inside her head.

"Mom, come on," Kate coaxed.

Mom laid the hickory logs in a stack inside the wood-burning stove.

"Hand me the newspaper please," she told Kate.

Kate picked up the Ogemaw County Herald and gave it to her mother, who wadded several pages and stuck them randomly between the logs. She ran the match alongside the rough strip on the side of the Diamond box and held the orange flame to the papers.

"Do you see this?" Mom asked. "Do you know why I'm lighting the stove?"

Kate pulled the blanket closer around her. Jutted her lips out in a pout. It wasn't fair. Mom had promised they could have a picnic at the lake before the fireworks that night.

Narrow whorls of smoke started to spiral their way between the logs. Mom turned and, with a smile, rumpled her white-blond curls.

"It's too cold, Katie-bug," she said. "The water will be freezing. You'll be miserable."

"It'll warm up by this afternoon. Please, Mom, you said we could go to the lake today. You said I could go swimming."

"That was before this front blew in, Kate." She gave a defeated sigh. "Okay, maybe. We'll just have to wait and see."

It was late afternoon when her mother pulled out the wicker basket and began loading it with picnic items. Kate hopped from one foot to the other, unable to contain her excitement.

"And I can go swimming?" she asked, already rummaging through the chest of drawers to find her bathing suit.

Mom hollered over her shoulder, "I don't think so, Kate. The water will be way too cold."

Kate just smiled to herself and wiggled her t-shirt over the red, white and blue striped suit. She knew her mother would change her mind once they were there.

A veneer of fog covered the lake. The beach was abandoned, except for the handful of families huddled around driftwood fires and charcoal grills. Determined not to let the cold front spoil their Fourth of July plans.

Mom stood next to the car. A gust of wind puffed wisps of hair across her face. She swept them aside and looked down at Kate, who was hanging out the window, waiting for the verdict.

Her forehead creased.

"I don't know, Kate." Mom's tone was doubtful.

"Mom," Kate wheedled, "you promised. You promised!"

It wasn't the lake Kate was thinking about anymore.

It was that night three years ago.

Her muscles tensed as the unexpected reaction bubbled up inside her like hot lava.

Why Mom?

Why did you promise to come that night?

Why didn't you just stay home?

You were the adult. I was the stupid teenager.

If you hadn't made that stupid trip, you'd still be here today.

Her breath caught, and she slammed her mug against the stone, scattering shards of ceramic across the patio floor. She watched dark rivulets of coffee stain the white limestone slab and remembered Aunt Cass's words.

"Anger is hurt lashing outward instead of inward. Forgive yourself..."

She turned her face up toward the heavens. Tears trailed her cheeks, down her neck, soaking into the collar of her shirt. Her shoulders slumped, and she held her palms out in supplication.

"Mom, I don't know what to do. I miss you so much. There are so many things I never got to tell you. So many moments I never got to share with you. Won't ever get to share with you." Her words caught in her throat, and she almost doubled over from the ache that squeezed her heart so tight she could hardly breathe, but she had something she needed to say. "I'm sorry for all the times I hurt you and let you down. But you were always there for me. Always loved me no matter what." The rest of her thoughts came out in a whisper. "And I'll always love you, too, Mom."

The willow shivered, allowing ribbons of blue sky to peek through its branches and a finger of shimmering sunlight to pierce its canopy. Kate wiped her eyes on the sleeve of her shirt so she could follow the light's path. It pinpointed a glint of something wedged in the narrow crevasse at the bottom of the stone. She leaned to pick it up.

Kate remembered her grandmother's diary.

"The gold band forms into hands that clasp a heart in the center. A crown perches atop the heart."

Kate exhaled a long, deliberate sigh. She slid the band onto the third finger of her right hand, facing outward.

"Thanks, Mom," she said softly. "I guess that means it's time to let the healing begin."

Mike came home that afternoon with a grocery sack full of all kinds of goodies. Hot dogs with all the fixings, chips, cokes.

That homemade-style ice cream he loved. He had another large brown bag, but when Kate asked about the contents, he hid it behind his back.

"Oh no," he baited her, "this is a surprise for later."

His enthusiasm was infectious. Kate chopped onions, grated cheese and opened a can of chili to warm on the stove. Mike wanted fullout, no-holds-barred chili dogs, as he put it. She even found the appetite to eat one herself.

After sunset, Mike spread a quilt for Kate. A short distance away, he opened the large paper bag and proceeded to pull out fireworks, lighting one after another. Spinning discs whizzed dizzily around and shot out golden flames. Roman candles lit up the night with red, blue, and green showers of sparks. A rocket exploded and released a colorful parachute that drifted away in the wind. And no Fourth of July was complete without sparklers. Mike lit several for her, and she twirled them around, making yellow zigzags in the air. He set off a whole package of Black Cats that sounded like a rapid-fire machine gun, still echoing in their ears long after the last one exploded.

After the fireworks had been spent, Mike said, "I'll be right back," and disappeared into the house.

Kate wrapped her arms around her legs, rested her chin on her knees. She couldn't help but wonder how their relationship would change after she told him about the bargain she'd made with Darcy. Would he despise her for it? Mike just didn't seem to understand her resolve to keep her promise to Grandma.

He emerged from the house a few minutes later carrying two bowls full of ice cream. Kate reached for the smaller bowl.

"That's cool," he said, pointing to the ring.

"I found it today. I think it belongs to Grandma," she replied. "I think it's the Claddagh ring that Aidan gave her on her birthday."

Mike sat down beside her and dug into his ice cream.

"What's a Claddagh ring?"

"It's a romantic story," she said. "About a fisherman named Richard Joyce who was captured by pirates and sold to a Moorish goldsmith, who trained him to be a master-craftsman. While he was a slave, he designed this ring for the true love he left behind." She set her bowl aside and held her hand out while she explained. "The hands stand for friendship, the heart symbolizes love, and the crown stands for loyalty and fidelity. Anyway, when Richard finally became a free man, he returned to Claddagh with the ring he'd made. When he found out his sweetheart was still waiting for him, he gave her the ring, and they got married right away."

Then Kate explained the symbolism behind the wearing of it.

Mike took her hand and examined the ring. After a moment, he looked up at her. His brows furrowed.

"The legend," he said thoughtfully, "the legend says when you wear it on your right hand turned outward it means your heart is open."

Kate met his eyes and gave him a solemn nod.

Mike glanced up towards the night sky and ran his fingers through his hair. "Do you believe in love at first sight? Because I do. I was in the grocery store one day when I spotted this beautiful girl with the most amazing green eyes I'd ever seen. She was quiet and self-effacing, but I wanted to get to know her. I couldn't get her out of my mind. In fact, I wanted to spend every minute I could with her. The more time I spent with her, I began to see that she was brave and selfless and loving and forgiving. Just the kind of girl I figured she'd be. The kind of girl I've dreamed of. The kind of girl I want to spend the rest of my life with."

He looked her way again.

Her heart was in tears. She wanted to speak the words he sought to hear. But her mind refused to tell her mouth what to say. She glanced down at her hands and picked at the cuticle of her thumb. She shook her head slowly.

"I just... I can't give you what you want right now." She looked up at him. Large tears rolled down her face. "I'm sorry," she whispered.

Mike tilted his head. His expression waffled between sadness and something else. Something indefinable. Pity? "It's okay. I understand. I love you, Kate, and I'm staying with you, no matter what."

They sat listening to the distant barrage of fireworks celebrating the country's two-hundredth anniversary. Occasionally, they'd catch a glimpse of colorful, sparkling explosions above the treetops. Mike attempted to spoon-feed Kate a bite of ice cream. She grabbed his hand to push it away. Spilled the half-melted confection down the front of his t-shirt.

"Oh man, look what you've done. You're gonna have to pay for that."

He peeled off his shirt and tossed it aside. Encircling Kate with his arms, he drew her onto the blanket next to him. There was something seductive about the warm scent of his musky patchouli combined with a light sweat from the summer heat. How was she supposed to resist? Her lips brushed his neck and nibbled along the curve of his ear.

"Kate." He mumbled her name in a low, husky voice and raised her chin to meet his eyes. She could see the hunger behind them and felt her resolve begin to crumble. She closed her eyes, her lips parted. Mike gave a slight shiver, and she heard his swift intake of breath as she ran her fingers down the curve of his spine and pulled his hips to meet hers.

His lips brushed hers for a fraction of a second then he kissed the top of her head and abruptly repositioned her beside him, resting her head on his shoulder. His chest rose and fell in a strained rhythm. A few minutes passed before he asked, "Are you trying to make this harder for me?"

Kate gulped and shook her head no.

"You still think I'm a brat."

He pulled her closer and whispered in her ear, "Yes, but you're *my* brat."

As they watched the last burst of color that signaled the grand finale of the fireworks show, Kate twirled the gold ring on her finger. She was becoming more comfortable with what they had together and Mike said he'd stay with her no matter what.

But would his feelings change after she told him about the deal she'd made with McMurray?

Chapter 15

Mike came home from work on Monday with news about preparations for the Founder's Day Festival.

"You oughta see it," he said. "They've built this big performance stage on Main Street. McMurray is offering cash prizes for the top three best decorated storefronts, so you can imagine the whole town is scrambling to come up with ideas. I've seen more tricolour flags in one day than I have in my entire life. And they've got a carnival scheduled to set up on Friday. Jake said he heard Old Man Donovan telling someone they might even hold a Miss Ardee contest this year."

Mike was surprised that MacMurray had become so magnanimous. Kate wasn't. She gnawed her lower lip. Of course, Darcy could afford to be generous now that his whole world was about to improve dramatically.

Thanks to her bargain.

On Wednesday, she woke with a new resolve.

Tonight she would tell Mike about what she'd done. The thought of it made her stomach twitch like a Mexican jumping bean. Would he walk out the door in anger? Disappointment? Would her worst fear come true? Now that she'd finally begun to let down her guard, would he leave her? It was a risk she'd just have to take.

After he left for work, Kate made a brief visit to Donovan's. She'd discovered Grandma's charcoal grill while rummaging in the barn for the tool box. Since Mike always said he could think better on a full stomach, she decided a cookout might be just the thing to help him understand why she did what she did. At least that's what her crossed fingers wished for.

That afternoon, as she wheeled the grill around to the backyard, her thoughts traveled back to the last time it was used.

Her sixteenth birthday.

Sweet sixteen.

Mom had splurged and bought thick steaks, enormous potatoes for baking, and a fancy chocolate cake decorated with loops and swirls of buttercream frosting, and clusters of pink fondant roses. Grandma had set the table with her best china and silver, and they toasted Kate's birthday with lemonade poured into cut-crystal glasses.

It was the year Mom gave her the silver pendant.

Today it felt like a lifetime ago.

As usual, the sound of tires crunching on the driveway signaled Mike's arrival. Kate looked up to see his face brighten as he rounded the corner of the house and spied the grill. He sniffed the air, then gathered Kate up in his arms and gave her a bear hug, lifting her off the ground.

"Mmm," he buried his face in her hair. "Somebody must be feeling better. This is great."

Kate couldn't help but smile, pleased with the effect the cookout was having on him.

"What's this? Baked potatoes, corn on the cob?"

He noticed the steaks on the platter waiting their turn.

"T-bones? My favorite. Mind if I...?" He nodded his head towards the grill.

She handed him the tongs.

"Knock yourself out."

After dinner, Kate poured the remainder of the mead into two glasses and asked Mike to sit with her on the front porch.

"I sense this has been a prelude to something." He paused to take a sip of the honey-colored liquid. "Don't think I haven't enjoyed it. That was the best steak I've had in a long time. And it's nice to see you smile and eat again. But I know you, Kate." His face wore an odd grin. "And you have something to say. So go ahead."

Mike was bracing for her to tell him something he didn't want to hear. He didn't think she'd changed her mind about him, did he? Ironically, it might be the other way around after he heard what she'd done.

"I should have said something earlier, but I just couldn't. I didn't think you'd understand how important this is to me."

Mike's face remained expressionless throughout her explanation. When Kate finished, she looked down at her lap. The flash of gold on her right hand reminded her of the stakes of her confession. She rocked slowly back and forth. Waiting.

The silence was agony.

"Say something, will you?"

He made a noise that sounded like a muffled laugh.

A burst of anger flared inside her.

There was nothing funny about this.

She raised her head to say so when Mike spoke up.

"Kate, you're a smart girl, but this time you've got it all wrong." He shook his head. "You've allowed MacMurray to intimidate you into giving him power. That's not how it is. Don't you get it? It's *you*. *You are the one with the power.* You could have put a curse on him at any time, and he could be writhing in agony right now. Or be dead broke rotting away in some jail cell. Except MacMurray knows you aren't the type of person who would do something like that. And you played right into his hands."

Mike locked eyes with Kate.

"But he's not going to win this one. We are."

We.

He wasn't deserting her. Still, his tone spoke volumes as he continued, "Why didn't you tell me about this from the beginning?

Instead of keeping it all in and making yourself sick. That's what you've been doing, isn't it? That's why you can't eat or sleep and walk around like a zombie all day."

She hung her head. Mike's next words were barely audible. "You still don't trust me, do you?"

Kate's head snapped up. Her eyes were wide as she answered a vehement, "No. It's not that at all. I was afraid of your reaction. I made a horrible pact with the evilest man I know. Someone willing to kill to get what he wants. And I'm going to help him. Doesn't it make me as despicable as he is?"

"No, it makes you a big-hearted person, willing to do anything to keep her grandmother alive. But Kate," his eyes were pleading, "if this relationship is going to go anywhere, you are going to have to learn to trust me."

"I was wrong. I know that now. I should have told you from the beginning. I was afraid to because I couldn't bear the thought of you hating me for what I had done. You're the only friend I have, and I'm," she sucked in a ragged breath, "I'm so afraid of losing you."

Holding her face in his hands, Mike kissed her. Gentle at first. Gradually, the pressure intensified. Kate's lips parted, and she drank in the sweet outpouring of his love.

"How can I convince you I'm here to stay? You're just going to have to believe in me."

He held her close for a moment then pulled back so he could look at her.

"Now, about your grandmother. Have you ever discussed this with her? Your idea of calling Aidan back from the Land of the Young?"

She hadn't. She was waiting for Grandma to get stronger, afraid the information about Darcy's involvement would have a negative effect on her recovery.

"But she'll have to agree to it," Kate insisted, "once I tell her Darcy was the one behind her illness. That he'll try to hurt her again. Surely she'll see she has no other choice."

"I hope you're right. In the meantime, we need to find a way to take back control of the situation."

Kate lowered her head and bit at her cuticle. Then it came to her.

"I think I know how to pull this off."

Saturday. The Founder's Day Festival. They would bring her home while the mayor was pre-occupied with the evening ceremonies. Her grandmother and Aidan would be reunited, and Kate would be on her way out of town before Darcy had an inkling of what was going on.

Later as they nestled together in bed, Kate felt happier than she had in weeks. Sleep was going to come easy tonight. Especially after Mike's reassurance.

"I love you, Kate McKenna. Everything's going to be okay."

The next day, doubts started to plague Kate's thoughts.

What if Grandma *didn't* want to go along with her plan?

What if she *didn't* want to be reunited with Aidan?

Kate was convinced the mayor would stop at nothing to gain the stone's power. If she failed to persuade her, her grandmother's life would be in mortal danger. And Kate had made up her mind that after Saturday night, the stone would have to be destroyed.

She parted the willow's draping curtain, touched the slab with fingers that trembled like the leaves ruffling overhead.

All these summers I spent here sitting under the willow. Never once did I suspect this old limestone rock would shape the most defining moment of my life.

She picked up the smaller stone once more. Felt its weight in her hand. She placed it in one of the bullauns and rotated it clockwise.

"I don't know whether someone can wish luck or good fortune on themselves. But if it's possible, please let my visit with Grandma be successful. Please let her agree to my plan. It's the only way to ensure her safety."

Kate had made arrangements with the hospital staff to take her grandmother outside to get some sunlight. Her real motive was to have a secluded place where she could tell Grandma her plan without the possibility of anyone eavesdropping. Lately, she'd begun to question how many people Darcy might have in his pocket. She'd never considered it before. Now, she suspected he had a much larger scope of influence. How else could he have continued to poison her grandmother with the monkshood toxin?

Kate pushed the wheelchair to a remote corner of the patio. Scooting her chair close by, she took her grandmother's hand.

"Grandma, I want you to listen before you say anything. I met your friend, Cassidy Quinn. Mike introduced me to her. She gave me the pages from your diary, so I know all about Aidan and the gift."

Pearl raised her eyebrows and opened her mouth to speak, but Kate held up her hand.

"Grandma please, let me finish. I know you had to make a really tough decision a long time ago. You walked away from the love of your life. And it must have been painful. But now you have a chance to be with him. I can call Aidan. I can use the stone just like he wanted, and he can come back for you. He promised to take you to the Land of Forever Young, and now you can go with him and be young and in love again. More than that, though, you can be safe." Kate lowered her voice. "It was Darcy MacMurray. He was the one who made you sick. And I'm convinced he'll do it again. But he can't touch you if you're with Aidan." Kate was begging now, "Please Grandma, please. I already lost Mom. I can't bear to lose you too. Not this way. Not at the hands of Darcy MacMurray."

They sat in silence for several minutes. Pearl looked at Kate with watery eyes.

"You can't imagine how hard it was, making such a decision so long ago. I was crazy about Aidan and those days in the Land of the Young were amazing. But I just couldn't leave my life here, my family, friends, my profession..." Her voice faltered. "I couldn't turn my back on this world, even with all its faults and failures. Believe me, I did think about using the stone. Many times. But then I became involved with nursing school and the more time I spent away from Aidan, the more itf felt like just a dream. Then I married your grandfather. Your mother came along. By the time, she was twenty-one it was absurd to think about using the stone. I didn't see much point in telling her about the power to bring Aidan back. I had another life now, with a daughter and prospects of grandchildren and great-grandchildren. I would never want to give that up."

Her shoulders drooped, and she shook her head as she continued. "Your mother was always cynical of the stone. I explained about the blessing and cursing, but she refused to have anything to do with it. And you cannot imagine how upset I was when I found out she had shared the story with Darcy. I never trusted him and tried to warn her, but she ignored me. Then she disappeared without a word to anyone. I was utterly sick. It was my fault. I should have destroyed the stone a long time ago. But in my foolishness, I preserved it."

A stray tear coursed down her cheek. "Your mother... I never knew exactly why she left like she did. Eventually, we heard from her. Kathleen was in Rose City, where you were born." She squeezed Kate's hand. "You were her saving grace, Kate. When she showed up with you in her arms...well, we all could see how much she adored you. Spent her whole life trying to keep you safe and make a decent life for the two of you. I know you always wondered about your father. I'm sorry to say I don't know who he was. I never met him. And your mother wouldn't talk about him, except to say that he rescued her at the lowest point of her life, and she would be forever grateful."

Grandma's lips quivered slightly as she continued.

"I was wrong for assuming your mother had explained to you about the stone. I'm so sorry you had to find out about it this way. Bless dear Caireanne for trusting Cassidy with the secret. So now you know the whole story and that the power of the stone is yours." She inhaled deeply. "And my answer is yes. Call Aidan and I will go with him." She patted Kate's hand. "I'm glad you met the grandson of my dearest friend. Mike's quite an upstanding young man."

Kate nodded absentmindedly, her attention focused on the orderly standing in the doorway, arms crossed, eyes trained on her. She gave her grandmother a big hug and spoke into her ear. "I'm taking you back in now. It's possible we're being watched."

The orderly helped her grandmother back into bed. After he left the room, Kate told her their plan.

"I talked to Dr. Anderson. He's supposed to sign your release papers tomorrow afternoon. Said you'd be free to leave anytime after that. We'll wait until evening when everyone is preoccupied with the night ceremonies. Mike is going to pick you up and bring you to the house. I'll summon Aidan, and we'll be waiting for you. Oh, I almost forgot. Look what I found."

She pulled off the Claddagh ring and placing it in her palm, offered it to her grandmother.

Grandma closed her hand around Kate's.

"You keep it dear," she said. "Something to remember me by when I'm gone."

Gone.

When she said it like that…

Kate flung her arms around her grandmother's neck.

"I'm sorry I wasn't here when you needed me. When you were hurting over Mom's death. We could have helped each other through the pain. I was stupid. I was so stupid. I've made so many mistakes," she shook her head, "so many bad decisions. Grandma, I don't know what to do. I'm so sorry. What can I do to make up for what I've done?"

Grandma hugged her tightly.

"It's okay, Kate. Mistakes are a part of life. Even an old goat like me still makes mistakes." Her voice softened, and she stroked Kate's hair. "It's the way we handle them that makes all the difference. We learn from them and move on. Don't punish yourself for things you can't change. The past is only a gateway to where we are at this moment. You're here. We're together again. And if it took those things to get us to where we are right now, it's not so bad after all, is it?"

They spent the rest of the afternoon talking about old times and new dreams. Laughing. Crying. Kate didn't let go of Grandma's hand once. When the orderly came with dinner, Kate stood reluctantly.

"I'll go so you can eat," she said, leaning over to kiss her grandmother's cheek. "See you tomorrow." She started to say more, but another nurse had arrived to take vitals, so she gave a little wave and a thumbs-up and left the hospital feeling better than she had in a long time.

That night, Kate lay on her side in the feather bed, Mike's arm draped heavily across her. His breath brushed across her neck as he exhaled the soft rhythm of sleep. On another night, it would have been comforting. Tonight, it did nothing to dispel the sliver of fear that had begun to splitter her confidence.

What would happen tomorrow night? Would Aidan show? What would they do if he didn't?

It has to work, Kate argued with her internal pessimist. *This is the only way to ensure Grandma's safety.*

And perhaps bring absolution for the guilt she'd felt so long about her mother's death...

ENOUGH.

She willed her mind to silence.

As her body drifted into a half-awake, half-asleep limbo, an eerie sound pierced the night. Something like a cross between a woman's cry and a screech.

Just the old barn owl, she told herself and buried her head further into the pillow.

Before Mike left for work, he made Kate promise to attend the Founder's Day festivities that evening.

"You have to see it. All the stores are decorated, balloons and streamers are everywhere. And there's a little carnival in the park." He took her hand, "Please. We won't stay long." He gave her a tight hug and a lingering kiss. "I love you, Kate. Everything will be okay."

The El Camino kicked up dust in its wake. As Kate watched him leave, all she could think was, *I hope he's right.*

She'd written Robert a note thanking him for his help. Explained that she was leaving but would look him up if she ever made it back to Ardee. As she picked her way along the path toward the greenhouse, she recalled the first time she met him-

Wait.

She gave a soft chuckle and shook her head. Why had it taken her so long to figure it out? The greenhouse wasn't their first encounter. Robert was the one who'd helped her that night of the hailstorm. No wonder he'd seemed so familiar.

Lost in thought, it wasn't until she stepped onto the first plank of the bridge that her eye caught sight of the envelope secured to the handrail by a ribbon.

Her stomach took a dive.

A pink-and-white striped ribbon.

The one Mom had tied around her baby things.

That's what had been out of place the day they'd returned from their campout.

Peg knew that she and Mike had gone out of town. She must have rummaged through the cedar chest. But why would Peg leave her a note like this? She untied the ribbon. The envelope fluttered downward to land on the bridge beside her.

Her name was scrawled across the front. She broke the blood-red wax seal and pulled out a thick sheet of expensive bond paper folded precisely into thirds.

Dear Miss McKenna,
I have completed my end of our bargain. Now it is time for you to fulfill yours. I cannot think of a more glorious way to end the Founder's Day festivities than to begin our newly established relationship. Please meet me at the bridge at nine o'clock tonight. I will be waiting anxiously.
Until we are reunited, Darcy

Bile crawled up the back of her throat. It was Darcy, not Peg, who'd been in the house. What else had he done while they were away? She'd been too self-absorbed to notice if anything had been misplaced or taken. And what arrogance. He'd deliberately used Aidan's words from the note when he'd arranged to meet her grandmother–

Kate's back stiffened, and she drew in a tenuous breath.

If Darcy found the note from Aidan that meant he'd also found the diary pages. Now he knew something even her mother didn't know.

The stone could be used to summon Aidan.

Had he figured out her plan?

Better call the hospital, just to make sure things were still on schedule with Dr. Anderson.

Kate's fingers twitched as she dialed the number. Broke into uncontrollable tremors as she hung up the phone.

This can't be happening.

Without signed release papers how could they bring Grandma home? Kate rubbed her temples and tried to devise an alternate plan. The whole third-floor staff knew her grandmother. How could they get her out without raising suspicions?

Mike said there would be a fireworks display after the mayor's speech. He could tell the nurses that Grandma wanted to go outside and see them. That was innocent enough. Once outside, he could just roll the wheelchair out to the parking lot.

Kate felt marginally better now that she had a plan B. As she slumped against the wall, she realized her tongue tasted like iron and her thumb throbbed. She looked down, shaken when she saw that she'd unconsciously chewed the skin around her thumbnail until it was in bloody shreds.

Later that afternoon, her suitcase lay open on the bed, packed only with absolute necessities, but she made sure to include Grandma's diary and the books Robert had given her. The silver pendant she wore securely around her neck. Mike had jammed his duffle bag with as many of his belongings as he could. It leaned against the ladder-back chair. After Grandma was safely away with Aidan, and they destroyed the bullaun stone, Kate would have to disappear. Mike was determined not to let her go alone.

"When we find a safe place, I'll come back and gather the rest of our things. I've already cleared it with Mr. Clarke to be off for a week, so disappearing after work tonight is no problem."

She lowered the lid to her battered blue suitcase. Started to snap it shut when she remembered one more item.

She slipped the gold cord off the nail above the headboard; ran her fingertips over the embroidered surface of the tapestry. Maybe she'd found a way to redeem herself and uphold the Barrett creed after all. She rolled it up and placed it on her pile of clothes.

There was nothing to do now but wait.

And the waiting was interminable.

At seven-thirty, Kate slipped on her favorite peasant skirt and donned an off-the-shoulder dark green peasant blouse. Large, silver loops hung from her ears. She evaluated her reflection in the mirror.

Not bad. But I look like a gypsy. Which is probably what I'm about to become after tonight.

Now Kate understood why Mom had moved them from town to town so frequently. She must have been afraid of Darcy's wrath. Worried about what kind of revenge he might exact against her for not sharing the bullaun stone and...

Revenge?

Her thoughts rewound back to the night of Mom's accident. Something she'd forgotten until she told the story to Mike. About the second set of tire tracks Andy Collins said he found at the scene. She couldn't recall ever reading anything about it, or for that matter anyone questioning it again.

"He'd have to get your grandmother out of the way in order to coerce you to use the stone on his behalf," Mike had said.

Tiny shocks of electricity exploded through her body like fireworks as she realized –

Darcy would've had to get her mother out of the way too.

Chapter 16

Kate scrambled for her purse and keys. Shoved the note from Darcy in her skirt pocket. She had to show it to Mike. It meant they were on a tighter deadline with their plan. And if her hunch was correct, it was more important than ever to get Grandma out of the hospital tonight.

The engine turned over a couple of times before it engaged. Kate ground her teeth together. This was not the time for car trouble. She gunned the motor. A spray of pebbles pelted the hackberry tree as she spun the Nova around in the driveway and sped off toward Ardee.

As she neared town, her pace slowed. Parked cars lined the grass alongside the road. She inched past the festival attendees that trooped their way toward the square.

The muscles in her back strained, and her fingers drummed a wild beat against the steering wheel.

Please, please let me make it before the library closes…

After what seemed like an eternity, she pulled into a parking space close to the library entrance and ran up the steps. Mrs. Stewart was locking her drawer at the front desk when Kate entered.

"I'm sorry dear," she apologized, "but we're closing now."

"I know, Mrs. Stewart, I know, but please. I need to look up one thing on the microfiche machine."

Tears welled up unbidden, as Kate found herself explaining. "Please, it's…it's about the car wreck that killed my mother three years ago. It happened just outside of Ardee, and I hoped the newspaper had carried the story. I know the exact date, so it's not like I have to hunt through the slides or anything. Please," Kate implored, "I promise it will only take like, maybe five minutes."

Mrs. Stewart eyes narrowed. Then softened.

"Fine, but make it quick."

Kate thumbed through the slides until she found the one she was looking for and inserted it into the machine. After searching through several months' worth of articles, she located the newspaper dated July twenty-third. She flipped through the subsequent pages. Nothing about the accident. Her shoulders sagged.

It was a dead end.

Kate reached to flip the switch that shut off the machine when something in her gut prompted her to look through the pages one last time. Something was out of sync.

Page numbers.

Page three was missing from the record. Kate examined the slide several times, to make sure there wasn't a mistake. That the pages hadn't been scanned out of order. But it was clear that page three was missing.

As an afterthought, she scoured the next few weeks' worth of articles until she came across a single commentary. Buried near the back of the paper. Just a few sentences.

Accident Investigation Concluded

After an extensive investigation, newly promoted Police Chief, Andy Collins, has determined that the accident that killed former resident, Kathleen Barrett McKenna, was a single car incident triggered by the condition of the road due to the severe weather.

The Mayor of Ardee, Darcy MacMurray, a former classmate of Ms. McKenna, expressed his condolences to friends and family. "Death is always a difficult tragedy to face. Our prayers go out to the members of the McKenna family and those left behind who must carry on in the face of tremendous loss."

The librarian's footsteps tapped across the wood floor, heading in her direction.

Kate stuffed the slides back into the envelope and handed it to her.

"Thank you so much for staying open just a bit longer."

She spun on her heel to leave.

"Wait," Mrs. Stewart said in a low whisper. "I knew your mother. We graduated from high school together." She beckoned, "Come with me."

They ducked into a room beneath the staircase. The bare light bulb swayed precariously on its frayed cord, causing their shadows to dance in erratic patterns on the wall behind the row of oxidized file cabinets. Kate shifted from one foot to the other, biting the inside of her lip as Mrs. Stewart rummaged through the bottom drawer and pulled out the thin newspaper. After briefly thumbing through the pages, she laid the newsprint, reeking with the musty smell of decay, on the wooden worktable, and silently pointed to the right-hand corner. Kate took a tentative step forward and leaned in to read the date.

July twenty-third, nineteen hundred and seventy-three.

Hit and Run Investigated in Local Fatality Accident

A car was forced off the road by another vehicle that fled the scene in an alleged hit-and-run incident that took place outside of Ardee late last evening. Police are appealing for witnesses to the accident that took place off of Highway 82 and CR2605. A member of the public called the police, who confirmed an accident had occurred.

Investigating Deputy Andy Collins said evidence at the scene indicated the Ford Galaxie left the road and drove down a nearby bank, where it crashed into a tree. Collins cited finding two sets of skid marks at the scene, suggesting the presence of another vehicle.

Police confirmed the driver of the Galaxie, Kathleen Barrett McKenna, was taken to the hospital where she died shortly thereafter from multiple injuries.

Investigations are ongoing at this time.

"I was told to omit page three and destroy the hard copy when I recorded the newspaper on microfiche. So there you have it. Make of it what you will."

"Who..." she began, but Mrs. Stewart's brows contorted into a scowl, and she shook her head vehemently from side to side, cutting off the question. She snatched the newspaper off the table, folded it in half, and stuck it back in the file cabinet.

Mrs. Stewart hurried Kate from the room. Kate watched her eyes dart from one end of the great hall to the other as she secured the door behind them.

The woman is scared to death, Kate thought. Mrs. Stewart escorted her to the library entrance and pushed the front door open, firmly nudging Kate forward. Kate stepped across the threshold, hesitated, then glancing over her shoulder, locked eyes with the librarian.

"Thank you," she mouthed.

Mrs. Stewart gave her a terse nod.

Kate maneuvered the Nova through the foot traffic to the parking space Mike had reserved for her behind his apartment. She turned off the motor and sat, lost in thought, contemplating the magnitude of what she'd just read.

Andy Collins had gone from investigating officer to chief of police in, what, a matter of weeks? Someone wanted to make the investigation of the hit and run disappear from history.

And she was positive she knew who that someone was.

Kate made her way down the congested sidewalk, jostled by partyers blowing horns and waving green, white, and orange flags. Tricolour bunting draped the awnings of many of the storefronts. A few of the merchants displayed their coat-of-arms. Darcy MacMurray's blue and white family crest hung above the entryway to the city hall, boasting its hypocrisy – "By Virtue and Faith."

Kate dug what was left of her chewed-off fingernails into the palms of her hands as she walked past.

The square had been transformed. Flea market booths were gone, replaced with an eating area, surrounded by ropes of twinkling lights that swayed back and forth in the hot summer breeze. Dozens of people sat at makeshift tables devouring bowls of Irish stew, plates of Ulster fry and drinking Guinness. Bright orange, white, and green balloons danced around the head of the elderly gentleman selling ice-cream from a cart. The air was thick with the aroma of cotton candy, hot dogs, and the cacophony of music dancing its way from the carnival rides in the park through the cobblestone streets downtown.

On a large platform in the center of the square, several men wearing kilts played a lively tune. Four young girls took the stage, dressed in ornately embroidered dresses and performed what Kate concluded was a traditional Irish step. The precision of their footwork was mesmerizing. She joined in with the other onlookers as they clapped appreciatively at the conclusion.

Kate spotted Mike waving to her from across the crowd. He had changed out of his starched pharmacy coat and black slacks into jeans and a white cotton t-shirt. When he reached her side, he put his arm around her waist, pulling her close.

"See? This is why I wanted you to come."

Kate did her best to reign in her apprehension. Told him it had been entertaining so far. Mike's first thought, as usual, was on food. Kate's stomach roiled at the thought. She hadn't been able to force anything down all day.

"I'm not hungry, but you go ahead and get something. I'll just wait here."

Mike headed off towards the refreshment stand as another band took the stage and began playing a tight rendition of 'Black Water.' Kate sang along under her breath, trying to relax as her eyes swept the crowd.

Where was he?

Beads of sweat dotted her forehead at the sight of the figure poised to take the platform. He was dressed in a black tuxedo and white pleated shirt. Pinned to his lapel was a bright purplish-blue boutonniere. His snowy hair, unbound from its usual ponytail, brushed his shoulders. He wore white gloves. Carried a top hat, which he donned as he ascended the steps to the stage. One of the band members offered him a microphone.

Mayor MacMurray waited for the spattering of applause to subside.

"Welcome everyone to the hundred and third celebration of the founding of our wonderful little town."

Mike was back with a corndog and beer for each of them. Kate opened her mouth to protest when her heart nudged her in the ribs.

Why spoil Mike's fun?

She thanked him and plastered on a smile while the mayor continued.

"We are indebted to our Irish ancestors. Their emigration to America represented a new opportunity for many. In turn, our people have made, and will continue to make, an invaluable contribution to the social, commercial and political development of this country. By doing so, we bring honor to ourselves and our beloved Ireland."

Whistles and enthusiastic clapping followed. The mayor gave the crowd a benevolent smile and signaled for the hubbub to quieten down.

"Our Founding Fathers left behind their cherished country to expand to a new world. But they did not leave behind their culture and traditions. That is what makes Ardee strong. That is what we celebrate tonight. Will each of you raise your glass in a toast?"

Someone handed the mayor a tulip-shaped whiskey glass. As he lifted it into the air, Darcy's eyes fastened on Kate.

Her blood turned to icy slush.

"Here's to our ancestors and their traditions. May we be ever grateful for what they have done for us. And may we always use our gifts with wisdom and thankfulness. Slàinte. To your health."

Darcy downed the drink and wiped his mouth with the back of his gloved hand. The kilt-clad band began playing 'My Wild Irish Rose' as the mayor left the stage.

"Did you see his face when he made that toast?" Kate's jaw tightened. "He was mocking me."

She threw her uneaten meal in a nearby trash receptacle.

"That's it," her voice quavered. "I'm leaving."

Mike followed as she stormed down the sidewalk, weaving in and out of the crowd. When they were alone behind Clarke's, she paused to lean against the building, bent over and balanced her hands on her knees. If this was going to happen, she had to calm down.

Mike stood beside her, quietly rubbing her back.

"It's okay, Kate. You're gonna be okay."

She shook her head, rolled her shoulders and rose to face him.

"Mike, this is much worse than I thought. I'm sorry I don't have time to explain. I promise I'll tell you the whole story later, but right now we have a big problem."

She whipped MacMurray's note out of her pocket and thrust it into his hand.

"When I called the hospital this afternoon, Doc Anderson hadn't signed her release papers. It's him. It's Darcy. He's onto us. I just know it."

"Not necessarily," Mike soothed and wrapped her up in his arms, pulling her close against his chest. "But it's a sure sign we need to get her out of the hospital and back to Aidan tonight." He thought for a minute. "Everyone at the hospital knows me. I doubt they'd suspect anything if I were to take Mrs. Pearl for an evening stroll. Then I just roll her right on out to the truck."

"That's what I was thinking," Kate said and let out a shallow sigh.

Mike took her shoulders and held her at arm's length, looked directly into her eyes.

"It'll work," he reassured. "Just remember, Kate. You're the one who controls the stone's power. Not MacMurray." He handed her back the note and gave her a quick kiss. "Try not to worry."

Moments later, the tail lights of Mike's truck disappeared around the corner.

It was time.

Kate climbed into the Nova and turned the key. The engine chugged momentarily before sputtering to a stop.

"Oh, come on," she coaxed and turned the key again.

Same thing.

On the third try, the only sound was a clicking rattle. She hammered the steering wheel with her fists.

No, no, NO!

Her heart beat in double-time as she raced back to the square. Standing under the gaslight at the street corner, Kate closed her eyes.

Please, she raised her face toward the heavens, *please help me.*

Chapter 17

Salvation came walking down the sidewalk towards her carrying a tricolour flag in one hand and a bottle of Guinness in the other.

Callie smothered Kate with a hug.

"Hi, sweetie, how ya doin'?"

"Not so great right now, I could use some help."

Kate explained her dilemma.

"Oh, we can fix that." Callie waved to the crowd and bellowed, "Luke, honey, can you come here?"

A tall, lanky teenager sauntered toward them.

"Sure, Mom, what's up?"

"We need to help this young lady with a dead battery. It should only take a few minutes to jump-start."

Luke yelled at a couple of his friends, "Hey Roger, Connor, come 'ere."

Two teens separated themselves from the crowd. The shorter boy had oily hair the color of coffee that fell in a tangle below his shoulders. He wore bell-bottom jeans with frayed hems, and his torn t-shirt boasted AC/DC High Voltage. The other boy was dressed similarly in a Dark Side of the Moon World Tour t-shirt. His long, auburn hair was cut in a precise, layered shag and his emerald eyes smoldered in a James Dean way.

That kid's gonna be a ladykiller someday.

But it wasn't his looks that grabbed Kate's attention. There was something different about him. Something that made the hair on the back of her neck bristle and the tips of her fingers throb.

Callie and Luke trooped down the sidewalk after Kate while the other two went to get their car. Luke tried to start the engine one more time, just to verify it was a battery problem.

"Oh yeah," he announced cheerfully. "It's dead all right. But we'll fix it."

The Plymouth Cuda Hemi rumbled around the corner. While Luke connected the jumper cables, AC/DC edged up to Kate. Introduced himself as Roger. Inclined his head and gave her a nod.

"Haven't seen you around before. Think maybe I could buy you a beer after this?"

His come-on would have been amusing if she'd been in a better mood. Tonight she had way too much on her mind.

"Sorry. I have other plans."

Roger shrugged, "Hey, you don't know unless you ask, right?"

True.

She decided to ask.

"Your friend," Kate nodded toward the redhead. "What's his story?"

"Connor?" Roger snorted. "He's just a kid. Doesn't even have his license yet. We let him hang with us 'cause he's got a job at his dad's furniture store and he buys us gas. And his sister, Jessica? She's smokin' hot."

That sounded pretty normal. Still, Kate couldn't shake the feeling that there was something unusual about this Connor. She was about to pry further when the engine revved, cutting their conversation short. Kate thanked them all profusely and crawled into the Nova.

Sweaty palms gripped the steering wheel. She'd have to step on it now to get home ahead of Mike. It didn't help that fingers of doubt squeezed her lungs, making it hard to breathe.

The El Camino was already parked under the carport when she pulled into the driveway.

Kate experienced the flush of exhilaration. Then a crushing fear smothered her.

The house was dark.

Everything was wrong.

She threw open the kitchen door and flipped on the light switch.

"Mike," she yelled.

A hollow echo repeated his name back to her.

She crossed the kitchen and turned on the floor lamp beside Grandma's recliner. Took a quick glance around the room, even though she knew it would be empty. And something else was off-kilter. It only took her a minute to figure it out.

The grandfather clock had stopped ticking.

Why?

Her heart whispered the answer but she shook her head in refusal, and her pace quickened as she headed down the hallway to her room.

The night air was thick with the cloying scent of sunbaked honeysuckle and faded roses. She leaned against the doorpost, fixated on the willow tree bathed in the light of the full moon. Its leaves, usually rustling about in the breeze or dancing to the music of cicadas or tree frogs, lay limp and unmoving, emphasizing the finality that no one waited for her at the bullaun stone.

Her feet were cemented in place and her thoughts flat-lined until the loud jangle of the phone split the silence. Kate's stomach pitched as she raced back to the kitchen to answer it.

"Miss McKenna, this is Dr. Anderson from Memorial Hospital."

The receiver fell with a loud crash against the kitchen tile. Kate reached out to the wall to steady her legs and tried to process what she'd just heard.

It was a slow build.

From the bottom of her feet, she could feel it burning upward. Outward. Until her fingers tingled with its fire, and the hair on her head singed from its heat.

Kate charged through the house and kicked open the garden gate, knocking it off its hinges. She tromped her way across the garden, dragging up basil and thyme plants that clung to the hem of her skirt and tangled in the straps of her sandals, almost as if they were trying to hold her back. She brushed them off.

"You're not stopping me," she muttered through clenched teeth and climbed the fence, undeterred when the frayed chicken-wire sliced through her hands. She glanced down at the small droplets of blood that began to drip from her fingertips, but the pain barely registered. Her attention fixated on the silhouette across the creek.

Kate stopped short of the bridge as he stepped out of the shadows, still dressed in his festival attire. Her words were slow and steady.

"You son-of-a-bitch."

He crossed his arms. An arrogant sneer spread across his face.

"Oh now, now," Darcy clucked in a condescending tone. "You didn't think I was going to be hoodwinked by a couple of kids, did you? You made promises you were never going to keep, so, unfortunately, I was unable to keep mine."

He took a step towards her.

"You're just like your mother after all."

"And you," Kate's eyes narrowed, "you were the one who ran her off the road that night. You were the one who killed her."

Darcy's pitch rose with each word.

"Your mother was a lying whore who got exactly what she deserved."

Closing his eyes, Darcy jerked at the collar of his shirt. Relaxed his shoulders. When he spoke again, his voice was calm and restrained.

"This time I have a guarantee that no one will renege on their promises."

A new fear impaled her heart.

"Where is he?"

"Oh, yes. Mike," Darcy drawled lazily and removed the boutonniere from his lapel with a gloved hand.

"Mike had an encounter with a nasty flower. Seems he's trying to recover at the moment."

He stepped aside to reveal Mike's body, slumped against the door of Robert's greenhouse. A dark bruise colored his cheek. Blood smeared across his face.

"Oh, he's not dead," was Darcy's offhand response to Kate's expression. "I need him for leverage. You wouldn't want him to be the victim of an unfortunate accident too, would you? I can see that you have become rather fond of him. He must be enamored with you as well. It took quite a bit to subdue him, even after he was exposed to the monkshood."

Darcy dropped the flower and crushed it into the ground with the toe of his shoe.

"Now it's time to keep your promise."

He smoothed the lapel of his coat.

"Shall we proceed to the bullaun stone?"

Kate's mind screamed for help. There had to be a way out of this. As Darcy made his way onto the bridge, she took a step backward. Her sandal touched something hard. She looked down. Silver handles glinted in the light of the full moon. The lost garden shears. How had she not noticed them before? Kate pulled them from the ground just as Darcy reached her. She lifted her arm and slashed downward with all her strength.

Blood spurted from the gash that split his face.

"You little bitch," he bellowed and grabbed Kate's arm, which was raised to deliver another blow.

Darcy was stronger than she anticipated. His sharp fingernails ripped the flesh of her arm as they wrestled for possession of the weapon. Kate grappled until she found the scissor handles. She gathered her energy for one last effort to arrest his assault.

Darcy stumbled backward.

His eyes widened.

Kate followed his gaze. Dark, sticky liquid had begun to spread downward, staining her skirt.

Pain hit the same time as the realization.

It took her breath away.

Kate sank to the grass, her hands wrapped around the silver handles that protruded from the green fabric of her blouse.

The mayor's scream reverberated through the woods.

"NO!"

A sickening crunch and a thud, and he was gone from sight. As she lay there, it occurred to her they had thwarted Darcy's plan after all. If she was gone, the power of the bullaun stone was gone. And, as Mike always said, everything would be okay.

Kate closed her eyes. The shallow breaths weren't enough to fill her lungs. She had a weird feeling she'd lived this before.

It was the dream. The dark mist was enveloping her. Suffocating her.

She coughed, and the searing pain wracked her body.

Please, just let this be over.

In answer to her prayer, strong arms wrapped around her, cradling her tenderly in their warmth. There was something comforting about the vaguely recognizable scent of bourbon and caramel. It reminded her of a line from a song her mother would sing to her at bedtime – "The night draws near but have no fear, you're sheltered in the arms of love."

Maybe dying isn't so bad after all.

She began a soft fall into oblivion until a low voice spoke her name. She recognized its lilting cadence. Something about its urgency empowered Kate to fight her way back into consciousness.

"Katherine – Kate, listen to me. Many years ago, I happened upon a beautiful young woman who had been brutally beaten and raped. Left for dead. I took her home with me. Healed her wounds. Protected her. Cared for her. Loved her. But she was uneasy; frightened that the one who hurt her would find her and finish what he'd started."

Kate felt the arms tighten around her.

"I planned her escape. I had friends up north who would keep her safe. I begged her to let me accompany her, but she refused. If the circumstances had been different, I believe she would have stayed with me. As it was, she let me hold her the night before she left. It was then I gave her a special gift."

His voice caught.

"You, Kate. You were the gift I gave to Kathleen."

Kate felt the grass, cool and soft against her back as he laid her carefully down.

"Your mother never told you the truth. That I am Aidan Kavanagh's brother."

Carefully, he removed the scissors from her chest and gave her a light kiss on her forehead.

"And you, dearest Kate, are my daughter. And there is no way I am going to let my daughter die."

She opened her eyes, just enough to see Robert kneeling beside her, a golden glow emanating from his palms. It spread in an ever-enlarging circle that encompassed her whole body with its peaceful warmth. After a few moments the light faded. Robert pulled his hands away.

Kate propped herself up on her elbows. With one hand, she lifted her torn shirt. The skin was smooth and flawless. She mashed around the area.

No pain.

She looked up at him, eyes wide.

"You... Are my father?"

"Indeed I am."

"But how... Why?"

Her mind was dizzy with questions. And then there was–

"Mike! We have to help him," she said and tried to stand, but the horizon began to sway. Robert caught her and eased her to the ground.

"I'll take care of this. You stay here."

He sprinted across the bridge.

Father. That'll take some getting used to.

As the reality of the situation started to sink in, Kate buried her face in her hands. Darcy was right. She had underestimated him and the extent of his greed. It had cost both her mother and grandmother's life. And it could have cost Mike's.

Her only consolation was the dark, crumpled figure nearby. Darcy MacMurray's opaque eyes stared sightlessly while a pool of crimson spread across the grass beneath his head. That, too, must have been her father's doing.

Robert returned with a dazed Mike, who showed no sign of the injuries Darcy had dealt him. She watched as Mike briefly registered MacMurray's immobile form then his eyes met Kate's. He rushed to kneel beside her.

"Are you okay?" His voice was charged with emotion.

"Oh, Mike."

She dissolved into tears, threw her arms around his neck, and buried her face against his chest. Several minutes passed before her heaving sobs diminished.

"I'm so sorry about your grandmother," Mike said, stroking her hair. "When the hospital told me she was gone, I was so furious with MacMurray, I rushed him. Nearly got myself killed, too."

She brushed away the remaining tears with the back of her hand. Attempted a weak smile.

"Good thing for both of us my father has some remarkable powers."

"Your father?"

Robert seemed content to keep his distance while Kate explained what had taken place with Darcy and revealed Robert's true identity.

Mike ran his fingers through his hair. "Aiden Kavanagh's brother? Who'd have thought..." His sentence trailed off and he gave her an intense look.

She recoiled slightly.

"What?"

"You realize what this means, right?"

Kate shook her head, puzzled.

Mike's mouth slowly shaped into a sly smile.

"You're part Faerie. You *do* have a little magic in you."

Kate glanced over at Robert, who stood with his arms crossed, nodding. An affirmatory grin rested on his face.

Mike helped Kate to her feet. One hand remained around her waist. The other he thrust towards Robert.

"I hate that we had to meet this way. But thank you for what you've done."

Robert took Mike's hand and gave it a hearty shake.

"No thanks necessary. It's what any father would do."

Kate and Mike looked at each other. Kate mouthed the words 'any father?' with a raised eyebrow. Mike gave a quiet chuckle and pulled her in closer.

"I know you have many questions," Robert said, "but there's plenty of time to answer them. Shall we leave here and go someplace where we can talk?"

"I'd like that," Kate said. "But, can you give me just a minute?"

Mike and Robert stepped away.

The stars spread like a smear of glitter across the dark sky. Kate watched as one blue star, larger and brighter than the others, exploded into view. It arched downward to disappear behind the silhouette of the weeping willow tree in her grandmother's backyard.

Make a wish, a voice inside her head prompted.

Hot tears streaked their way down her cheeks as Kate closed her eyes and let her heart express its desire.

Another minute or two passed before she exhaled a measured sigh. She glanced one last time at the lifeless body beside her then strode to where Mike and Robert waited. Standing on her tiptoes, she gave her father a kiss on his cheek. Then she turned to Mike.

"You know, you were right."

Mike's arms enveloped her. He kissed the top of her head as she rested it against his chest.

There it was.

Thumping its reassurance through her whole being.

"You've been right all along. Everything is going to be okay."

Epilogue

She watched from the shadows.

Not even Darcy knew she was here. But after he showed her the note, there was no way she was going to miss this. Not even when the thorny mesquite trees tore flesh from her palms. Stabbed through her denim shirt, sprinkling it with red dots as she clawed her way through the underbrush. She didn't mind. After Darcy got control of Kate, he would use the stone to heal her.

That's who Darcy was.

A man of his word.

A man who always rewarded loyalty.

A slight moan disrupted her reverie. She glanced to her left, brows furrowed. She'd always liked Mike. Even flirted with him a couple of times. But that was back when he was new in town, and she was digging for information. He seemed harmless enough. Guess that's why she felt a wave of compassion. She hoped he understood this wasn't about him.

He was an innocent.

Only here because of Kate.

She ground her teeth together.

It was all Kate's fault. If she'd just done what she was supposed to, none of this would have happened. Now Mrs. Pearl was dead, and Mike lay propped against the greenhouse, struggling to breathe after his exposure to the monkshood, barely conscious from the blow Darcy gave him.

Her ears picked up another sound. From her vantage point, she could see Darcy, the bridge and the clearing between Mrs. Pearl's garden and Boyd Creek. She trained her eyes toward the voice.

Kate. She had climbed the fence. Stood across the bridge from Darcy, accusing him of murdering her grandmother and her mother. Well, Kathleen had screwed him over by backing down on her promise and her daughter had just tried to do the same thing.

Who could blame him?

As she watched him cross the bridge towards Kate, a flutter of excitement tickled her stomach. It was really going to happen. Darcy would finally have the power of the bullaun stone. He'd spent years talking, planning, waiting for this day.

Suddenly, her heart cried out. She covered her mouth with her hands to keep her voice from doing the same.

That little bitch had sliced Darcy's face open with a pair of scissors.

She rose from her crouched position, poised to help when she caught the glint of silver that protruded from Kate's chest.

Wait. That wasn't part of the plan. Kate had to be alive. What about the stone? How would it work if she…

The next few minutes were a blur. As Kate crumpled to the ground, a tall man burst onto the scene. She heard Darcy's blood-curdling scream as the man tackled him, picked up a nearby boulder and–

She squeezed her eyes shut. Her breath came in short bursts. What went wrong? The plan was flawless, yet now…

Open your eyes, her brain ordered. *You need to see what's happening.*

Darcy was a dark, motionless mound in the grass. The tall man hunched over Kate. As she watched, a golden cloud engulfed

Kate, its light so bright that even from a distance she had to shield her eyes. When it subsided, Kate sat up and raised her shirt.

Her heart beat wildly against her ribs, like a caged hummingbird. She'd seen the scissors. Watched the blood darken Kate's blouse and skirt. And now the stab wound was gone? What kind of devilment was this?

Now the tall man was heading across the bridge toward the greenhouse. She cowered closer to the rain barrel, praying she was sufficiently hidden. He stooped to touch Mike with the same golden glow. Then he helped Mike to his feet, and together they crossed back to where Kate sat.

A few minutes passed before the three of them left the field, headed toward Mrs. Pearl's house. She waited in the darkness for what felt like an eternity. Finally, convinced they weren't going to return, she crossed the bridge.

She knelt beside him. Her hand touched something warm and sticky. Blood. A pool of dark red spread across the ground beneath his head. The flesh on his cheek puckered around the jagged gash the scissors had made. His eyes were icy, gray marbles. She kissed her forefinger and gently closed one eyelid, then the other. Then she wrapped her arms around her chest and rocked back and forth, allowing herself a low keen.

It didn't make sense. She'd consulted the ogham staves. There was no indication of any turmoil today. The staves were never wrong.

What kind of magic had taken place here tonight?

She settled into the grass beside Darcy and eased his head onto her lap. Stroked his beautiful white hair, unmindful of the burgundy clumps that stained her clothes.

Now he would never know.

Never know how much she loved him.

Nay worshiped him.

Bitter tears splashed Darcy's forehead and cheek. Tendrils of hair fell like a chestnut-colored curtain, surrounding his shattered face as she bent her head. Tenderly, she kissed his cold lips, then lifted her eyes toward the heavens and spoke.

"De réir an bandia Macha, beidh mé dhíoghail do bhás mo ghrá."

She patted the almost imperceptible bump that strained the waistband of her jeans.

"Oh yes," she whispered in his deaf ear, "you will be avenged. No matter how long it takes, my love, you will be avenged."

A Note from the Author

I've spent my life in love with books – mysteries, romances, historical novels, fantasies; you name it. So when I set out to write this book, it became a blend of all those genres.

I hope you've enjoyed The Bullaun Stone. It's the first in a collection of stories based on Celtic folklore and legends. To learn more about The Bullaun Stone and upcoming novels and novellas, please visit my website at www.janflynnwhite.com.